R

FEY BORN

Gold Imprint
Medallion Press, Inc.
Printed in USA

DEDICATION:

This book is dedicated to the guardians of nature and
all her creatures —
And to Carol Ann and Michael, my faery godmother
and her husband — with appreciation and love.

Published 2006 by Medallion Press, Inc.

The MEDALLION PRESS LOGO
is a registered tradmark of Medallion Press, Inc.

Printed in the United States of America

Typeset in Adobe Garamond Pro

10 9 8 7 6 5 4 3 2 1
First Edition

ACKNOWLEDGEMENTS:

To Dov for hinting, "This needs a little more work."

To Mom and Bill for saying, "We want to read it!"

To Edward for taking all those author pictures.

Thank you.

Previous praise for PREDESTINED:

"Everything that deceives may be said to enchant."
~ Plato

FORWARD

With the passage of time and memory, many names of historical heroes, Gods and Goddesses have been stripped into imitation figures, fitted into ancient culture and lore. However, every so often, a great guardian is lost to the ripples of time . . .

    . . . and is found once again.

PROLOGUE

Eire
Long ago

In nightshade and legend, they linger, a forever trespass into the past and present, a forever warning to those who would defile and ruin the living lands and waters.

Deep in the ancestral memory of the faery realm, they reside, answering to the given name of *Guardian*. Remote beings of just cruelty, they are intolerant of weakness and flaw, intolerant of ugliness, rules, and falsity. Intolerant of most things, mortal men believe, knowing a guardian's punishment to be swift, sure, and lethal.

They are like no other.

Beautiful.

Selfish.

Male bred.

They are fey born, primordial, powerful, and none have ever changed . . . *until now*.

CHAPTER 1

Drumanagh, Eire
Spring

HE STOOD AT THE EDGE of the high ranging meadows where the horses of the tribe grazed. Darkly lashed eyelids closed in exquisite pleasure. Slowly, his head tilted back, long brown hair flowing down his bare back in dampening glints of red and gold. It began to rain, a gathering of gray clouds muting the light of the late afternoon. He sighed deeply, tasting the sweet air of *Meitheamh*, June, in his lungs and savoring the touch of cool raindrops upon his naked and responsive flesh.

He was fey born, a purebred creature of sensations and selfishness. A legendary guardian of the waters, he was crafted of cruelty and enchantment, a being to be feared; a being whose true form must remain secret. He knew he should not be here and thought of the olden ways with a sharp surge of resentment. There was no sense in being bored, he thought rebelliously.

Wearing his mortal appearance, he lived among the tribe of the *Tuatha Dé Danann* now. A fierce, loyal, and constant warrior — he slowly grinned — answering to the given name of Keegan. The name meant "highly spirited." An admirable name, he chuckled darkly. *If only they knew . . .*

Lana, a farm girl of unimpressive worth, at least that is how she thought of herself, stumbled back behind the ancient oaks and nearly dropped the druidess's basket of herbs. She had been making her customary visit to see Lightning, the aged sorrel stallion, when fat raindrops plopped and splashed upon the land. Dashing into the tall oaks for cover, a short-cut back to the village, she had never thought to see *him.*

Like that!

Lana set the basket down on a dry spot beneath a thick canopy of branches and took a moment to catch her breath. Swiping a drenched blond curl out of her eyes, she peered around the thick tree trunk, unable to help herself. The fading light caught the silver glint from the cuff he always wore on his right wrist.

She looked at the lines of his body and blinked to clear her vision. Lightning and three black mares calmly grazed around the naked warrior in acceptance of the afternoon rain showers. From what she could see, Keegan's silvery gray eyes were closed, his angular face tilted upward as if listening to the rain's chant of faery whispers. The corners of his lips slowly curved and Lana had the impression the raindrops sang to him of their joyous journey from the stormy clouds to the green land below.

She watched him in silent fascination as any female would. His lean, well-built body was turned slightly away from her, offering a splendid view of long limbs and curved buttocks. If she leaned right, she might get a glimpse of that very impressive male part of him. Good sense took hold, however, and she decided to stay under the protection of the trees. Besides, she could see him well enough from here, she reasoned. He looked taller without clothes. All that smooth skin she could just imagine running the tips of her fingers over the ripple of muscle and strength.

Lana drew back. She must learn to curtail her over-active imagination. She might be impulsive, but she was not stupid. The gentle sound of the rain pattered consistently in her ears, and she tugged the laces of her damp tunic closer with cold fingers. Never could she hope to know the remote Keegan in that way, or any warrior, given her frail condition.

He stood not ten horse lengths from her, his dark hair falling in wet plaits down his broad back. He was not born of her tribe. However, he had earned the right to belong to the warrior class of the *Tuatha Dé Danann*. He came during the time of shadows only two summers before. A freeman, he worked hard and trained hard with sword, spear, and shield. Last year he fought bravely in the battle of Kindred, the re-capturing of their ancestral home from the invaders, yet still he was considered an outsider by many.

He did not partake of their ways, and did not seek

payment for his fine skills. Instead, he offered to help her father in the fields. A warrior on a farm? She shook her head in bewilderment and rubbed her wet nose. If she remained much longer, she might catch a chill, but feminine curiosity took hold of her and she could do nothing else but look.

"Caught in the spring showers, too, Lana?"

Lana straightened abruptly in surprise, her hand clenched across her chest. With flushed cheeks, she stared guiltily at the white-haired druidess, Derina.

"Your heart bothers you?" the druidess asked in concern.

"Nay," Lana choked, embarrassed at being found gaping at the naked warrior. She took a recovering breath, feeling the familiar twinges inside her chest. Everyone in the village knew of her weak heart, lack of stamina, and occasional fainting spells. However, unlike some others, the ancient was always helpful and sympathetic, which was odd since most members of the druid class were callous. She heard so, anyway.

"Come to visit that mean-tempered stallion again?" the druidess prompted, moving under the protection of the canopy. "What be his name?" Her white brows drew together and then she answered her own question, a common occurrence. "Lightning, methinks."

"Aye." Lana bristled slightly at the description of her friend. "Lightning is not mean-tempered, at least not to me," she whispered, hoping the naked warrior could not hear them. "He has mellowed much over the years."

The druidess was not listening to her.

She shifted right and appeared to be looking, if looking could be used to describe one who had no eyes and yet could see.

"Ah," the ancient said in a hushed tone, understanding immediately. She pointed her walking stick. "You be visiting another kind of stallion today."

Lana turned apple red. "I am not visiting," she said firmly in a hushed tone.

"Watching then."

"I am not watching," she protested.

The ancient smiled. "I would."

Lana looked away, wondering how the blind druidess could possibly know.

"He fascinates you, Lana?"

"Please lower your voice. I doona wish him to hear us."

The druidess nodded and hunched her shoulders, leaning forward. "He fascinates you?" she repeated her question with less volume and more emphasis.

"Aye, he does." Lana admitted grudgingly. Keegan captivated her interest since he first came to the tribe two seasons before. He always smelled clean and fresh like the rain even when soiled with toil and sweat.

"I know," the ancient replied as if reading her mind. She tapped a bent finger on a wrinkled cheek. "I may be one hundred and . . ."

". . . three," Lana offered.

"What?"

"You are one hundred and three summers."

"I know how old I am," the ancient grumbled. "Now, what did I want to say? Ah, I may be one hundred and three summers, but my fey sight remains strong. This gift be from our fey brethren."

"I know."

"It allows me to see shapes and movement; otherwise I would be walking into trees and tumbling into lochs."

"I know," Lana repeated patiently.

Empty eye sockets crinkled in merriment. "Now tell me, why does he interest you?"

Lana shrugged. "He is different, ancient."

"Different how?"

She wished the druidess would keep her voice down. Taking a moment to stem the flow of her tumultuous thoughts, Lana found she could not describe what she felt and instead blurted, "He looks perfect."

"You think so, do you?" The druidess laughed and Lana quickly motioned her to lower her tone.

The druidess nodded and then whispered, "I would not call him perfect, young Lana. His voice is too deep."

"Nay, 'tis not."

"His hands and feet look a wee bit large, methinks."

She shrugged. *Mayhap.* "His eyes are the pale gray color . . .

". . . of rainstorms," the ancient continued with hushed gaiety.

"Aye," Lana answered in all seriousness. "And his ways

are different than ours, too."

"This be true, yet has he not earned honor among us?"

"Aye," Lana acknowledged easily, having seen the quickness and strength of his battle skills.

"What else be bothering you about him, young Lana?"

She took a breath. "Derina, a warrior does not work on a farm."

"That one does."

The druidess made her answer sound so simple. Lana pointed over her shoulder. "He stands in the rain unclothed."

"Mayhap he needs a bath." Leaning heavily on the walking stick, the ancient looked around her, lips curving in what seemed to Lana a bold appreciation indeed.

"I have decided the shape of those hands and feet be perfect. Our fey brethren could not have crafted a finer male form." The ancient laughed softly at a secret known only to her. "Do you wish to discuss another part of him then?"

Lana shook her head self-consciously. Thank the goddess the warrior could not hear their conversation.

"Then I be curious and ask, did you find my linseed, Lana?"

"Aye, I have it here in my basket." Lana walked back to where she left the basket. "It is still early yet, but I have found a good patch." The blue flowering herb soothed the coughs and problems of the chest several members of her tribe occasionally suffered.

"Good," the ancient remarked, and followed. She tapped

her walking stick against the tree trunk. "The spring shower has paused for us so you may walk back with me. Come, my robes be damp, my bones be aching, and my stomach pains me again."

Lana could not help but smile. "Your stomach grumbles, does it now?" All in her tribe knew of the ancient's complaints. She picked up the basket and settled it on her hip.

"Lana, has your father made more of his sweet mead?" the druidess asked nonchalantly.

"Aye," she said and laughed softly, "I will bring some to you this eve."

✳ ✳ ✳

Keegan let a smile curve his lips as he listened to the ancient one's inner thoughts.

"I have fetched her away," Derina remarked in her mind so that he heard.

"I am in your debt, ancient."

"You should be." She gave her thought to him in a huff.

The druidess kept his secrets, an olden pledge always to serve the fey. She came as he bade. Being fey blooded herself, she responded to his mind call and claimed his inquisitive onlooker from the small grouping of trees beside the meadow. Lana was a lovely, sickly female of little worth. He valued strength and had little tolerance for fragility and weakness. Still, she was pleasant to look upon and he enjoyed the way her nose wrinkled when she smiled.

He turned away, his nostrils flaring in recognition of a familiar scent.

He did not want Lana to see the golden territorial goddess who also came to the rain drenched meadow and now stood in silent splendor, watching, waiting, her sweet fey scent filling the air.

Lana and Blodenwedd, though mortal and faery goddess respectively, were crafted of the same sunlit hues. Lana's mortal shades were softer than Blodenwedd's and he found her black eyes strangely alluring, certainly more so than the goddess's piercing amber.

Keegan felt wisps of gold in the air touching his skin and heard the horses move away.

"RAIN," the golden perfect one said.

He did not answer, did not move.

"RAIN," she hissed at him in exasperation, using his faery name.

Keegan lowered his head and stared down into flashing amber eyes with silver tipped lashes.

"Blodenwedd," he replied, bowing his head respectfully to the territorial goddess.

She pulled back the white webs of her robe's hood and Keegan once more looked upon the excellence of her features.

"WHY DO YOU STAY AMONGST MORTALS AND NOT YOUR OWN KIN?"

Boredom, he thought and arched a brown brow at her

reproachful tone. The fey born always believed themselves superior to mortals, though they themselves were not immortal, only extremely long lived.

"Foolish," she spat when he did not answer.

"Not foolish," he said very slowly. The tedium of life had led him to their mortal brethren, an inner curiosity, an interest to be part of their responsiveness to the land.

"I say foolish."

She was in a foul temper, he mused, nothing new. He adjusted the cuff on his wrist. "Foolish is the territorial goddess who continues to desire the Dark Chieftain of the *Tuatha Dé Danann* for her own when the Faery King has pledged her to another."

Her gaze slid away and he felt a twinge of regret for his harshness.

"I no longer desire him," she murmured.

"Good."

"I doona like the new one either."

"If you doona like the king's choice for your mate, Blodenwedd, then you should tell him."

"Tell? He doona listen to me," she said with an impatient turn of her hand.

"Who did he choose for you?"

She looked back at him, a dark light in her eyes. "You."

He smiled only slightly at her mischief. "Why are you really here, great goddess?"

"You doona believe me, Rain?" There was an open

challenge in her voice, a menacing quality to her tone.

"Careful, Blodenwedd," he warned silkily, his resentment aroused. He could detect the fragrance of her, the changing scent meant to dull his senses. "I am not like mortal men who bow to your every wish."

"You are male bred," she said, her eyelids lowered, and he felt the inspection of his man-parts.

A flicker of annoyance gleamed in his eyes when he saw appreciation light her face. He waited for what he knew was coming.

"Rain, I wish you to be my consort."

He placed a finger under her chin and lifted her gaze to his. "The king dinna pick me, did he, Blodenwedd?"

"Nay," she grumbled, admitting to the devious lie, and whirled away.

"Blodenwedd."

"I want you instead." She tossed her silken mane.

"You doona want me."

She turned back, her gaze hot and expectant, roaming boldly up and down his naked body.

"I can make you want me, *Báisteach*."

He did not like it when she used his olden fey name. *Báisteach* meant Rain. Keegan locked his hands behind his back in rebuff and looked up at the clouds. He could feel her anger and resentment brewing just below the surface. "Goddess," he said with extreme patience, "you canna make me want or do anything I doona want to do."

"BE YOU SURE OF THAT?" she murmured coyly.

He looked into her cold, lovely face. The game she played no longer amused him. "Be you sure, Blodenwedd?"

At his returned challenge, she pulled back in stunned silence. He guessed his defiance rankled her a wee bit. The look she bestowed on him was filled with such hatred he felt his only recourse was to . . . chuckle.

"HOW DARE YOU!" she spat in a full temper, the urge to kill shining in her eyes.

He peered at her with a strong conviction. "Why did you come here?"

She made a distasteful sound in her throat. "WANTS YOU NOW TO COME."

"Who wants me?"

"THE HIGH KING. COME NOW." She turned away, expecting him to follow like an obedient slave.

He did not move.

She stopped and looked over her shoulder, golden tresses glimmering with raindrops. "RAIN," she said in irritation.

"Blodenwedd," he cajoled.

He saw she struggled with his sweet and patient tone. "COME NOW!" She actually stomped her foot at him.

"I will come after the storm abates and twilight passes into night."

"Now, I SAY."

"After."

Her wraithlike body stiffened, her face turning cruel.

"YOU NOT BE SPECIAL, NOT EVER, GUARDIAN OF THE WATERS.
I DOONA KNOW WHY I WANT YOU."

A passing fancy, he mused. Whenever Blodenwedd did
not get her way, he knew from experience she could become
malicious.

"After," he said calmly, which only infuriated her more.

"YOU SHOULD HAVE DIED AT BIRTH."

"Then who, lovely goddess, would you dream about?"

Her slender chin jutted out and she hissed at him.

He arched a brow.

She shimmered then, dissolving into threads of golden
light and nothingness, or as the piskies would say, winked out.

Spoiled, self-indulgent goddess used to having her own way.
He knew her infatuation with him would pass in time, as it
had passed when all she could talk about was the Dark Chieftain of the *Tuatha Dé Danann*.

Taking a deep, calming breath, he closed his eyes and
threw back his head.

"Drench me," he called out to the clouds. Heavy rain
fell from the sky. He could not command rainfall. Only
when the clouds were full with moisture could he beseech
them. Being a full guardian of the waters, he sensed all
things having to do with water and always knew when rain
was about to fall.

"More," he whispered and fell to his knees, arms outstretched in entreaty, hands open. He glimmered in the
way of his faery brethren, his body changing, eyes tilting at

the ends, ears pointing. Gossamer wings unfolded from his back, forming into a webwork of shimmering silver, gray, and black filaments.

He stretched out his magnificent wings fully, relishing in the freedom of his true fey form.

CHAPTER 2

STANDING UPON A HILLTOP BATHED in a new moon's light, Keegan watched the fey woodlands shimmer out of a wall of white mist. A faery place seen only to some and hidden from most, he considered it a shadow place far from the sky.

The mist curled around his bare feet in a cool beckoning. He walked down the hill and disappeared into the woodland's night and vapor. Yellow balls of faery light winked in and out among the moon-kissed darkness and the tall ancient oaks. It was a haven of muffled sounds, of life-giving dampness, and of haunting enchantment left over from the before-time. A pulsing of life making him feel trapped. He much preferred the openness of the lochs and sea, so he took the long way, walking along the edge of a small creek for his own comfort, the sound of the clear water music to his ears.

To his left lay the sacred *nematon*, a circular clearing in the woodlands with a stone well at its center. It was a place of divine and earthy union for both the fey and their mortal kin.

He paused to look at the square stone well, feeling the silence of it. Rising before a thicket of silver thorns, four stone columns grew out of the well at each end, rising high with tips blunted at the end. At its base, brown vines and white roses twisted providing both protection and sweet fragrance.

Beauty must be in all things faery, he knew, and here it was at its most dangerous peak. He turned away from the sacred well and walked down a path lined with green and lavender ferns. The feathery plants parted for him in greeting.

After a time, he came upon two identical oaks whose massive trunks were thick with age and threads of silvery fey light. Long, knobby branches stretched outward, clutching the cool night air in silence. Within the leaves, silver glittered with the breath of tiny, watchful, and invisible piskies.

"I have come," he whispered, ignoring their scolding at his delay. Piskies bore the souls of the virtuous so Keegan always treated them respectfully. In spite of their prankish ways, they more often helped those who were aged rather than caused havoc.

"WHY DO YOU NOT TAKE YOUR TRUE FORM?" they asked in melodious voices. "WHY DO YOU NOT WINK AS THE OTHERS?"

Why indeed? he mused. It seemed his preference for the ways of the mortals spilled over into this as well. However, when the need required, he assured them he would wink in or out like any other proper faery.

They were not at all satisfied with his answer, but Keegan knew they would question him no further. Guardians of the fey did as they pleased without explanation.

He continued walking. To his right, he caught sight of a white owl perched on the end of a long branch. *Blodenwedd*, he mused, and dipped his head in acknowledgement of the territorial goddess. Circles of pale, golden, radiating feathers surrounded her forward-facing eyes. She turned her head away in silent disdain.

He grinned at her rebuff and walked beyond the trees. A boundary of black boulders led to the entrance of the hallowed place. The temperature dipped to coolness all around him and he felt the gleaming of the in-between, the place where mortal and fey met. A clearing of lush green grass rose up before him, spreading outward to a sacred waterfall tumbling from a tower of shiny rocks to a small black pool. Considered a sacred place of revealing, the Falls of Orchids was known only to his brethren, a secret kept from all mortals except the tribal chieftain of the *Tuatha Dé Danann*.

He looked around, finding it odd the Faery King bade him here instead of to Tara, the faery's new grassy hill fortress.

Keegan breathed in the new, clear night. A full moon bathed the land in eerie glow, casting shadows as if it were day. He came and stood before the edge of the rippling pool, drawn by the sounds of the water. Lichens and mosses clung to the fissures in flat rocks and along either side of the moving waters.

Around him, thousands of fragrant orchids grew. They were white and creamy blooms borne on stems surrounded by fleshy leaves.

"RAIN," a male voice said with displeasure. "AGAIN YOU HAVE COME TO ME IN YOUR MORTAL FORM AND DRESSED AS THEY."

Stepping back from the pool, Keegan looked to the right. The High King of the Faeries sat atop a boulder, watching him. While he wore simple dark green breeches and tunic, King Nuada gleamed in a long coat of silver, silver breeches, white stockings, and silver shoes buckled with diamond drops. Jeweled eyes stared unblinkingly down at him.

"You know my preference, Great King." Only then did he drop down on one knee and dip his head respectfully. "I have come as you bade."

"STAND, GUARDIAN."

Keegan stood.

"YOU SPEAK LIKE OUR MORTAL BRETHREN, TOO."

He nodded. "Would you prefer I speak like the fey?"

"I PREFER YOU COME WHEN I SUMMON YOU." The king gestured him close with an impatient wave. " STAND BEFORE ME, RAIN."

Keegan moved in front of the boulder. A few summers ago, he set aside the faery inflection to speak as a mortal. He felt a strong presence move with him and then materialize behind the king, and immediately recognized the powerful faery warrior, Lugh.

"REBELLIOUS," Lugh offered in a bold tone so that he heard.

He could not agree more.

"KNOW WHY I SUMMONED YOU, RAIN?" the King asked.

Keegan shook his head and glanced at Nuada's false silver hand. During the *Tuatha Dé Danann*'s conquest of the *Fir Bog*, the king lost a hand. Considered blemished, he relinquished his throne to Bress, a hero of the battle. For seven years, the vain Bress ruled in a tightfisted and inhospitable fashion, demanding unfair tributes. The guardians experienced many disputes with the new king.

All that changed when Nuada returned with a new silver hand, reclaiming his sovereignty and casting Bress out. Like many of his fey kin, Keegan was curious about the magical silver hand, but out of deference for Nuada, he never inquired. Only the whispers remained of a dark enchantment, *joint-to-joint of it and sinew-to-sinew*, performed by a gifted and mysterious healer.

"Do you summon me because of a problem with Lord Bress Mac Eladan, your predecessor?"

The king shook his head. "BRESS HAS RETURNED TO HIS FATHER'S PEOPLE, THE FORMORIANS." He waved his hand. "ACROSS THE SEA."

"He ruled unfairly."

"AGREED."

Keegan waited for his king to explain his summons.

"YOU BE THE FIRST GUARDIAN OF THE WATERS, RAIN."

"I am first guardian." Keegan nodded in concurrence.

"LAST EVE I DREAMT OF MY SWORD DROWNING IN DARK WATERS."

An image of the fey's great sword talisman flashed in his mind. "Is the Answerer not safe?" he asked.

"ANSWERER BE SAFE AT TARA WITH OUR OTHER THREE TALISMANS," his king replied.

The Answerer was the fey name given to Nuada's magical sword. When drawn, it would inflict only mortal wounds.

Keegan frowned. "My king, if the Answerer is safe with our other talismans then of what sword do you speak?"

"I SPEAK OF VALOR."

"Valor?" He stilled at the mention of the sword spirit of dark enchantment. Very few even knew of its existence and he saw it only once, a glimpse of bronze and spiral-cut bone.

"THEY HAVE STOLEN MY DEFENDER FROM ME," the king hissed, pounding his fist into his thigh.

"Do you know who has stolen Valor?" Keegan asked with great care.

The king shook his head, eyes glinting with outrage. "LAST EVE I DREAMT OF HER DROWNING AND WHEN I AWOKE SHE BE GONE."

"In your dream, did you see the waters? Was it loch or sea?"

"ONLY MIST AND DARKNESS. I HAVE ENVISIONED HER DROWNING YET I DOONA FEEL HER THREATENED, ONLY . . ." The king shook his head, unable to form further words to describe his strange dream. He looked up. "FIND VALOR, RAIN."

"I will."

"FIND HER AND TELL NO ONE."

He found the request unusual, but agreed. "As you wish."

In the next instant, the High King of the Faeries was gone, leaving only silver shards of light flickering in the air.

"No one must know Valor be missing, Rain."

Keegan looked up at the warrior Lugh and was cautious in his objection. "Would it not be wiser to gather the other guardians and have them aid in the search?"

Lugh shook his head. "Nuada wishes secrecy."

Keegan nodded slowly in acquiescence. Yet, he could not help feeling this secrecy was ill conceived. He bowed his head. "As you wish," he replied in a tone of disagreement.

"You oppose the king's desires, Rain?"

"Aye, I do, but I will find his dark sword nonetheless. He fears her drowning, yet senses no threat. I suspect whoever took her knows her worth, knows what they have, and will be cautious."

Keegan took on his fey form and dissolved into silvery threads of mist and starlight, winking out, leaving behind only vapor and misgivings.

He would never know Lugh believed him right, that the secrecy was indeed ill conceived.

In the darkest black of the predawn hours, Keegan returned to the land of men and shed his fey form. He stood outside the blind druidess's round, candle-lit cottage, inhaling her favored rosemary scent. All was quiet. A yellow glow spilled from the open door onto his feet.

"Doona stand there like an old goat, come in then," the druidess called at him from inside. The crone might have no eyes, he mused, but there was nothing wrong with her other senses.

He entered the cottage. "I have come for my weapon, ancient one."

The druidess turned to him, holding an empty goblet in her hand. "I know. Blodenwedd has already visited me." She tugged at her long brown robe, common cloth for her faith. "That goddess shows interest in things she should not," she complained. "She tells me the king dreams of his dark sword drowning, yet senses no threat to her."

He simply nodded.

"Odd dream," she remarked. Her white hair fell down her back in wild disarray as if she had risen abruptly.

He agreed.

"He has chosen you to find Valor?"

"Aye."

"Why? Because you be first guardian of our blessed waters and be sensing the blade when the waters touch her?"

"If you know this, why then do you ask me?" he asked impatiently.

She snorted at his tone then looked away. Turning left and right, she peered up at him with those empty eye sockets again, her mouth thinned in concentration. "Why do I stand here?"

Keegan blew air out of his nostrils and glanced at the long wood table, at the three white candles in the center, at the two plates of food, and at the single bronze goblet filled with goat's milk. "I doona know. Mayhap to fill the goblet you hold."

"Aye." The druidess grinned as if remembering just that. She headed back to the long table, a slow shuffle of age and lack of sleep. "Come and break fast with me. I have two plates and food enough to fill the belly of even a large faery as you."

"I doona have the time. Where are my things?"

She dismissed his question and said, "Sit down with me."

"Ancient," he warned.

"Sit and listen to what I have to say, fey guardian of the waters."

Disgruntled, Keegan walked over to the dark wood table at his right and sat down on a bench. A druid knew many things and this particular one committed all knowledge to memory. She did not believe in painted images and spoke her mind without care.

"Eat," she commanded with all the authority of a fey queen.

He looked down and wrinkled his nose at the offending smell. The ancient had a fondness for tripe, which was sheep's stomach. She would cook the stomach in goat's milk for many long hours and season it with herbs. He pushed the plate aside.

"You doona like tripe?" She sat on the bench opposite him.

He shook his head.

"Even faeries must eat."

"We do."

She pushed the goblet of milk across the table and under his nose.

He grimaced. "I doona care for milk either."

" 'Tis not only milk," she argued softly, and Keegan had the impression that if she could, she would have winked at him.

Reaching for the goblet, he sniffed at the contents and tasted the offering. "You mix mead with your milk, Derina?" he said with an approving smile and took another sip. He developed a deep appreciation for mead while living among the tribe of men.

"Aye, I do," she replied smugly. "How else do I live this long?"

He chuckled low. "You live long because you serve the fey."

"Aye, I have served the fey, but my remaining years be dwindling and I have much to say."

He set the goblet aside. "I listen, ancient one."

"Valor be missing."

All amusement left him. "I will find the dark sword."

"Will you, First Guardian of the Waters? And where, may I ask, do you look?"

"I will look toward the waters."

"Loch or sea? Do you also consider the black pools of

our Otherworld below, where your senses are dullest?"

"I will sense the sword when the waters touch her," he retorted.

"Too late, you will be."

For several long moments, Keegan toyed with the stem of the goblet while he regarded the lined face of the ancient. "How do you know this?"

She shrugged.

"Share your thoughts with me."

"You must take the *claíomh host* for your guide."

Sword Host? He went rigid inside at the reference to the olden fey legend.

"Do you even know what you speak of?"

"Aye, I do," she snapped in defiance. "Being old doona make my mind weak."

"I never said your mind was weak, Derina."

She huffed, not completely appeased.

"Tell me," he soothed, lacing his low tone with the soft compulsion of a fey guardian.

"You doona need that easing voice with me."

He smiled, bowing his head in acknowledgement of the fey coercion. "Tell me what you know then," he urged in a normal voice.

"The sword spirit, Valor, can only exist within a female host. When the union takes place, the female host gives up her humanity, transforming into the immortal blade." She took a sip of her mead-laced milk.

Keegan waited then asked, "What else do you know?"

"I know if the enchanted sword tastes fire for too long a time, the host will burn and die. I know if the enchanted sword lies beneath the surface of the waters for too long a time, the host will drown. I know Valor gives incredible strength to whoever wields her."

"You know enough," he grunted.

"In every generation, it be said, a rare few be born with the chosen host mark," she continued.

His eyes narrowed.

"She bears the birthmark of the sword spirit, Keegan, and I have seen the *duil*, desire, in your faery eyes."

"I feel no desire."

"You have the *teastaigh*, the madness and want."

Keegan scowled at the druidess. The *teastaigh* spoke of intensities, of yearnings, and of bone deep feelings. A guardian experienced none of these things.

"Know of whom I speak?" she prompted in a taunting tone.

His mouth thinned in concentration. A vision of fair-haired loveliness formed in his mind despite his inner protest. "Not the frail Lana?"

"Aye, Lana." She grinned triumphantly.

Keegan shifted in his seat, a feeling of unease settling within his being. "I doona believe it."

"Why?"

"She is weak. A sword host is strong."

"True," the druidess agreed.

"She is pure mortal," he argued, "untouched by faery blood."

"True," she answered again. "Yet, there be another olden legend that says the sword host be not born of faery blood."

"I have heard whispers of it," he grumbled.

"Do you believe it?"

"I believe the host canna be pure mortal, bear the mark, and be so . . . so scrawny."

The ancient grinned, showing gaps in her teeth. "Well, she be."

"You make no sense," he said in open quarrel.

"Your fey body hungers to lie with her."

Keegan's eyes narrowed at her swift change of subject. He pushed the goblet away from him, the sea waves etching on his cuff scraping along the table's slightly uneven surface. "If I like a maiden, I take her, but I doona hunger," he corrected her through clenched teeth.

"Horse dung."

He released a frustrated breath. "I am forbidden a mortal bride, Derina. There can be no mixing of the olden blood. You know this."

"I dinna say bride, guardian."

He had an urge to whisper a few words of enchantment so she would remain silent for the rest of her days.

"Lana be one of the rare *claíomh hosts*."

"What of the older sister, Rianon?" he asked, finding that one's curves more pleasing.

"Rianon's skin be unmarked. Only Lana bears the sacred birthmark."

"How do you know this?"

"I attended Lana's birthing and saw the mark on her pale skin."

Keegan looked away, mulling over the possibility of such absurdity. Both sisters born with the same bloodline, yet only the youngest bearing the sacred mark. "How can one daughter of the house bear the mark and not the other?"

The druidess shrugged. "It be."

He frowned at her. "If Lana is a true host, I must have her with me. Her instincts will guide me to Valor."

"If Valor does drown before you get to her, the spirit of the enchanted sword must have a new host near or all will be lost."

"I need no reminder." Keegan glanced to the open doorway once more where a new light formed across the horizon. "I will see this sword birthmark myself."

He felt the blind crone's pleasure at his assent.

"Lay your claim upon her with the mating bite," she urged, taking another sip of her drink.

That caused him to blink. The mating bite of the *Tuatha Dé Danann* was a confirmation of life, freely given by a male and freely accepted by a female. It was a binding promise to mate, which seemed to lead to handfasting ceremonies and babes.

"The fey guardians doona participate in such as this," he

said firmly.

She ignored him, which did not surprise him. "You must here. After you initiate the mating bite . . ." Her white brows drew together in open suspicion. "You do know how to initiate a mating bite, do you not?"

He glared at her.

"Well," she held up a hand, "I dinna know since you say guardians doona participate in this."

He spoke very slowly, struggling with his irritation. "Say what it is you have to say."

"After you initiate the mating bite, say the Claim of Binding."

"Claim of Binding?"

Her white brows drew together. "I thought you said you know the tribe's mating rituals. Stop scowling at me." She put both hands on the table and stared directly at him with those empty eye sockets. A lesser faery would have been intimidated, but he was not a lesser faery.

"Guardian, you initiate a mating claim by nipping her jaw without breaking the skin. Then you suckle the slight bruise using your saliva to heal. This leaves your scent upon her, warning other males away. The binding words come next. Do you know them?"

"Aye," he said tightly. "I know of them."

"Good. After the binding words comes the promise to handfast." She scratched her cheek in thought. "You may have to go through the handfasting ceremony in order to take her with you. Aye, that be the way of it, methinks. You should handfast with her quickly. Then she be free to accompany you on your quest for the sword without challenge."

"Who would challenge me?"

She shrugged. "Other males might and the parents most certainly. You have chosen to live among the *Tuatha Dé Danann*, so you must follow their ways, guardian."

"What males?"

"I have noticed a few of our males watching her. She be lovely."

"Watching is not taking. I can also cast an enchantment so no one will miss her and then take her with me."

"You could." Her dismissive tone indicated she did not believe he would.

His right hand fisted on the table. "Let me understand this. You expect me to bruise her jaw with my teeth, marking her as my possession?"

"Aye, the mating bite."

"And then I should use my saliva to heal the bruise."

"Mating bite, not bruise," she corrected. "And a male faery's saliva has the same healing and scent marker as our males. The faeries are blooded kin to the Tuatha tribe. We have the same ancestors."

His jaw clenched at her words. "I know this." Fey males and mortal males were not so different in many things.

"Guardian, if Lana's true destiny be a sword host, then she belongs to the sword spirit, yet . . ."

Keegan grew impatient with her pause. "Finish your words."

". . . other males may try and claim her."

Again, she brought up the interest of other males.

"What males?" he demanded. "Give me their names."

She shrugged noncommittally and he had the distinct feeling of being led to where she wanted him to go.

"If Lana be marked," he stated, "she belongs to the sword spirit and only to the sword spirit."

"Our males doona know she be marked, for none of their hands have caressed her flesh."

Caressed. The thought of another male touching Lana irritated him.

The druidess leaned across the table and patted his arm. "You must make a mating claim and protect her for the sword spirit."

"Protect her?"

"Aye, guardians doona have . . . hunger and yearnings as you say. They take what they want. Why should it matter to you? She be frail, after all."

A knot of frustration coiled in his stomach. "You wish me to make a mating claim upon one who the sword spirit may have already claimed. 'Tis forbidden," he growled in strong objection, "not to mention madness. I could be castrated by the Gods and Goddesses."

" 'Tis a simple enough answer to your problem: doona share your body with her. Doona take her virgin sheath and you doona trespass upon the sword spirit's claim. You be knowing our handfasting ceremony. It be a trial marriage, a temporary arrangement for a year and a day to ensure an heir."

Keegan muttered forcefully under his breath. "I know the tribe's handfasting ceremony. If no heir is born within that year and a day, both the male and female part without shame."

"By handfasting with her, you protect her for the sword spirit."

"If she is this *claíomh host . . .*" He pushed away from the table and stood, but the conniving old crone was not done with him yet.

"Make a mating claim upon her and doona forget the binding words, or Lana be wondering why your claim be unfinished."

"By the white moon, you strain my patience, Derina."

"I know," she said, grinning at him with those gaps in her teeth.

He stalked out into the growing light.

He was going to have to initiate a mating with a frail mortal female . . .

One he could never have . . .

Then, if she had the birthmark, he was going to have to go through a tribal handfasting ceremony to protect her from other males. He shook his head.

He should just cast an enchantment upon the whole tribe and take her, but deep down he knew he would not follow that path. It felt wrong and he was not a creature to go against his instincts. He realized he should have asked the manipulating crone the location of Lana's birthmark, but it was too late now. He would have to search her for it. Lifting his face to the new morning light, he inhaled deeply, searching for Lana's heather scent.

CHAPTER 3

MINUTES LATER, HE FOUND HER where the low tides surged relentlessly against the shore, sculpting and mating with the land. She looked north, a frown creasing her lovely brow. He lifted his face and sniffed. The scent of her carried to him on the warm air currents, and the scent of her moon time was not present. If she suffered her womanly courses, he would never have approached her with this intent. His lips thinned, yet he had to know if she bore the birthmark.

She stood quietly looking out to sea, her body turned slightly north, unaware of the teeming life just a short distance from her small bare feet. There was an abundance of life here; lobster, eel, salmon, shark, and the sea pig made these coastal waters their home.

His gaze skimmed the pinking horizon. To his right he could hear the joyous sounds of the gray seals hunting the sweet flesh of squids this morning.

He looked at the brown and red clusters of seaweed moving gently back and forth in the shallows in a feathery dance. A misleading tameness, he thought. For, beneath the surface lay a ruthless hide and seek existence of which his brethren were well aware. Far-away kin dwelled in the living, liquid depths, protecting and guarding the bejeweled waters that would turn bluer in the spring and summer months. Often times a white light shined out upon the far away waves, a sign from them all was as it should be. No light this morning, he mused, a dark omen of disquiet. He listened to the waves gently lapping over pebbles and broken shells. The salty scent of the sea filled his lungs in treasured coolness. The dampness lying upon his skin was familiar and welcome.

His focus returned to Lana, returned to the long blond hair cascading down her slim back. The breeze moved the green cloak about her dainty ankles and he felt the *duil*, desire, coil in his loins. He was a guardian born of the Good People, those faeries who protected all living things. His distant kin were the prankish Piskies who were no taller than a mouse, the nasty Spriggans with large heads, and the versatile Knockers who worked underground, to name a few. Only the Good People were still tied to mortality's fate, only the Good People could still mate with a mortal and be bound by that destiny.

Though a first guardian faery, Keegan learned to appreciate the ways of the mortals, the emotions they felt, the surprise and wonder in their hearts. He was curious about it, and in rare moments he actually ached for the memory of it, which had been forgotten when his ancestors crossed over into the magical world of in-between and became faery.

But not now.

Now, he needed to know.

Claíomh host.

Sword host.

"Keegan." His lovely quarry smiled. "I dinna see you there." She turned back to the calm sea, unaware of his sordid intentions and the danger she was in now. The druidess's words echoed in his mind. *"If Valor does drown before you get to her, the spirit of the enchanted sword must have a new host near or all be lost."*

" 'Tis a fine morning, 'tis not?" she murmured in an agreeable voice which carried swiftly to his sensitive ears. "The sky be bright with pink light."

He did not answer, did not stir.

Lana looked back at him and frowned slightly.

He remained silent in response to her greeting, an unusual occurrence. He watched her with light gray eyes, which were fixed and unblinking. Her heart picked up a beat. He stood unmoving in a green tunic and breeches. A strange intensity marked his handsome features. "Keegan?"

In the next moment he was beside her, as if wings had given him speed. Large hands cupped her face possessively. She could not escape even if she wanted to.

Lana stared up into smoldering eyes that swirled with hot streams of amethyst fire. She grabbed hold of thick wrists, the curve of his silver cuff cutting into her fingers. For the first and only time in her life, she felt a slice of fear. Always before, he remained remote, but now . . . "Keegan?"

"So fragile you are, how can it be?" he rasped, his face a mere breath from her own.

How can what be? She stared up into his uncommon eyes, the rich clean scent of him filling her lungs along with . . . "You smell of my father's mead."

A mocking smile curved his lips. "Derina's milk is sweet."

"Her milk has been much sweet of late. I dinna know you favored the drink before the day begins."

"You are not frightened of me, Lana?" he asked.

"Nay." She bit her bottom lip in nervousness.

His potent gaze lifted and locked on hers. "You should be fey daughter of the sword."

"What did you call me?"

"Daughter of the sword," he said with soft menace.

She tried to pull back, but he would not allow it.

Warm lips lowered and lingered over hers in wetness. "You said you were not afraid," he breathed.

"I am not."

White teeth tugged gently at her bottom lip.

"Have you been kissed before, my fair one?"

"Nay," she admitted softly. Never could she have imagined this.

His satiny tongue pushed inside her mouth.

Her heart lurched and Lana closed her eyes against the

growing excitement and fear.

He tasted of mead and of the clear essence of rain.

Something ancient and mysterious combined in her bloodstream, silver threads entwining into a new yearning, a coercion of spirit.

Strong arms tightened around her.

Lana felt her legs weaken under her, but he held her steady, his mouth feasting on hers, igniting a new found feminine hunger in her bloodstream.

Her mind became clouded with images of him, a compulsion of need.

The silvery tint of his eyes across the glows of the fire . . .

The gleaming sweat of his flesh in her father's fields . . .

The perfection of his form, unclothed in a rainstorm . . .

His mouth slid moist passion along her cheek and settled over the right side of her jaw.

He suckled and wild pleasure rippled through her . . .

Lana clutched at his powerful arms, holding on.

His teeth scraped along her flesh causing her to gasp and drag air into her lungs.

"So sensitive you are," he murmured with male pleasure.

Strong fingers locked around her chin and slid down her neck, caressing every inch of her heated flesh, searching. She felt enveloped in wantonness, her mind succumbing to a power of some unknown force. She couldn't seem to think beyond the craving of her body and the fervor of the male pressed up against her.

"I must see." His voice was hypnotic, mesmerizing.

See what? she thought in a jumble of imagery.

The bronze brooch holding her cloak closed landed in the sand with a thud. Then her cloak came away from her shoulders as if caught in a strong wind. Powerful arms slid around her back and under her knees. Lifting her, he laid her gently upon the soft folds of the cloak, his large body following her down.

His mouth was hot against her neck, sipping at her collarbone, and then he ripped the green morning gown from her shoulders, exposing her breasts.

Startled, Lana struggled against him but his mouth was insistent and covered the dusky center of her left breast. She choked back a cry of shock and pleasure, swept away by the sensitive agony of it. Eyes closed, she flung back her head, holding him to her. His large hands slid around her ribs, supporting her back, moving up and down her quivering flesh. He continued to suckle at her breast, sending ripples of desire through her. Then he latched onto the other nipple, his tongue firm and caressing, stealing her breath away. Never had she felt such a joyous yearning. Her hands tangled in the thick brown hair, holding on to him as if caught in a dream. The cauldron of flames within her grew while he continued to stroke and suckle her. She moaned, low and soft, fighting to have more of his hot mouth on her. He licked the underside of her breasts, her ribcage, and the flatness of her stomach. His mouth returned to the place on her jaw, creating an aching need. For a breathless moment, Lana thought he was going to initiate a mating claim upon her, her spirit eager and willing.

His mouth moved away. Large hands skimmed the woolen gown up over her hips and then . . . he abruptly stopped, his thumb resting on the raised birthmark above her woman's place.

Lana froze, caught between womanly desire and genuine dread.

She waited for his rejection, well aware of the mark of wickedness upon her unattractive flesh.

He did not move.

Her eyes fluttered open.

His head was flung back, veins pulsing in his corded neck. His long hair, a soft sheen of brown, fell about his broad shoulders. He looked wild, feral, like a predator suddenly ensnared.

Above her, his chest expanded as if with suffering and labored breathing.

"By the white moon, a true host," he said brusquely, and looked down, the harsh lines of a frown arching his fine dark brows.

His eyes gleamed critically as she stared up at him.

Lana blinked in confusion.

His eyes.

They seemed to be changing.

Light grays swirling into cool fires of amethyst . . .

The almond shape, elongating at the end, tilting upward . . .

His lips parted.

He snarled, baring white teeth.

Lana's eyes widened in maidenly fear. "Keegan?"

Then he leaned down, gently crushing her, his mouth clamping on her jawline in the mating bite embrace, teeth sinking ever so lightly ...

She went rigid in surprise and quick discomfort, her hands clutching the tunic across his sturdy shoulders. She had expected a disgusted dismissal, not a mating bite, never a mating bite.

Never this total seizing . . .

Her heart thudded in her breast and the discomfort slid away, forgotten in the new bold stirring in her quaking limbs. Eyes closed, her head tilted back against his arm, his mouth remained insistent upon her. She felt the tantalizing heat of him through his clothes melting into her flesh, the scent of male, the scent of rain strong in her lungs.

His mouth dropped away, the whisper of breath near her temple.

"To you am I bound." He took a ragged breath, the Claim of Binding echoing harshly in her ear. "To twilight. To honor. To land."

His decadent mouth returned to the throbbing in her jaw. The sensation was not unpleasant. She could feel the hard slope of his chest, warm and muscular, beneath his clothes. He suckled greedily at her jaw, forcing her head back further. Her world collapsed in upon itself. Her neck strained from his demands then a large hand wrapped around the back of her head in support.

A few seconds later he released her.

Breathing heavily, her eyelashes lifted and she froze at what she saw.

In glorious majesty, a male faery rose slowly above her, his handsome face formed of firm male angles in the palest of shades. Dark brows arched over catlike, amethyst eyes that watched her without tenderness. Gleaming hair shone with the darkest of golds, reds, and browns, as if drenched in rainfall. The thick strands danced in the air, curling around pointed ears.

He wore the silver webs of a moonlit night upon his body, showing the perfection of his male shape. Enormous wings of silver lace and black webs beat at his back in obvious agitation, spraying water upon her. He hovered above the white waves just in front of her, feet bare and humanlike.

"You are mine now, daughter of the sword spirit."

Lana struggled to collect herself and sat up in the looming shadow of him. With quivering hands, she held the torn morning gown over her bare breasts. She retreated, scooting back a bit, her mind slowly clearing from the compulsion of desire. She had heard tales of maidens being swept into passion with male faeries. Never had she believed it until now.

Eminent danger studied her, yet a familiar silver sea cuff of fine metalworking gleamed upon a right wrist.

"Keegan?" she whispered with barely a breath, unconsciously touching her jaw.

He nodded and landed gracefully at her feet, his magnificent wings drawn close to his back. Unblinking eyes
continued to regard her.

She forced down her fear. *Think. Doona let emotions
rule. He shows his true form to me for a reason.*

"You are faery bred." She stated the obvious, glad to
hear the steady tone of her voice.

He nodded, his eyes never wavering from hers. "Purebred."

Purebred. A new trembling gripped her. She heard many
stories of the ancient purebred faeries and they were not at all
comforting. She stared into his tilted eyes, feeling a long ago
past, a glimpsing into a magical and predatory creature. She
could not fathom him in any of the fearsome legends, which
spoke of intolerances and spitefulness.

"What have you done to me?" she asked in barely a whisper.

His cool gaze slid to her jawline. "Made you mine."

Lana shifted uncomfortably, the rising sun warming one
side of her face and bare shoulder. The rest of her felt chilled to
the bone. Tales of male faeries lying with mortals never mentioned a mating claim, never mentioned anything like this.

"Does my mating bite hurt you still?" he asked.

She shook her head, mesmerized, and pulled back when
he knelt beside her.

But he only lowered his head and then before her very
eyes, transformed back into the familiar form she knew.
Silver light glowed around him and a green tunic and breeches

replaced seductive silver webs. His wings vanished as if they had never been.

When he looked up, she found his eyes returned to their normal shape and color. The amethyst marker of his fey kin was gone. Slowly, he reached across her and picked up the old brooch where it had fallen. Brushing the granules of sand away with his fingertips, he placed it gently on her lap.

Lana held perfectly still.

"I will not hurt you, Lana."

The urge to laugh hysterically locked in her throat.

He seemed to be waiting for her to respond. She said the first thing that popped in her head. "Why do you hide your true form?"

"My own reasons."

A large hand reached out and gently caught her chin, tipping it sidewise for inspection.

"Why did you initiate a mating claim with me?" She looked at him from the corner of her eye.

"You are a *claíomh host*," he answered simply as if she understood what he meant.

She took in an uneven breath, unable to help herself. His touch was blistering on her skin, stirring the female places within her.

His other hand slid over the place of her birthmark and Lana felt the heat of it through what remained of her morning gown.

"Above the sacred woman place, you bear the fey mark of

the sword host." He sounded almost reverent.

"You initiated a mating claim with me because of my . . . birthmark?"

She could not believe it.

Keegan could not believe it either.

He felt lost in the haunting depths of her black eyes.

" 'Tis the sword spirit, Lana," he explained softly, and saw she did not understand. An innocent mortal bearing an ancient magical mark did not sit well with him. Legend always said the *claíomh host* would be strong, would have some faery blood in the veins, even if but a drop. She had none.

As he looked into her eyes, he felt a desire to comfort her, to touch her, emotions he never felt before. He blinked, letting them settle and dissolve within him, but still this strange yearning remained and his arms froze with indecision.

Never did he feel.

Not like this.

Not hot and hurtful.

He looked at her, confused by what she did to him.

"Keegan?" she whispered, lighting a liquid ache in his blood.

She seemed fragile to him, a creature easily broken. The sweet heather scent of her, like the sea itself, filled him with longing. She was unbled, a virgin waiting to be claimed by a male, or by a sword spirit.

His hold tightened on her chin. "Who has seen this birthmark?" He needed to know.

"The druidess and my parents."

"Anyone else?"

She frowned. "The head simpler too, long ago, when I was young."

"The simpler Rose, the tribe's healer?"

"Aye." She tried to pull out of his hand. "Birthmarks are wicked and should be kept hidden."

"Your parents told you this?"

"Aye."

"It is an old belief that these marks are the marks of evil. They are not."

"What are you doing?"

Bending her back with casual ease, he sniffed at his first ever mating mark, feeling a wave of possession. "I must finish what I have begun. You should feel no discomfort from my touch." He held her close, small breasts full against his chest.

"Stop."

His mouth lowered over his mating mark again. She belonged to him now. This daughter of the sword would guide him to Valor. He must take good care of her.

"Keegan, stop!"

He stilled her struggles. "Let me finish."

"This mating claiming is forbidden," she cried out, pushing against his chest. "You are purebred faery."

True, he thought, somewhere in the unseen reaches of his mind. "I have made my claim for you," he breathed against her sweet flesh. *In spite of the sword, in spite of what we will face. I will protect you.*

He hadn't much time. Pulling back, he looked into her wide, night-hued eyes. "Lana," he breathed, tasting the saltiness of tears staining her cheeks. "You must trust me for I need your help in finding the sword."

He needs my help to find a sword. What sword?

Lana stood beside an open shutter in Derina's thatched cottage, her eyes focused on the northern horizon. She was alone with the druidess. In her right hand, she held a goblet of water mixed with the blackish root of a supportive herb for her heart. It was late afternoon, the dark memory of Keegan's touch still warm in her blood.

It was not until after, when he brought her back to the druidess's thatched cottage, the resentment and bodily weakness had come. She was careful to keep the fatigue hidden, but the druidess noticed all things.

She looked down at the familiar old brown tunics and breeches Derina retrieved from the back room. She spent so much time helping the druidess with her chores that she always left a clean change of clothes here. Despite the warmth emanating from the fire circle at the center of the cottage, she continued to battle the trembling over what happened and the knowledge that came after.

Keegan is a purebred faery and wants to handfast because he needs my help finding. . . the sword. Not *a* sword, she thought in dismay, but *the* sword. *Whatever that meant.*

She finished her heart tonic and set the goblet aside. Lana wrapped her arms around herself. Ancient shadows and dangerous obscurity permeated Keegan's presence, something best left hidden, except now she knew.

Now she knew.

Knew exactly what had watched her with an unemotional gaze.

Knew exactly why he was so swift.

Knew exactly why the perfection of his features lured her. *He is faery.*

She continued to look out toward the northern horizon, trying to clear her mind and calm her fears.

Hours before, Keegan brought her here and then left with a promise to return. What was she going to do?

"I must go home," she murmured to herself, turning away and walking over to the fire circle, unconsciously seeking its warmth.

"You will," the druidess replied from her right.

Lana glanced over her shoulder into the withered face and felt a sense of dread.

"He has claimed me," she said in dismay, touching her jaw where the mating mark could still be seen. "He said the Claim of Binding to me."

"Aye, he has," the ancient agreed. "A fine claiming it be, too."

Lana frowned at the druidess's pleased tone. "He wishes to handfast."

"Aye."

"He doona know about my heart."

"I doona think so."

Lana bit her lip. "I should tell him."

"If you must."

She stared at the druidess. "This claiming is forbidden."

"Why?"

She was unwilling to reveal Keegan's secret, but something in the druidess's face gave her pause. Her eyes widened. "You know what he is," she accused.

"I know."

"Ancient, he is a purebred faery," she said aloud to make it real. "A faery," she emphasized, still caught in disbelief.

"Aye, young Lana, he be faery," the druidess said gleefully. "I doona think you know how distinctive and dangerous he be."

Lana did not understand.

"Do you know the legend of the fey guardians?" the druidess prompted.

"The legend speaks of the fey guardians as being living shields. Many believe they served the Gods and Goddesses in the long ago time but now serve the High King of the Faeries. They are deadly and fiercely protective of the natural ways and of all living creatures. They are among the oldest of the faeries, yet something far more mysterious and magical.

All my tribe believes in them."

"And wisely so." Derina scratched her chin.

"They live in mist and shadow," Lana added, "rarely seen except in matters of justice."

"True."

"Are you saying Keegan is a guardian then?" she asked.

"Aye, Keegan be a first guardian of the waters."

"A first guardian of the waters?" she echoed in amazement.

"Do you know what that means?"

"He protects all of our waters, the lochs, seas, rains, all of it."

"Aye, he does," the ancient said, satisfied by her knowledge.

Lana shivered, hugging herself tighter. No mortal ever survived a battle with a guardian, let alone a first guardian.

"A first guardian of the waters," she said again, more softly this time, still unable to believe it even though she knew she must. Derina never lied. First guardians were the wisest and most powerful of the fey guardians. They were also the most intolerant of weakness.

The ancient motioned her to sit at the long table where a small pot of stew waited.

Lana glanced at the table, feeling slightly sick.

"Come eat," the druidess said. "You must stay strong."

"Why does he want me?" she said, voicing her thoughts aloud.

"Sit, young Lana."

"I am not hungry."

"You will be."

Reluctantly, Lana walked over to the table. Her mouth watered at the tantalizing scent of stew stock, mutton, and herbs. Beside the cooling pot, a long round loaf of spotted barm brack bread rested on a plate, waiting. She remembered the flavor of the light and spongy texture of the bread. The last time she had a slice had been in *Deireadh Fhómhair*, the end of autumn, October, during the celebration of *Samhain*. The festival of the dead welcomed the onset of winter's darkness and of in-between, a time when boundaries were broken and the dead roamed the land. She much preferred the smell of flowers and spring. Reluctantly, she sat down at the table.

The druidess cooked whatever she wished, whenever she wished, regardless of the season. Even though everyone else waited for *Samhain* to prepare bram brack bread, the druidess made it all year long. Sitting with her back to the wall, Lana ran a finger along the smooth edge of the plate holding the bread.

"Eat. You will feel better," the druidess encouraged.

Reaching out, Lana took a slice of bread and found she was ravenous. Derina poured some of the stew onto a plate and Lana ate. After a time, when her hunger was sated, she looked up. The ancient had taken a seat across from her and waited, watching with empty eye sockets.

She pushed the plate aside, feeling better.

"My food be tasty?"

"Always." Lana smiled.

The ancient nodded and folded her hands on the table. "Now, I answer your questions."

"Tell me why this has happened."

"The guardian does the telling."

Lana curtailed her frustration. "Tell me then, why does a fey guardian live among us?"

The druidess rose, retrieved a bronze goblet, and returned to the table. She sat back down, her face grave. For a long moment, she tugged on her white plaits as if settling things in her own mind and then reached for the goblet to take a sip of its contents.

"I canna say, Lana."

"Please, Derina. He has initiated a mating claim with me and wishes to handfast."

The druidess took a deep breath and nodded to herself. "Keegan yearns for that which be lost to him."

"I doona understand."

A strange sadness curled the edges of the druidess's mouth. "He yearns for those things mortals take for granted."

"Like what?"

"Surprise and wonder, for sure. Imagine standing among some the trees. Suddenly a tiny songbird lands on a branch just above you. Would you not be pleasantly surprised?"

"Aye, I would."

"The guardian would not. He senses the bird's approach, hears the flutter of wings, and therefore knows of its coming. He sees the delicate beauty of the feathers and hears the bird's song, but the wonder and simple awe of it escapes him. Can you understand this?"

Lana nodded.

"He be the first fey guardian of the waters and one of the oldest of our fey kin. Long ago, as is the way of the olden fey, he lost the feel of things. Yet, methinks, he hungers for it. "

"He hungers for emotions and feelings?"

"Aye, but 'tis dangerous for him. He canna be both fey and mortal, both knowing and unknowing."

"I am fey," Keegan replied firmly, standing in the doorway. "Doona make me out to be something other," he reprimanded the druidess.

The ancient waved a hand in the air to silence him. "Doona let it be said I offend a guardian."

"Would you even care if you did, ancient one?"

"Mayhap, mayhap not."

The fey guardian took the druidess's comments in stride, Lana mused, with no displeasure crossing his features.

"I would speak with Lana," he said, stepping into the cottage.

The druidess pushed up from the table. "Do the father and mother know of your claim? Have you promised to handfast?"

"I have spoken with them."

"And?" the druidess prompted.

Lana looked up at the handsome guardian with mixed feelings and waited.

Keegan realized the druidess would not leave him alone with Lana until she knew all of the details. "I told them I have seen Lana's birthmark."

"I suspect they were not pleased," the ancient said with glee.

His gaze narrowed at the meddling crone. "Not at first, but they soon realized I had come to ask for their daughter in marriage and to receive their blessing. Both agreed with me that a quick handfasting was needed. Does that satisfy you, curious one?" he prompted tolerantly.

"It does. When be the ceremony?"

"Day after tomorrow," he answered. "Now, I must ask that you leave us, Derina."

Reaching for her crooked walking stick at the doorway, the ancient grumbled something about being kicked out of her own home and shuffled out into the warm sunlight.

Lana sat very still at the table. She soon found herself the sole focus of that hypnotic fey gaze. Even though he told her parents he had seen her birthmark, she found it difficult to believe they would agree to her handfasting with a faery.

"We must talk, Lana." He gestured to the table. "May I sit?"

She nodded and watched as he took his seat across from her.

He looked like the Keegan she knew.

"The druidess has made stew and bread. Would you like some?" she inquired politely.

He shook his head.

She stared at him, unable to help herself, searching for what lay within.

"I have not changed since last we met."

An understatement, she thought. Her hands locked in her lap. "What do you want of me?"

"First, I want your word to handfast with me."

"Why?"

"Because I have made a mating claim upon you and it must be willingly accepted."

"You have my parents' blessing," she rebuked softly.

"I want yours."

"You are a faery."

He arched a brow at that obvious fact and she found herself frowning. She realized quickly that desire and passion had not prompted the mating claim. Something else stirred him, and her jaw grew rigid with resentment. Why did he not value her for who she was? She had so much to offer, if only given a chance. For the briefest of moments, she wanted to hurl a variety of caustic insults at that handsome face and tell him what he could do with the mating claim.

"I suppose you claimed me because of a birthmark you believe will somehow help you find a missing sword," she said.

He conceded, which only added to her bitterness. "I need your help to find the sword, Lana."

"How can I help you find a sword?" she said, barely managing to contain her fury.

"You bear the birthmark of the sword host above the

sacred female place."

" 'Tis only a birthmark, a wicked thing," she snapped.

"Not wicked, I have told you this."

Lana looked away, the fury leeching out of her. "What is a sword host?"

He did not answer her question, but said instead, "I need your help."

She looked back at him, feeling wretched and hollow inside. A heavy sadness settled around her heart. "You are fey born, Keegan. Why did you not just take me, whisk me away into mist and shade." Her voice sounded despondent even to her own ears.

"I will not dishonor . . ." he seemed to hesitate, ". . . the sword."

"I am not a sword," she spat in anger.

His head tilted, eyes slowly searching her face as if seeing the hurt reflected there. "True," he said softly. "You are not."

"Nay, I am not."

They sat in silence looking at each other and Lana felt warmth rising in her cheeks at his continued perusal. She looked away and still she knew he continued to watch her.

"What has Derina told you about me, Lana?" he asked.

"You are a fey guardian, the First Guardian of the Waters. I doona know what that means." She looked back at him.

"I am fey," he said. "I am first guardian of our blessed waters, of the rains, lochs, and sea. I am protector. I battle and defend all that would harm and malign that which gives life to life."

"Why would the waters need protection?" She could not fathom anyone not valuing the waters.

"There are some who doona respect. I remind them." He sat back, folding his arms across his chest. "What else has the druidess told you about me?"

"You hunger for the wonder of things, for the surprise, and the not knowing."

A brow arched in disdain. "Did she now?" he challenged, and Lana wished she had remained silent to his question.

"Do you always listen to an ancient druidess who smells of mead?" he prompted.

"I always listen and then make up my own mind."

"A wise decision." He continued to look at her, searching for something known only to him.

Lana looked away. Out of the corner of her eye, she saw his gaze turn silvery and bright. His arms unfolded and she slowly faced him, feeling a strong trepidation at his continued scrutiny. He leaned forward, his face stark and intense.

She pulled back.

"Why do you look to the north, Lana?"

"North?" she echoed in relief. She thought he used his fey senses and found out about her flawed heart.

"You look north, Lana. Even now, as you sit before me and turn away, your eyes strayed to the cottage's northern window. What is there?" he urged softly. His dark velvet voice slid through her blood in warm compulsion. "What do you sense?"

She felt her body melting into mist and yearning.

"Tell me."

She blinked. "Tell you what?"

His eyelids lowered a fraction and she abruptly pushed up from the table, regaining control. "Stop that!"

"Stop what?" he murmured innocently.

"The compulsion in your voice. You are trying to steal my will."

After a brief pause, he nodded his acquiescence. "Methinks you would fight me much anyway."

"I would." Lana moved around the table and turned to leave. Her breath caught sharply at his touch.

He grabbed her wrist, holding her gently but steadfastly. "You have not agreed to handfast with me, Lana."

"Would it matter?" She spoke meekly despite the anger. "You have my parents' blessing. You could probably cast a spell upon me anyway."

He released her wrist. "I suppose I could. Do you wish me to conjure a spell? I would much rather have you willingly."

The air became heavy in the druidess's cottage as she stared at him. She could not win. A long sigh slipped from her lips and she reluctantly agreed. "I accept your claim."

He stood then, looming over her, and Lana stepped back, the scent of rainstorms strong in her lungs.

"We will leave after the handfasting ceremony," he said brusquely, turning away from her. "The druidess will pack food bags for the journey."

"Leave?"

"Aye." He headed for the door.

"Where do we go?" she asked, feeling even more uncertain than before.

"North, Lana. We travel north."

CHAPTER 4

It was morning, the day before her handfasting to an emotionally remote fey guardian. Lana felt vaguely terrified, angry, and restlessly excited. Placing her dried heather sash back in its wooden box, she walked into the main room. She wore her working clothes, a long sleeve green tunic, breeches, and worn leather boots.

A fire circle lighted the center of the main room, above which a gap opened in the top thatching, allowing smoke to escape and amber sunlight and blue sky to shine through. Outside, a blackbird's song greeted a sunny new day.

"Morning," she greeted her mother, Cara.

"Morning, daughter," Cara replied, taking a sip of goat's milk from a bronze goblet. "Come join me, Alana."

Only her mother called her by her given name. Alana meant fair among her people. Lana took a seat at the long table opposite her mother. "Where is Father?"

"He is out in the fields inspecting what Keegan has

ploughed for him. Did you sleep well?"

"Aye," she reassured, though she did not.

"Methinks we need to talk, Alana."

Lana thought to explain about Keegan and wisely kept silent instead.

"When you were born early, tiny, frail, and wheezing for air, I thought the rock faeries would steal you away and give me one of their bigheaded children instead."

Lana laughed softly, some of the tension easing from her shoulders. "They steal only healthy and special children."

"You are special, my daughter." Her mother's gaze took on a far away look, a look Lana had never seen before. "The sea calls to you and every morning you go to greet her. When twilight descends, you visit the high meadows where sky and land are closest."

Like him, Lana thought, studying her mother's tender yet sad expression. It felt as if her mother wanted to say, *like him.*

"I visit the sea because I love the sounds of the waters, unending melodies of silence and soft echoes. In the eve, I walk the high meadows where Lightning and the other horses end their day grazing. It calms me."

"Aye, I know your fondness for that horse, but you be full grown and must look toward other pleasures and calming, Alana." Her mother focused back on her and asked, "Would you like some milk?"

Lana startled at the question. "What?" Her mind had caught on the word *pleasures.*

"Milk, would you care for some goat's milk this morn?"

She shook her head.

Cara stood and retrieved a clay bowl of raw honey to mix with her milk. "Keegan came to visit us last eve while you were out."

"I know."

"Aye, I know you do."

Lana waited for her mother to retake her seat. "Are you and Father upset? Does he wish to speak with me?"

"Nay, Alana child, we are pleased by Keegan's claim. Your father considers Keegan to be one of the tribe's most skilled warriors. He is proud of you."

"He is proud of me?" she said in helpless disbelief. Her inability to attract a mate had been a great burden to her father.

"Aye, Keegan mentioned he has seen your birthmark."

That is not all he has seen, Lana mused, and looked down at her hands in discomfort. "I know."

Her mother smiled in understanding. "It is all right, my daughter. Sometimes desire overwhelms our better instincts, and Keegan is a fine looking male."

Blushing, Lana refused to comment.

"Keegan told us he believes the Gods and Goddesses have blessed you. He has convinced your father and I he will care and provide for you and we have given him permission to handfast with you."

Lana wondered if he also happened to mention he was fey born. She met her mother's blue eyes and thought not.

"You have always told me to keep the birthmark hidden. Does this birthmark make me special now?"

"Your . . . your father has always believed it to be the mark of darkness and I never went against him."

"Is that what you believe?" she inquired.

"Nay, I believe as Keegan does, that you are blessed by the Gods and Goddesses."

"I wish you had told me."

"I wish I had too, Alana child, but it is done. Now I need to know if you have mated with Keegan."

Lana choked. "Nay," she said.

"So he has touched but not taken."

Blushing profusely now, she nodded, her body tingling in remembrance of his touch, his mouth...

"Then let us speak of intimate things."

Lana averted her gaze.

"Keegan is full grown and probably has much experience. Methinks he knows to be slow and gentle with a virgin maiden when planting a seed in her belly. Daughter, look at me."

Lana lifted her gaze. Her mother conveniently forgot her moon time came but rarely and the simpler said she could not bear children without threat to her life.

"The mating hurts the first time, sharp and quick. Doona fight him. His root may seem threatening at first, but soon you will learn the passion of him and ride him well. Do you understand?"

She gave a quick nod, opened her mouth and then closed

it shut like a fish.

"Do you wish to say something, my daughter?"

Lana swallowed and then asked her question. "Do you think Keegan fey born?"

"Fey born? Nay, I have seen no amethyst marker in his eyes. Why do you ask?"

She shrugged.

"Alana child." Her mother reached across the table and caressed her cheek. "Talk to me."

"Keegan does not know the weakness that lives in my heart," she mumbled instead, her palm resting on her breast.

"There is no need for him to know."

" 'Tis not truthful. The not telling feels like a lie to me."

" 'Tis not a lie and 'tis a verra small weakness, Alana." Her mother's eyes filled with tears. "You are so beautiful and full of spirit like our fey brethren. I think most of our males are afraid to come near you for fear of rejection."

A painful ache settled in her breast.

"Keegan is a bold warrior and has seen the wonder and truth of you. This should be a happy time for you."

"I am happy."

"You doona look happy."

Lana pasted a smile on her face and her mother laughed again, shaking her head. "After the wedding night, this fear that grips you will subside. Then you will know the fullness and ardent mating with your mate. 'Tis a wonderful. . ."

"Would you like me to help you mix the honey with the

milk?" Lana interjected.

Her mother took the hint. "Nay, daughter. I would like you to finish your chores and then visit the druidess as she wishes to speak with you."

Lana stood and kissed her mother on the cheek, glad to end this conversation. Turning, she started to walk away when her mother called her name softly.

"Alana."

Pausing, she looked expectantly over her shoulder.

"I know you have always wished to be found valuable and worthy in our tribe. Because of how frail you look, few have given you the chance."

She had not known her mother understood.

"Keegan values you and finds you worthy."

"I know," she replied for her mother's benefit. "I love you."

"And I you. Now go, my daughter, for I have much to do this day before the handfasting ceremony tomorrow."

Lana strode out of her family's home and prepared to do her chores before visiting with the druidess.

A small meadow spread out before him, the late afternoon sunlight washing the grass in a blaze of gold. Behind Derina's home, Keegan practiced with his double-edged sword, mortal skills he felt would serve him well in the journey to come. He held his weapon up to the sunlight for inspection. It was simple and well made, the handle crafted from solid wood and flanked with a bronze guard to protect the hand. The blade flowed just under the length of a man's arm and the blood grooves on either side were crafted well. It suited him, a fey guardian who must be able to defend a *claíomh host* both in the fey and mortal places.

His gaze slid to the lone, bow-legged cow standing beneath the rowan tree. He supposed the druidess would be asking him for a bull next.

Turning to lay the sword upon the old wooden table behind him, he was unprepared for the cutting slap across his cheek.

"They doona know you are fey born!" his fair one cried, her voice hurtful to his sensitive ears.

He stumbled back in shock, unable to respond. He simply stared at her, no outward change to his features, his breathing under control, yet inside, inside. . . his very existence had been ripped out from under him.

She surprised him.

Surprised *him*!

It took a moment for Lana to see what she had done. A slash of red blood dripped down his right cheek where she hit him, open handed, and with full force. *Why did he bleed?* she wondered, staring at his cheek. *Red blood?* He did not bleed the white blood of the faeries? And why was he bleeding at all? She did not have a blade in her hand when she hit him.

"Your anger slashes deeply, *claíomh host*."

She glared up at him. "I dinna mean to hurt you."

"Did you not?"

"You lied to my family!" she accused, feeling shame for hitting him, yet knowing he deserved it.

"I dinna lie."

"Did you tell them what you are, guardian?" she demanded, her fists clenched at her side.

He shook his head slowly.

"Not telling is like lying," she said tightly.

"Not telling is lying?" he questioned in an inquisitive tone as if he did not know it.

"Aye!" she exclaimed, and felt a wave of guilt at her own secret.

"You know what I am. Why did you not tell them?" he asked quietly, his eyes watchful beneath the long dark lashes. Ice and fever battled there, emotions he kept hidden and closed off.

Lana turned away, unable to answer.

"You have no response?"

"Why are you bleeding?" she asked in avoidance.

"You cut me." He sounded slightly amazed, his long fingers trailing blood along his cheek.

"I slapped you," she corrected fiercely. "Never would I cut you."

He reached over and took her right hand in his, the one that hurt him.

"No rings on your fingers to accidentally cut flesh, just a

small, lovely hand." He frowned for several seconds, lashes hiding the shadows developing within him, and dropped her hand. "Your anger seems to cut fey born flesh."

"How can you say that? How do you know that? Never have I hit or slapped a faery."

His head tilted, blood dripping down his cheek. "Not only have I felt it, but I sense it as well, *claíomh host*."

"Stop calling me that."

He nodded, but she had the vague feeling he would call her as he saw fit.

A droplet of blood paused at his jaw line then fell to his collarbone. "Why is your blood not white, Keegan?"

"Would it please you if it were?"

"Faery blood is white," she stated stubbornly.

"Not all of us have white blood. Does this please you better?" he asked.

Lana blinked. In a moment's breath, his blood turned from crimson to the white color of snow.

"How . . .?" She looked up at him in amazement.

"Men anticipate colors, textures, and scents in a certain way, and I can influence to meet expectations. You see red blood because you expect to see red blood."

She rubbed her forehead. "So you have white blood then?"

He nodded. "I am purebred. We have white blood."

She understood that at least. "Who in the fey has red blood?"

"Why do you wish to know?" His tone turned cautious.

"I am curious only."

"Crimson flows in the veins of some territorial goddesses. There are others, too."

He held up his hand to halt her next question. "It simply is. Why do fish swim and birds fly?"

"Because that is the way of things." Lana understood and exhaled. "We need to stop the bleeding."

"Your anger has ended, thus the bleeding will end."

She had no idea what he was talking about, but the gash looked like it hurt. She stared up at it, willing it to stop bleeding and then unexpectedly it did.

He bowed his head. "My thanks."

"I dinna do that."

His mouth twisted. "As you wish." He turned back to the table and that was the end of it, no more discussion.

Lana sighed quietly. He might sense magic within her, but she did not. He looked young, this fey guardian of olden times, a graceful body, which was lean and sculpted with natural male perfection.

"How old are you, Keegan?" she inquired in a strong study of him.

"Old enough." He slid the sword into its brown leather scabbard and flung it over his back. Lana watched the way his body moved as one strap slid over his right shoulder and the other went around his lean waist.

"Where are your wings, guardian?"

"Where they always are."

Lana looked at the emptiness beyond his shoulders. "I doona see them."

"In this form, they are invisible to the eye, yet they are there."

"Does the scabbard impede your invisible wings?" she asked.

"Nay, it falls down the center of my back." He rolled his shoulders, adjusting the strap of the scabbard, and Lana moved forward to help.

He immediately stepped back, his eyes narrowed in wariness.

"I was going to help," she explained.

"I doona need help."

She locked her hands behind her. "Why do you even need a sword?"

"You ask a lot of questions."

"I am curious."

"You said that." It was obvious he was not going to answer this question.

"My father asked me if you would stop by our home this evening. He wishes to pay you for the work you did in the fields."

"I need no payment."

"No payment?" His response amazed her. All in her tribe sought payment in some form or another for work performed.

"Nay," he affirmed.

"Why do you plough fields? I mean, a creature such as you, sweating over soil."

"I like to sweat. I like my hands aiding the growing of

things."

"You do?"

His lips tilted in scorn. "Do you find that hard to believe? A creature such as I?"

"You are fey born."

"I am, Lana. Never forget that," he said with finality, and cupped her chin firmly, catching her by surprise.

He sniffed at her as if she were some fragrant herb on a stalk. "You are free of your moon time. We can handfast." In the next instant, he was gone.

Lana stepped back, startled. She was going to have to get used to this winking out, she surmised. It took a moment for her to regain her balance then she turned and walked around the two muddy holes belonging to the druidess's fattened pigs.

The familiar pail of water caught her eye at the entrance of the roundhouse. A week before the arrival of *Aibrean*, April, the primrose month, the druidess placed a pail of water outside her door at night to catch the reflection of the first warm rays of the sun. It was now the beginning of *Meitheamh*, June, and the pail of water would remain where it was, refilled often, until the chill of winter returned.

Holding onto the door frame, she called inside, "Derina?"

"Come in, Lana," the druidess replied from within. "I be over here."

She entered. The druidess stood near her long table, dressed in a gray robe. Twigs of dried, fragrant herbs hung on the walls filling the air with a calming fragrance.

"Have you seen the guardian outside?" The druidess turned toward her.

"Aye, we have spoken."

"Doona let his thick-headedness dictate to you. Listen to your heart and instincts and all will be well."

Lana's lips curved. "I will. You have always been a dear friend to me, Derina, and I value your counsel."

"A wise child you be." The druidess laughed smoothly and turned back to the table. "You will stay here for the night."

"I thought I would prepare for the ceremony at home."

"Nay, you will spend the night with me. Your mother allowed my request, fine woman that she be. We must talk of your new mate, Lana, and I doona want to feel rushed by those meddling women in the morning when we prepare you for the sacred bathing."

A faint sensation of longing and dread welled up inside her at the mere thought of handfasting with Keegan. "As you wish."

"Lana, bring me three white candles. They be in the large basket by the door. Three this night I need, all the same size, one for the maiden, one for the mother, and one for the wise crone. All these you will be."

Lana walked over and knelt by the basket. She knew the color of candles to be very important. White symbolized peace, protection, and strength through the moon goddess. Reaching into the basket, she picked the three closest in size, carefully lit the wicks from the center fire, and placed them in the center of the table.

"Good," the druidess said with pleasure, and carried plates of cheese and bread to the table. "Sit now and we eat."

With the wall comfortably at her back, Lana took her seat on the bench opposite. The scent of the dried fragrant herbs behind her and the cheese and bread in front should have made her mouth water. It did not.

"Let us eat now and give thanks to the Gods and Goddesses for all they have given to us. We talk more of your guardian after food fills our bellies."

"He is not my guardian," Lana protested.

"He be yours," the druidess argued kindly, and pushed a goblet of hazelnut flavored mead in front of her. Next came a small bowl of drisheen, common blood pudding.

"Derina, I mean no disrespect to you, but I am not hungry."

The druidess pushed her plate aside. "In truth, neither am I. Shall we talk then of tomorrow's happenings?" she asked warmly.

Lana felt a wee bit reassured by her tone, and nodded.

"You will sleep late until the sun be high. Your mother and our head simpler, Rose, will attend your first meal of the day. Then we join the women of the tribe for your sacred bathing."

Lana folded her hands in her lap. "What of my birthmark? The women will see it."

"They will not notice it."

She tilted her head in confusion. "Why do you say that?"

"You be handfasting to a magical guardian. He will do a conjuring so no one notices the mark upon your flesh. Now, be your moon time near, Lana?"

"It comes but rarely."

The druidess scratched her white eyebrow.

"The simpler says I am too fragile to carry a child and this be my body's way of protecting me."

The ancient huffed in disagreement. "I am not arguing with that foolish notion now."

"Why is my moon time important, ancient? Keegan spoke of this to me as well."

"In your misgivings, you forget a handfasting be not allowed during the time of a bride's bleeding. Brings ill luck to a marriage."

"Oh, I had forgotten."

"It weakens a male's root to take a woman during her moon time." The druidess shifted and pushed up from the table. "Come with me outside. I wish to gaze upon the stars while we talk."

Gaze? It always astounded her that a druidess with no eyes could see. She rose from the table and followed the smaller woman toward the door. The druidess grabbed her walking stick and Lana trailed her outside into the cool, beckoning embrace of blue tinted darkness.

The stars were out, sharing a white luminosity across the land. She wrapped her arms around herself to ward off the slight chill of the springtime night.

"You wed fey born, Lana. A powerful guardian he be, knower of secrets and long ago ways, a dark conjurer of magic and defender of the waters."

Lana wished it were not so. She wished Keegan were merely a man, but then, would he have wanted her?

"Doona worry, young Lana. You have your own magic to tame him."

"Tame him?" She stared at the druidess. "I canna even look at him without trembling inside."

"An excellent beginning. Your body wants him."

"Ancient!" she admonished in a hushed tone of forcefulness.

The druidess laughed. "Patience, young Lana, 'tis just the musing of an old woman. Shall we talk then of secretive and important things? You must listen carefully to all I have to say now."

She nodded, exhaling. "I listen."

The ancient looked up at the stars. " 'Tis a clear night for such a talk as this; the moon goddess gives us her blessing." She held up a bony finger to make her point. "There be three rules you must always follow when dealing with a fey guardian, Lana."

"Three rules?" Lana waited anxiously.

"Rule one, never challenge a fey guardian or dire things will happen. Do you understand?"

Lana nodded that she did.

"Rule two; never lie to a fey guardian."

She paled slightly. "I doona lie."

"Or dire things will happen," the druidess said meaningfully with a quick turn of her head.

Lana wondered what dire things would happen to her when the powerful guardian found out she had a weak heart.

"Rule three . . ." The druidess held up three fingers. "This be the most important rule. Never touch the magical part of a fey guardian."

She had a good idea as to what part of him was magical.

" 'Tis his wings I speak of, not the other parts," the druidess murmured with mirth.

"Why may I not touch his wings?"

"Doona touch them, that be all. The guardian will not respond in the ways you expect him to. He be different, Lana. Heed my warning in this. He be fey born and you know they follow different rules than men."

"Our tribe's chieftain wed a territorial goddess," Lana argued. "She be fey born and most wise and sweet."

"That be different. Long ago the Dark Chieftain line of the *Tuatha Dé Danann* be predestined to take a fey mate to return bounty and loyalty to the lands."

Lana looked down at her hands and gave a quick nod. "And I am not predestined to mate with a fey guardian," she added, unable to keep the edge out of her voice.

"I will not lie to you. This handfasting be unlike any other that has come before. He be a male guardian, a creature of great cruelty, and also great gentleness. You be a mortal born female. Let us see what happens before we say destined and fated. Now, think no more of it. 'Tis time to take our rest. You have a long day of preparation tomorrow before the twilight handfasting. Come, I have made a soft bed for you."

Lana started to follow the druidess back into the candle glow of the cottage, but paused at the shifting of a shadow to her left. "Keegan?" she murmured.

The guardian stepped from the shade of night and her heart quickened with a mixture of pleasure and fear. She wondered how much of her conversation with the old druidess he overheard.

"Good eve, Lana." He bowed his head in a formal greeting.

"Good eve, Keegan," she replied in kind.

He held out his right hand. "For you."

Lana took a hesitant step in his direction. A lovely brooch rested in his open palm. The gilded pin glittered with amber and golden granules.

"A small token from the fey." He placed the brooch in her hands. " 'Tis formed from the upland mists of Tara."

With her fingertip, she traced the round filigree surface and felt the weight of fine craftsmanship, felt the warmth of his flesh resonating still within the pin.

"Do you not like it?" he asked.

" 'Tis the most beautiful adornment I have ever seen, Keegan." She dipped her head in appreciation. "My thanks."

"What then bothers you?"

Besides handfasting to a fey born. . . She shrugged.

"Tell me."

"Tomorrow I bathe in the sacred Bridal Pool in the woodlands. The women of my tribe will see my birthmark." She shook her head. "Many among them continue to believe birthmarks are wicked."

He folded his arms across his chest. "Are you wicked?"

"Nay," she declared indignantly.

"And has the druidess not told you I will take care of it?"

"Aye, she has."

"Then doona concern yourself. They will not notice the birthmark."

Lana searched his face. "You can do this?"

He arched a sardonic brow at her and she immediately remembered their previous conversation about the color of blood.

"Men anticipate things and you can influence to meet expectations," she said.

He nodded. "The women will see what they expect to see — pale creamy flesh. Even your mother will not ponder upon it." He gestured to the brooch. "I ask that you wear this to the handfasting ceremony tomorrow to honor the fey."

"I will wear it," she promised quietly. No male had ever given her a gift before.

"I will bring my other gifts later."

Lana looked up in surprise, but he disappeared once again, leaving behind a simple sparkling in the air.

"Lana?" the druidess called impatiently from inside her home. "If that faery be gone, 'tis time to come inside."

Lana held the brooch closely to her breast. Turning away from the star-filled night, she headed back to the cottage.

CHAPTER 5

LATE AFTERNOON SUN SPILLED WARMTH upon his back, relieving some of the tension formed there. It was the day of his handfasting.

When twilight approached in a couple of hours he would take a lovely golden-haired bride, a bride he dare not touch, he reminded himself. He rolled his shoulders, a subtle movement masking the ruthless resolve forming within. Keegan took a deep breath and knelt silently at the edge of the loch.

"Tell me," he commanded. Dipping his left hand into the cool waters, his long fingers spread easily, seeking what he needed.

He donned a worn pair of green breeches, which rode comfortably low on his hips. Rarely did he wear tunics in the warm months, preferring nothing against his back. Closing his eyes, he bowed his head, listening carefully to the sounds of the waters, his thick brown hair falling over one powerful shoulder.

No sense of Valor did he feel, only a thread of anger, a sliver of dread, and then nothing.

It came as a small shock, that he, the great first guardian of the waters, a powerful and deadly faery, needed Lana . . . needed a mortal female to find the missing fey sword.

Lana.

A vision of slender beauty formed in his mind and his body immediately quickened in response.

Yearning.

Desire.

Want.

He remembered that long ago night, an unwelcome flash of memory, forever haunting him.

An expanding night sky awash in brilliant star clusters . . .

The black waters of a running stream, flowing in musical tones . . .

A pile of manly clothes at the edge, he thought nothing of it until he caught the faint scent of woman and heather . . .

A slender nymph knelt naked in the waters, washing the untamed mane of golden fire.

He remained in stillness under the cover of tree canopies, watching . . .

Moonlight spilling down upon her.

The swell of her breasts quivered with her movements, her nipples surprisingly large and pink.

She stood in graceful silence, her body full of slender womanly curves, her golden fleece far lovelier than any other he had ever seen.

He had wanted her then.

Brimming with lust, he took a step closer, wanting to ride between her shapely legs and thrust in her silken cave until the night ended, and still he knew it would never be enough.

He bared his teeth.

He had not taken her then.

He would not now.

In the shadow of a waning moon and lust, he had not noticed the birthmark upon her flesh. A failing, he admonished himself, before refocusing back on the present.

His hand fisted in the waters, hunger and tension spilling into his blood, his man parts thickening in response. Muttering an oath, he focused by strength of will alone, a sheen of sexual frustration coating his body.

If Lana guided him to Valor, he had no doubt the great sword spirit would reject her should the current host die. *What then?* he pondered. And why had the sword spirit chosen only Lana and not her older sister, Rianon? Both daughters were born of the same bloodline, were they not? He locked onto that one thought. *Were they?* Had Cara, Lana's mother, taken another male's seed into her womb? That would answer why only the fragile Lana bore the magical birthmark.

His thoughts returned to Valor. If the sword spirit did lose her current host, and did reject Lana, would she, a sacred feminine spirit, accept his male body as a host offering instead?

"Rain, what be this I hear?"

Slowly, Keegan looked toward the sweeping female voice of derision, his body reacting as if he had dove into a loch of icy water.

"Blodenwedd," he greeted the goddess evenly, and stood.

Dressed in a white cloak of webs and fanciful scrolls, the golden goddess bestowed him with a brilliant smile. "Who be lana?" she asked silkily.

He smiled in return. "My mate."

"Take her over me?" she demanded in a sudden scolding, her expression turning cold and deadly. "Gave her a brooch of Tara?"

Ignoring her spoiled outburst, he walked around her and replied, "The brooch was mine to give." Stopping, he looked over his shoulder and tried to explain without giving away the secret. "Blodenwedd, I want this female."

"Liar. You want me."

In the late afternoon light of the day, he drew in a patient breath. "I doona lie, goddess."

"Trickery then."

"You have seen the Tara brooch. You know of its high honor when given to an intended bride, yet you question me?"

Her gaze narrowed in response and he took that as an affirmation.

"This mating forbidden, Rain. You be guardian."

"I know what I am," he said in a lowered voice, "but I will have her nonetheless."

She frowned, searching inward, finding a cause for his breech and choice of a mortal bride. "WHY DID NUADA SUMMON YOU? WHAT DID HE WANT?"

"The why and want be none of your business, great goddess."

"BE THIS ABOUT A MISSING SWORD?"

He did not respond.

"I KNOW OF VALOR, RAIN."

He chose to end the conversation and bowed his head respectfully. "If you will excuse me, great goddess. I must make ready to receive my bride." He walked back to the edge of the loch and dove into the cool, blue waters, seeking relief from the turbulence of feminine influences.

Keegan was true to his word. None of the women noticed her birthmark at the late morning cleansing in the woodland's Bridal Pool. She disrobed quietly in the shade of the brown-black boughs of the large oak. The tree stood at the edge of the pool, branches extending outward across water and shore. While maidens in white robes chanted softly, she waded naked into the cool waters. Three respected women of her tribe followed her in and then cleaned her with fragrant soap. Afterward, the blessings were given and she was brought to the druidess's home for her bride's preparation.

Now, it was time.

As she walked across the green meadow accompanied by

her mother and the druidess, her legs suddenly refused to carry her forward another step. The food she had eaten in the afternoon settled like a rock in her slightly queasy stomach.

"Alana?" her mother questioned.

Lana adjusted the blue hooded cloak and gave her mother a reassuring smile. The delicate bracelets on her wrists chimed lightly and somewhere in the trees a bird chirped in response. She felt vulnerable, a willing sacrifice to the needs of the handsome guardian, and nothing in her life would ever be the same again.

She looked down at the bracelets. She wore all of Keegan's gifts, gifts he said were given to him by the faeries to honor their handfasting.

Sea green combs, embellished with wispy golden waves were at her temples, pulling her hair up and away from her face. On her body, a sheer aquamarine gown glided upon her skin in a clinging dance ending at her ankles. She touched the soft bodice beneath her blue cloak. It felt like nothing she ever touched before. A thick gold strand held the gown in place, gliding from her back over her bare right shoulder and ending in a faceted stone of seashore hues above her left breast.

"Alana, you canna delay any longer. Twilight comes soon and Keegan awaits, as do the elders." Her mother touched her arm to hurry her while the druidess waited quietly to her right.

"I know." Lana looked to where the tribe gathered. Her gaze settled on the tall warrior standing apart from all the rest. Swallowing her unease, she strode forward on bare feet, the bracelets on her ankles ringing softly.

✴ ✴ ✴

At the east end of the ancient oaks, Keegan waited, anxious to have the ceremony done with and begin the quest for the enchanted sword. Behind him the handfasting circle of gray stones and crystal rocks stood beneath a sky of fading clouds. He supposed he should have just taken her and not dithered with ceremony, but it was too late now. His decision had been made.

He walked to the northern end of the circle where the tribal elders stood in their long white robes. The leader, a man by the name of Dafyd, tapped the blunt end of his hazel-wood walking stick to the ground with impatience. Keegan knew the dark-eyed elder with the limping gait would be the one to perform the handfasting ceremony. He nodded to Lana's father, and turned back to wait.

In the distance, three women approached. Framed by the twilight sky, one wore brown druidess robes, the second wore colors the subdued quality of a mother's trepidation, and the third was cloaked in the moving colors of the sea.

Keegan quickly checked his clothes. The blue long sleeved woolen tunic fitted him well enough, he thought. The stringed placket opened down the center of his chest from collarbone to waist. Earlier, he cut slits in the back

for his own comfort, his long hair covering the minor altera-
tions. He shifted his weight. The form-fitted blue breeches
were snug on his legs, but not overly so. He adjusted his silver cuff, his fingers subconsciously tracing the interlacing sea
wave design. While he preferred to walk on his own bare
feet, he had developed a tolerance for the foot coverings. The
leather boots, a gift from the druidess, were acceptable if one
liked their feet so encumbered.

His bride stopped at the opposite end of the stone circle
while the druidess and mother faded into the background.
He was pleased that she wore his gifts.

A hush came to the land and sky and to his innermost
being.

Behind him, the elder Dafyd said, "Twilight has arrived
and so we begin the joining."

The tuneful sounds of three bells tolled, only slightly
hurtful to his highly sensitive ears. His bride gave him a
gentle smile meant to reassure.

He tilted his head slowly, a feral movement not lost on his
fair one. Her smile dissolved instantly and she turned away.

He continued his strong inspection of her while four
maidens tossed red rose petals along the perimeter of the
stone circle. He could feel her presence, the uncertainty of
her heartbeat, the small intake of her breath fueling his need
for possession.

She took an involuntary step back and then walked once
around the circle, lighting torches the maidens held for the

four cardinal directions, East, West, North, and South.

She is brave, he thought, and licked his lips in anticipation.

Lana felt her stomach drop out from under her. She could not keep her eyes from him. The druidess said the guardian might need guidance in the handfasting ceremony and that she should watch him for hesitancy, but there did not seem to be any hesitancy in his manner. In fact, he seemed to be transforming into his true shape.

She moved to stand in front of him. Gray eyes shifted into amethyst radiances, tilting at the ends as if he were having trouble maintaining his mortal form.

"Keegan," she warned softly, and he blinked, there was a sudden focusing, and the faery light within him faded once more to light gray.

White teeth flashed in a grin at her, and for a moment, she had an overwhelming image of a stalking hunter. With her heart fluttering in her throat, she reached and pulled back her hood. He remained in quiet observation, his features set in an unreadable mask.

With shaky fingers, Lana unclasped the Tara brooch, his first gift to her, and shrugged out of the cloak. The druidess stepped forward and took the brooch and cloak out of her hands.

Lana turned back to Keegan. His lashes swept low, hiding the iridescent glimmering in his eyes, but there was a stirring in his body, a rippling of danger and supremacy thickening the air she breathed.

One of the elders rang the handfasting bell, unaware of the sudden change in him. A clanging melody rose three times in the air and she caught him flinching slightly. He looked fey born, a cruel and untamed creature of ancient power and beauty, the *Daoine Sidhe,* the faery folk.

Lana moved a little away from him, feeling a bit like a sacrificial animal.

Then his head tilted again, showing his curiosity.

She indicated the handfasting circle. "Twilight has come," she said, struggling for calm.

He nodded.

Taking her hand, he led her once around the circle, with a domineering and imposing stride. Then, stopping and moving aside, he placed a hand on her lower back, a gentle force propelling her forward. They entered the circle from the east and came to stand in front of a small wooden altar in the center.

Upon the altar rested a silver knife, a single red cord, a small silver box, and a trowel. Lana saw her guardian eyeing the trowel questioningly.

The handfasting bell rang three times once more to mark the beginning of the ceremony and the elder Dafyd entered the circle. He faced them from the other side of the altar. Holding up both hands, he began the blessing.

❧৵

"Let us begin in the east. Here we ask for the
blessings of the element of Air, which brings truth,
wisdom, and vision. May East and Air bless
Keegan and Lana throughout their lives."

❧৵

"Now, we turn to the south. Here we ask for the
blessings of the element of Fire, home of passion,
pleasure, joy, and happiness. May South and Fire
bless Keegan and Lana throughout their lives."

❧৵

"Now, let us turn to the west. Here we ask for the
blessings of the element of Water, bringing tranquility,
peace, emotion, and serenity. May West and Water
bless Keegan and Lana throughout their lives."

❧৵

"Now, we turn to the north, where the element
of Earth resides, deeply grounded in strength,
comfort, and support. May North and Earth bless
Keegan and Lana throughout their lives."

❧৵

"And in the Center and all around us, above and below,
resides the Spirit who brings blessings of love, magic, friendship, and community. May the Spirit of all things divine
join us and bless Keegan and Lana on this sacred day."

❧৵

Lana turned and faced Keegan.

"Take my hands," she whispered, slipping her hands in his.

"Do any here challenge this joining?" the elder leader asked, looking around.

Keegan's features hardened, his focus on the men.

No one responded, and Lana breathed a small sigh.

"Then let us begin the joining," the elder said, and turned to them once more.

"Keegan, do you come of your own free will?"

He nodded.

"You must say 'I do'," the elder directed.

"I do."

"Lana, do you come of your own free will?"

"I do," she replied softly.

"Then state your vows."

She tugged on his hands. "Say these words with me."

He shook his head and something fearful tugged at her heart.

"Nay, my fair one. You say these words after me." His voice sounded almost tender.

Lana nodded, wondering what words he would use.

"We commit ourselves to be with each other in joy and in adversity," he began; his grip on her hands gentle but controlling.

Lana echoed the words, immediately recognizing the olden vows.

"In wholeness and brokenness," her guardian mate said,

in a deep dark cadence.

"In wholeness and brokenness," she said, staring up at him in wonder.

"In peace and turmoil."

"In peace and turmoil," she continued, feeling a sense of permanency washing over her.

"Living together faithfully all our days," he said. "May the Gods and Goddesses give us the strength to keep these vows. So be it," he ended.

She repeated the final phrase.

The elder stepped forward and placed a red cord over and around their right hands.

"Red symbolizes life and a handfasting commitment for one year and a day," the elder said. "If our faery brethren approve and your bodies join in a child, you may return and repeat the vows with the cord tightly knotted to show a permanent joining. If not, the trial-marriage ends and you may go your separate ways if you so choose."

The elder bowed over the red cord, said a brief blessing, and then removed it, returning it to the altar. Picking up the small knife, he handed it to Keegan.

Her guardian immediately reached for a blond curl lying on her breast and cut it cleanly. He placed the curl in the silver box the elder held.

He then held the knife out to her, his large palm open. Lana took the knife. She cut a lock of Keegan's brown hair and placed it in the silver box over her own curl.

The elder closed the silver box. "For the future," he said, and returned the box to the altar.

Keegan took both her hands in his again.

"Be understanding and patient with each other," the elder murmured, backing away. "Be free in the giving of your affection and your warmth. Have no fear inside your hearts and let not the ways of the unenlightened give you unease, for the Gods and Goddesses be with you always." He stepped out of the circle.

Lana turned to her guardian mate.

"Together we must bury the silver box in the center of the circle to safeguard our future."

He picked up the trowel and Lana placed her right hand over his.

He stilled and looked at her skeptically.

"Together, Keegan."

He nodded and she leaned forward with him.

They dug a small hole, her new guardian mate doing all the work.

Together they placed the silver box in the hole and covered it beneath a lumpy mound of dirt.

From outside the circle, the elder called out, "The circle remains open but unbroken. May the peace of the Old Ones go in our hearts. Keegan and Lana are handfasted."

The handfasting bell rang three times.

"For a year and a day, we are handfasted," Lana whispered.

" 'Tis more than enough time," her guardian mate

replied without merriment. He took her arm and led her out of the circle.

" 'Tis time to feast and celebrate!" Dafyd raised his walking stick high. A loud, joyous roar rose in the twilight air, but it did little to lighten Lana's heart.

CHAPTER 6

SHE BELONGED TO HIM NOW, every delicate eyelash, every blond curl, every soft breath, *his*. The scent of his mating bite on her sweet flesh made him sweat. Some primordial influence, he suspected, the *teastaigh*, the madness and want, a forgotten taint in his ancient bloodline, blazing now like an unexpected fever because of the handfasting.

He was *Báisteach,* Rain.

He was *Daoine Sidhe,* of the faery folk.

He was olden and powerful.

A deadly, fey born guardian.

Meant to be feared . . .

He found he could not move.

"Are you thirsty, Keegan?" With two hands, his lovely, fair-haired mate held a large goblet of bronze out to him. " 'Tis my father's mead," she explained, seeing his hesitation.

He was not thirsty for mead. Reaching out with one hand, he took the fine goblet from her anyway. Hefty and crafted with the metalworking swirls of a devouring whirl-pool, it seemed to intend the drinker to be sucked into the very depths of its contents. *A cauldron for a male's hand*, he thought admiringly, and brought the smooth edge to his lips. He finished the contents in one long swallow, enjoying the sweet burning sensation streaming down his throat. Wiping his mouth with the back of his hand, he looked down at his beaming bride and nearly flinched at the happiness he saw there.

The clinging bodice showed the swells of small breasts. He frowned, deeply regretting having given her the fey gown as a gift.

She touched the gown's fluttery webs above her left breast self-consciously. "My thanks for your gift."

He looked away and nodded, wondering when he could toss her over his shoulder and leave the infernal celebration.

" 'Tis lovely, Keegan."

He nodded a second time. Lovely would not be how he would describe the sea-hued gown, more like enticing, an alluring weave meant to destroy a male's willpower. What had he been thinking? She was not fey born, not water faery, never was she meant for the sheerness of webs his fey brethren wore. He looked back at her again, his focus moving downward in a slow perusal. Through the fey weave, he could make out the shape and color of her nipples. They were large, especially for breasts so perfectly small and shaped. He could fit his mouth over . . .

"Would you like some food?" She regarded him curiously, unaware of his growing displeasure, looking up at him with those night-hued eyes that would forever torment him.

He thrust the goblet back in her hands and said icily, "I still thirst."

Her smile faded a wee bit, a slight tremble in her chin, but she nodded bravely and took the goblet from his hands. With narrowed eyes, he watched her walk away, watched the seductive flow of her, his senses slowly shrouding in lust until all he saw, smelled, and sought was *her*. He muttered an oath and looked away. He wanted to lie down with her in a bed of sea foam waves and ride the tide between her legs until this terrible craving in his loins was sated, but she did not belong to him. He must remember that.

During the time it took her to return with his mead, his mood continued to turn dark. A single beaded strand was the only thing holding the gown in place. With a simple gesture of hand, the fey gown would respond to him and pool at her feet, freeing her body for his use. Dragging the warm air into his lungs, he angrily crushed down his lust and looked around at the merrymaking. The sword spirit claimed Lana long before he ever did, and he must abide by that decree or face the consequences. He was not a fool. If he took her virgin sheath, *there would be consequences*.

He moved away from where he stood to a small group of bushes. To mark the celebration of the handfasting, tar barrels were set ablaze in the spring night air, adding to the sense of life's promise and joy. Ropes, dipped in tar, hung from stakes, which were securely placed in the ground, but at a safe distance from the trees and homes. Even the animals were secured in their stables, mews, and pens. All precautions had been taken so the fire spirit would hurt no living creature while it gave blessing to their union.

He had watched in fascination while Lana lighted the ropes with a torch. An easygoing cheer echoed among her tribesmen as the fire, a tribute to both light and elation, raced across the ropes with the swiftness of lightning.

Her people milled about in their finest garments and adornments. Young revelers held twigs of oak high above their heads with streaming white ribbons. Maidens giggled curiously among themselves, reminding him that all females were alike in their feminine mystery. Locking his hands behind his back, he watched three boys play a game of tag and chase. He could never truly be part of this, he reflected darkly. Always, he would remain separate from them because of what he was. He scanned the tribe, noticing a few men who drank more than their share of mead and lay prone on the ground, muttering gleefully of their many conquests in love. He bit back a smile, remembering the tedium of his long life. He turned to the mortals for distraction, participated in their wars and in their ways, and found a strange contentment in it. The answers he sought for his restlessness remained elusive to him, and he reluctantly accepted it.

"Keegan? I have brought you your mead."

Turning to Lana, he resisted the urge to smile and took the goblet from her hands.

Lifting the goblet to his lips, he was surprised when a small finger inserted itself between his mouth and the fruitful drink.

He looked down at the foolishly naïve owner of the dainty finger.

"Would you care to eat something?" Her smile was faint.

"Remove your finger," he said in a whisper of breath, not at all amused.

Blushing pink, she did as he bade, dropping her hand to her side.

He followed the way her hands twisted in the folds of her gown, marking her anxiousness. Eyelids lowering, he lifted the goblet to his lips, and once more, a small finger came between him and his liquid intention. He experienced a peculiar urge to take her finger into his mouth.

"Keegan."

Tilting his head in acknowledgement of her, he waited for her explanation.

"My father's mead makes men . . . do strange things."

"Does it now?"

"Aye. Mayhap you should eat a wee bit."

"I am not hungry for food," he said with restraint. Taking a step back to dismiss any further intrusion on her part, he lifted the goblet to his lips and drank deeply of the golden liquid, enjoying the warm glow entering his bloodstream.

He handed the empty goblet back to her.

"More, Lana."

She looked at the goblet and then back at him in that female way of silent reproach and he knew, without a doubt, he displeased her.

"More," he said.

Biting her lip, she walked away and refilled his goblet. He drank that one too, eyeing her warily. She smiled tolerantly back at him, which perturbed him even more.

He thrust the goblet back in her hands. "More."

"I think you have had enough, Keegan. You are swaying on your feet."

He looked down at himself. Not only was he swaying, but he also felt exceedingly warm.

"You do not drink mead often, methinks."

"Nay," he mumbled, his upper lip feeling a peculiar numbness. The fine blue tunic and laces became uncomfortable against his chest and back. He looked around. Couples were forming, as was the tribe's manner. The scent of the desire and the lust in the air added to his boiling frustration.

With two hands, he jerked the tunic over his head and tossed it aside where it landed on a bush.

"Keegan, what are you doing?"

"I am hot."

"I can see that," she said, and grabbed his forearm for some reason.

He shoved her hand away. "I have waited long enough,"

he declared in a rather loud voice. Grinning faces turned to them and he knew what they all thought. "Time to go, Lana." Without further announcement, he flipped her over his shoulder and to the cheer of the men carried her off into the night.

Lana found herself dangling from a broad naked shoulder, the beads in her hair chiming lightly with her guardian mate's purposeful stride. The unsteady step and swaying were gone, her mate seemingly back in control. For a moment, she thought he was about ready to topple over on his face.

They were in the back meadows heading toward the druidess's home. Darkness and the silence of a starlit night surrounded them with false comfort.

"Keegan, please put me down. I can walk."

Immediately, he stopped. Leaning forward with scarcely a slip, he set her gently on her feet.

Lana looked up at the imposing presence before her. Her guardian mate stood in the moon's shadow, a tall, unmoving shape which smelled of rain, mead, and anger. Lana could just make out his face. "Are you feeling well?" she asked, leaning toward him, trying to see his eyes.

"I am well," he replied curtly, and stepped back.

Before she could say anything more, he strode around her, heading for the druidess's candle-lit roundhouse.

Hiking up the gown so she would not stumble on the hem, Lana raced after him. Weaving around the druidess's small herd of white goats, she tripped on a . . . man's boot?

Slowing down and picking her way more cautiously among the grass and rocks, she found the second boot, and then a few paces further she found a pair of fine blue breeches.

Reaching down, she picked the breeches up by the waist and felt his body's heat still contained within the weave. Keegan had shed all his clothes.

"Lana," he called from the amber darkness ahead.

She dropped the breeches guiltily. "I am coming," she answered, trepidation and excitement sweeping through her.

"Make haste for I wish to begin our journey."

She stopped in mid-stride. *Now?*

"Doona stop," he commanded.

Lana forced her legs to carry her forward and found him near the old table behind the druidess's home.

He stood naked and unconcerned, slipping the sword scabbard onto his back. He did not even acknowledge her presence.

"Keegan," she said after a long tortuous moment.

"The druidess has clothes for you inside. I wish you to change."

She held on tightly to the folds of the gown. "Do we not spend some time together before the journey?"

"Nay. Go inside and change. We leave now. "

With a solemn heart, Lana walked around the round-house to the front. For a few precious hours, she had forgotten the true reason for her trial marriage and why an enigmatic guardian had chosen to handfast with her, a lowly farm girl.

At the entrance to the roundhouse, Lana stepped around the pail of water and peered inside. "Derina?" she called out softly.

No answer. The roundhouse was empty. She entered and walked over to the table lit with five candles. Two food bags had been prepared for her journey, one large and one small. There had never been any intention of a wedding night. Tightness welled inside her chest. She did not know if she was happy or sad.

Sensing a presence behind her, she glanced over her shoulder.

In the doorway, her guardian stood in silent observation. He had donned a pair of worn green breeches; the strap of the scabbard lay diagonally across his muscular chest.

" 'Tis time to go, *claiomh host*."

He put distance between them by calling her that name. *And so it begins*, she thought sadly, and nodded in response. Turning away, she reached for the jewel clasp of the fey gown above her left breast.

"If I may?" he prompted.

She turned to see the sweeping gesture of his right hand.

A warm breeze suddenly flowed across her face, lifting her hair from her shoulders.

The fey gown shimmered gold and then pooled around her ankles; the golden beads in her hair tumbled to the floor one by one in a chiming melody, followed by the beautiful hair combs. The bracelets on her wrists and ankles came next, landing on the gown with dull thumps. Then, as she watched, all his gifts dissolved into the air, leaving her heart chilled and her body unclothed. For some unknown reason, she thought of her beautiful Tara brooch and wondered if Keegan had reclaimed it, too. She had given it to the druidess when she removed her cloak before the ceremony. Only the ancient knew now if the guardian had taken it back. Out of all the fey gifts, she formed an attachment to the brooch almost immediately. The thought of it being gone saddened her greatly.

She shivered, turbulent emotions locked in silence.

He left her nothing, his wedding gifts reclaimed.

Without looking at him, without showing how he had hurt her, she reached for the familiar brown breeches and tunic resting on a bench beside the table. Her mother must have brought another set of clean clothes for her as she had not found the time to replace those she usually left at the druidess's cottage. She dressed quickly, slipping her feet into her boots. Reaching over, she hiked both food bags on her shoulders securely. Catching hold of her resolve, she turned and walked past him, only to be pulled up short by a hand on her upper arm.

Without comment, he removed the larger food bag from her shoulder and released her. Lana forced back her tears and headed out into the night, her direction north.

✴ ✴ ✴

The air turned cool with the coming of the third twilight. They had walked for three days and Lana felt the weakness of her heart keenly.

"*Claíomh host.*"

She stopped. Her guardian mate paused near a small grove of trees. Dressed in a sleeveless green tunic laced up the front and sides, he looked more like a warrior of her tribe, than a creature of the fey. However, the odd diagonal slits slashed into the back of his tunic with his dagger to make way for his wings reminded her he was indeed a fey born guardian. His breeches, though worn, were made of the finest weave and his brown leather boots were snug on his feet, an item of clothing he sometimes complained about but did not remove.

"You are tired, *claíomh host*." He adjusted the single shoulder strap of his scabbard. "Come, let us rest here for the night."

She wished he would stop calling her a sword host. "My name is Lana," she said glumly.

"I know." He pulled out a blue blanket from beneath the food bag. Kneeling, he spread it upon the ground, checking for any offending rocks or pebbles, which would bruise her flesh. He was careful of her comfort, she noted, gestures that did not live up to the legends of spitefulness of the fey born.

She wondered what he would say if he knew she had a blemished heart. The fey valued beauty and strength above all else and were cruel in their rejection of the weak. She tried to imagine Keegan being harsh and cruel, and failed miserably.

"Come." He held out his right hand, beckoning her toward the blanket. "Twilight and shadows are all around the rolling hills, giving way to a full moonrise. It is time we rest."

She walked over to him, feeling used up from the long day's travel.

"Lie down." He took the smaller food bag from her shoulder and guided her down onto the blue weave. He had wanted to carry both food bags, but she refused. She would carry her own weight for as long as she could.

"Are you hungry?" he inquired in that aloof tone she had come to know so well.

"Nay." She shook her head. Lying on her back, her legs flopped open. The breeches allowed her ease, allowed her legs to fall open in rest.

From the corner of her eye, she watched her guardian mate remove the scabbard from his back and lay it on the ground within easy reach.

"I have never traveled this far north before," she offered by way of conversation.

He managed a wry smile. "It is land like any other."

The shine of the moon spilled down upon them in streams of amber. "The moon's brightness dims the luster of the stars this eve."

He sat down, nearly a man's length from her hip, and

looked up at the dark sky. "Do you like the stars?"

"Aye," she whispered, and her thoughts drifted homeward. "Sometimes at night I would walk out to the high meadows and stand on the hill with Lightning, my friend. If there are no clouds, you can almost reach out and touch the stars."

"I know that animal, big sorrel stallion with the jagged slice of white lightning down his forehead."

"Four white fetlocks and battle scars across his chest," Lana added in confirmation.

"A courageous spirit that one has."

"Aye," she agreed and then added, "he has a fondness for apples."

Her guardian mate chuckled unexpectedly, startling her. "An understatement for sure."

"Why do you say that?" she asked defensively, pushing up and resting on her elbows.

A small silence followed her outburst and then he shifted, a leg lifted, a wrist came to rest upon a knee, and Lana found herself staring at long blunt fingers.

"Sitting beneath the branches of a tree and admiring the moon goddess one eve," he explained slowly, "I was content to eat my apple drizzled with fresh golden honey."

"Bee honey?"

"Aye, I like my apples drizzled with raw honey and it appears Lightning did, too. That eve a horse's soft muzzle came sniffing around my hand. I looked up and found myself staring into the brown eyes of a very large horse. I have shared my apples with him ever since."

Lana relaxed. "He has his ways."

"That he does."

She sat up and pointed to the moon. "The moon wears her golden cloak of honey this eve as well."

"Aye," he agreed in a voice that seemed rough to her. She could feel his warm presence in the core of her being and Lana felt regret she had not even a small place in his heart.

They watched the sky and stars in silent harmony, a hush of nocturnal melodies surrounding them. A strange sense of peace came upon her and her attention unerringly moved to the tantalizing allure of him.

His face was turned to the nighttime sky, ropes of dark hair spilling down his back. Even in this light, she could see the gleam of reds and golds in the thick strands.

With a single finger, he pointed to the stars and moon as if to redirect her interest away from him. "The moon goddess returns near this position in the night sky every twenty-seven nights or so," he said with soft authority.

Lana looked up at the moon. "Every twenty-seven nights?"

"Or so," he added.

"How do you know this?"

"I have lived a long life," he murmured with mocking amusement. "She only returns to the exact position in the sky, in the exact same way, every nineteen years. So enjoy her splendor for she will not be this precise way again for a very long time."

Her lips parted slightly in breath and Lana studied the position of the moon against the stars. She probably would not be alive to see the moon goddess's splendor in this precise way again. The hair on the back of her neck stood up and Lana felt his strong contemplation of her. Her gaze slid to his and she saw a flash of yearning in his eyes before his long lashes lowered and he turned away. She could feel herself falling hopelessly in love with him.

It was a physical reaction, her body humming and responding to the maleness of him, his movements, his scent, his breathing. Her spirit coveted him now and never would she be able to give him up.

"Sword host," he whispered in a tone of ache and warning. "Doona look at me that way."

"What way?" she challenged softly.

"Needful."

She had a difficult time thinking with his harsh tone ringing in her ears and the fatigue of her body pulling her down. "I know you have handfasted with me because of this sword quest. I know you need me to guide you to something I doona understand. I will help you in any way I can, but I wonder, will we be sharing a bed together?"

"Go to sleep," he commanded sharply.

Hurt, Lana laid down on her back, reluctant but obedient.

"Take your rest. It has been a long day," her guardian mate said in the dimming reaches of her mind. Lana gave into the fatigue and closed her eyes, a veil of blackness quickly enveloping her.

Keegan felt his resolve slipping. He watched her with a strong inclination to do exactly what she so innocently asked for. She took a shaky breath now and again as if some mischievous faery had stolen her air. It unnerved him.

"What weakens you?" he murmured gloomily into the night. He frowned down at the dark shadows under her eyes, reaffirming the frailty of her.

"Keegan, the horses need feeding," she said barely audibly, idly dreaming in her own little world.

He drew in a deep breath. "I have fed them. Sleep, Lana."

She gave a little shiver, the chill of the spring night seeping in.

"Cold?" He moved himself closer and pulled the border of the blanket over her small form.

A feeling of disquiet settled inside him. He sensed her weakness, something inside, but could not name it. He briefly contemplated sleeping, but then decided to remain awake for the reminder of the night and guard her. He would take his rest on another night. Sighing, he buried his unwanted feelings for her deep within.

The days that followed remained uneventful, the endless hours, the endless walking north, Lana leading, guided by instinct, and, he suspected, misgivings.

On the seventh night of their journey and under the radiance of a crescent moon, she sat on her blanket staring at him in defiance.

"Do you ever sleep?" she inquired indignantly.

"Aye," he answered, feeling the impatient undercurrents of her tone. He suspected this inquiry spoke more of a mating between them than of sleeping.

"When?" she demanded in a rush, aware of his every move.

"Tonight," he replied meaningfully.

"Now?" she responded in exclamation, feminine interest showing plainly on her face.

Considering he only wanted to sleep this eve, he looked away from the temptation of moist lips. He did not intend to touch her, ever. *Ever.* "Lie down," he mumbled, removing his scabbard.

"Should I remove my clothes?"

He blinked at her, caught off guard. "Nay. We are sleeping," he replied, slightly dazed from his own lack of rest.

"Do you . . .?" she started. "What I mean to say is, do fey guardians . . .?"

He inclined his head for her to continue.

She straightened her spine and ploughed ahead. "Derina said guardians do not behave in the same ways that we, mortals, expect them to."

He sighed. "I thought we agreed not to believe everything a white-haired druidess said."

"Aye, but what I wish to know is, if you are shaped the same as . . ."

He cocked an eyebrow. "If I am shaped the same as?" He was very certain she could not turn a deeper shade of red.

He held up his hand to stop her tumble into utter embarrassment. "If you are asking me about my man root, I am shaped as any other mortal male in this."

"I thought so."

"Why?"

She shifted in her seat. "I overhead one of the maidens in the village say the man root of a fey guardian is as large as that of a male horse."

He snorted. "How idiotic."

"And then Derina said guardians doona behave in the same way as mortal males, and well, I thought since you doona appear to sleep, mayhap mating is different as well."

"You thought wrong. I take my rest when and where I need it, which is tonight. I mate when and where I desire, which is not now. So please lie down, be quiet, and go to sleep." A guardian could go for long days and nights without sleeping, but after a time, rest must be taken to reclaim strength.

She responded to his request without argument. Lying down on her side, she shifted to the edge of the blanket, making way for him, and patted the spot in front of her.

Not thinking clearly, he accepted her invitation and lay down on his back beside her. Immediately, she snuggled close, and he recognized his error. Her head rested easily on his shoulder, her small breasts pressed into his side, and a slender arm lay across his chest. He reclined there, mindless and tense as an untried boy.

"Keegan?"

"Now is the time for sleeping, not talking."

She shifted in closer, if that were possible. "I just wanted to say that I like sleeping next to you."

He grunted noncommittally while she pressed her nose against his neck. After a time, she fell into slumber and moments later, thankfully, so did he.

The next morning, Keegan awoke with a start. The scent of female was strong in his lungs. Lifting his head, he looked down his chest. She had shifted in her sleep and now lay face down atop him at a most odd and crosslike angle. Somehow, she found a way inside his laced tunic. Her face hidden, golden waves cascaded over the top of him. He felt her breath against his flesh and bit back a groan. One slender arm was flung over his chest, fingers twisted in the brown hair lying across his shoulder. The other arm lay across his thigh, an elbow grazing a part of him that it should not. He looked to his right. His own hand cupped a curvy bottom.

He jerked it away as if burned. With a bone deep unease, he laid his head back on the ground and took a deep breath. She was drooling on him, in his navel, of all places.

"*Claíomh host*," he called, staring up at the pale gray sky, feeling his body's unwanted response. He could not remember the last time he awoke with a mortal female draped all over him. Never did he remain once his lust had been sated.

"Lana."

"Mmm." She shifted, a knee came up, and an arm went down.

"By the white moon," Keegan choked as a pointy elbow jabbed him in his man parts.

Lana jerked awake, her hair caught in the laces of a male's tunic. Immediately she tried to scramble off him, only to be pulled up short by her hair.

"Stop," her guardian mate croaked, a leg drawn up and one hand cupping his man parts protectively.

She stopped her attempts at freeing and waited, breathing heavily in the damp morning mist, a chunk of hair good and caught on his tunic.

Slowly, he lifted his head. From beneath dark brows, he glared his anger.

She smiled in return, for what else could she do? "Are you hurt?"

His eyes narrowed with suspicion, the reason for which she could find no cause.

"I doona move," she said, holding on to the piece of hair which was entwined.

He looked down his chest and then with a flick of his wrist, her hair came free as if dancing in a breeze.

She sat back, pushing the offending strands away from her face.

Grimacing, her guardian mate rolled away and then

climbed to his feet, taking a long time to straighten to his full height. With hands on his hips, he took a slow, recovering breath.

"Keegan? What is wrong?"

"Give me a moment. 'Tis not every morn I have the wind knocked out of me."

"What wind? There be only a mild breeze this morn."

He scowled at her. "I am not talking about the wind."

"What are you talking about then?"

"You drooled on me," he accused.

She covered her mouth in dismay. She occasionally drooled in her sleep, especially when sleeping on her belly.

"If that were not bad enough, you jabbed me in my . . ." He winced and pointed to his man parts.

She tried not to show her shock. "I dinna jab you there."

His eyes narrowed to slits of annoyance.

"If I did jab you there in your man parts, I dinna mean to. I doona remember doing it."

He said not a word.

"Anyway, it must have been a light jab, not a hard whack."

His head tilted.

She decided now would be a good time to excuse herself and take care of her body's needs. Rolling to her hip, she climbed to her feet.

"For a farmer's daughter, you are sadly inexperienced, *claíomh host*. It seems I must instruct you on this."

She froze. "No need." She was not sure she wanted to

learn his lesson right now and besides, she had to find ...

"I disagree."

In the next moment, he sat on his heels in front of her, pulling her back down with a firm grip on her arm and then suddenly releasing her.

Scooting back, she stared suspiciously at him.

He did not move, did not give her cause to flee further.

"Come closer to me."

There was a fey command in his voice, a smooth compulsion of liquid velvet. She fought it, stiffening her back.

A smile slowly curved his lips.

She glared back, which only seemed to amuse him further.

"Forgive me. I forgot I have promised not to compel you." He patted the ground in front of him. "Closer to me."

His tone changed to ease, the coercion in it gone, so she complied.

Now practically nose-to-nose with him, the heat and scent of him cocooned her.

"Give me your right hand," he urged softly.

"Why?"

"Give me your right hand, Lana."

She extended it warily.

His large hands felt warm and strangely smooth for a warrior, but he was fey born, she reminded herself.

"A small hand," he said, holding onto her when she tried to pull away.

He cupped her right hand in his much larger one and

then with the other, wrapped long fingers around her wrist, holding her so she could not pull away.

She tugged once, a reflexive action at his overpowering proximity.

He smiled tolerantly, ready for her lesson.

"Last night you were curious about my male root. All males have a weakness, Lana. Mortal and fey born are all the same in this."

Slowly, he pulled her forward, so that the bridge of her nose touched him in the jaw.

"Keegan, what are you doing?"

"Learn."

He guided her hand forward and down, showing her how to cup him.

"Feel the shape of me?" he asked huskily.

She bowed her head, her face hot, and nodded.

"Am I shaped in size like a horse?"

"Nay," she mumbled in reply, the scent of rain and desire thickening the air.

His chin dropped close. "I am made for a female's pleasure."

She could not deny that.

His hand tightened around hers. "Here, where the seed of life grows, there is strength and weakness. A kick, punch, or jab here," his fingers curved more closely against hers, "will steal a male's breath and strength."

Within her hand, Lana felt the firm warm pulse of his

man root. Her fingers explored his shape, feeling, and forming his length instinctively.

He released her and stood up.

Lana scooted backward, caught in rolling waves of mortification.

He looked down at her. "Remember, 'tis always better to experience knowledge rather than to listen to it."

He walked away, leaving her flustered. Lana stared at her right hand. He was not as huge as the stallions in the field, but he felt large enough to her. She glanced in the direction he disappeared. Had he just taught her how to hurt him?

CHAPTER 7

THEY HAD TRAVELED FOR MANY days with her leading the way north, although Lana knew not the destination.

Keegan had been strangely quiet, which she considered a mixed blessing. Her right hand still tingled from the intimate feel of him several mornings before. The lesson ignited a profound curiosity to feel the shape and contours of his muscular body against hers. She supposed he knew this and that is why he kept his distance.

Lana returned her attention to the winding path they followed. They walked through a small valley of tall willow trees, leaving a green ridge of rolling hills behind them. The blue sky above smiled warmth upon them and she took joy in that. She knew her pace was slow, knew her guardian mate must suspect something. She would, if their roles were reversed. Yet not a complaint or accusation did he make.

Adjusting the strap of the small food bag, she looked

over her shoulder. As usual, he bowed his head in acknowledgement of her glance and gave her nothing more. Lana turned back to the gently rising path before her. The rain stopped hours before, yet underfoot the ground was still wet and soggy. The air smelled of earth and woods. They were common scents, reminders of home.

Off to their right, in front of an old hawthorn, stood an odd assortment of white pillar stones. They rose in varying heights to the waist and shoulder. She stopped to admire them, for they stood in the shade of the black branches of the tree. She heard Keegan stop silently behind her. This was an olden place, she surmised.

All in her tribe knew the hawthorn to be the resting place of the sidhe, and the faeries did not like to be disturbed. She glanced at Keegan and quickly determined since she traveled with a faery, she was probably safe. On impulse, she walked over for a closer look at the pillars.

"*Claíomh host?*"

"My name is Lana."

"I know. Where are you going?"

"To look at the tall stones." She stopped at a waist high stone and traced the smooth rounded top with her fingers. It seemed shaped from larger rocks. She had never seen anything like it before and ran her fingers down a carved edge. "Look at these notches, Keegan."

"I have seen such as they."

She continued her perusal and pointed to one of the inscriptions. "What are these?"

"Rocks with notches." He walked over and studied the indentation markings on the rocks. "Spriggans."

"The rock faeries with the big heads?" she asked.

He straightened and rested his hand on the surface of the rock, right next to hers. "Aye, have you ever seen a druid carve a note or signal into a wooden post or tree?"

"Aye, my father marks trees to show the boundary of his land."

" 'Tis the same thing." Leaning over, he ran a finger along the first set of five notches. Each notch looked a little different to her. They had varying bends, almost like the figure of a hand, a very small hand.

"These markings are spriggan," he said, and knelt down on one knee for a closer look.

"What do they say?" she asked, excited to learn something new, and knelt beside him.

"Mystical oaths," he answered, "and warnings not to trespass here."

He looked at her from beneath his lashes and Lana felt the world pause.

She could taste his breath with hers, the scent of rain strong in her lungs. His smoky gray eyes had slashes of amethyst light in them, beautiful and terrifying all at once. Her father often said although the faeries were their fey brethren they could not be trusted. To trust one was to be foolhardy. She wondered if it held true with guardians. She wondered if she could trust Keegan.

"Why do you go on this quest?" she inquired, seeking answers for this mysterious journey she found herself on. "What is this sword to you?"

He went very still.

"I think I have a right to know, Keegan."

"Valor will drown," he answered, without further clarification.

She studied his face. "Would that be the Faery King's dark blade?"

His head tilted in an equal study of her. "You are more informed than most."

"I have spent many hours listening to the druidess's storytelling. She knows many things about the fey."

He did not respond.

"How will Valor drown?" she asked.

"In water," came the reply.

Lana fought to control her annoyance and climbed to her feet. "Do you think me dim-witted, guardian? I can assure you I am not."

His jaw clenched, but she was not going to be put off. "Please tell me what is going on. Has the dark sword been stolen?"

He climbed to his feet, towering over her once again. "You have guessed correctly," he replied. "Someone has stolen Valor. What you could not know is that the Great Fey King has dreamt of her drowning."

"Who took her?" she demanded, and realized the stupidity of her question.

"If I knew who took her then I would not be here with you, would I?"

She would give him that. "Who else is looking for the sword, Keegan? Should we not have a plan, other than traveling north?"

"We travel north because that is the way you lead us and there are no others who look for the sword."

"Well, that is stupid."

His lips curved and Lana had the impression he agreed with her.

"It is the king's wish this quest be made in secret. We doona wish our enemies to know one of our fey defenders is missing. I am First Guardian of the Waters. I sense all things, which touch our sacred waters. I will find her."

Sanctimonious faery, she thought and then asked, "Why do you need me then? Will you not sense Valor when the blade submerges?"

"I may be too late."

How could he be too late? His answer made no sense to her. "Can you not just wink into the waters and save her?"

He shook his head and raised a hand for silence.

Lana frowned up at him.

And then . . .

With a quickness that startled her, he reached around the stone pillar and pulled out a small hissing creature with an enormous head and brown beard.

Lana stepped back and dropped her food bag in surprise. She could not help but stare at the distraught individual.

Dropping his food bag on the ground, Keegan held the creature high by the back of his thick neck. Spindly arms and feet waved back and forth in distress.

"The sooner you stop fighting, the sooner I will set you down, Master Spriggan."

The spriggan stilled and muttered in a gravelly voice, "Down now."

"First, tell me why you were watching us," Lana's guardian mate insisted, wrinkling his nose as if offended by the creature's smell.

"My place, not walk here."

Keegan set the creature gently down on his feet.

The spriggan adjusted his rock-crusted blue jacket and long pants. He gave the guardian a withering look and then turned beady black eyes upon her.

Lana took a step back, the bearded faery's inspection turning her blood cold. Dwellers of ruins and burial mounds, the spriggans were said to be the minders of the dolmans, sacred places of the Otherworld. Notorious child-snatchers, they also brought bad weather and general mischief wherever they went.

They had enough to contend with, Lana thought, and did not need any bad weather or mischief, or whatever else this creature had in mind.

The spriggan sniffed at her, his large hairy nostrils twitching rapidly. She glanced at Keegan. He nodded, understanding all too well. The rock faery had scented his mating bite upon her.

"Pretty," the ugly faery said.

Keegan adjusted the strap of his scabbard, rolling his right shoulder to relieve the ache there.

"Aye," he replied, feigning non-interest.

"I like sun-colored hair. Like white skin, too."

"Aye."

The spriggan scratched his coarse beard in contemplation, gesturing at her clothes in dislike. "Why she dress like that in man clothes? Not show enough of snow white flesh."

"Agreed."

Lana folded her arms across her chest in discomfort.

"Yours, guardian?"

"She is mine."

A ray of hope warmed her blood despite this peculiar conversation. Perhaps Keegan did feel something for her after all, she thought.

"Odd it is," the spriggan muttered in all seriousness.

"What is odd, Master Spriggan?"

"She be pure mortal."

Keegan's long lashes lowered, showing a glint of ice-cold silver. "She is pure mortal," he echoed.

"You be pure guardian."

"I am."

"Odd it is, a great powerful guardian marking a pretty mortal." The spriggan frowned and then grinned in sudden enlightenment. "Mayhap guardian likes pretty."

"Mayhap," her guardian agreed.

Lana knew Keegan would not explain about the claiming. "Share her?"

Lana gasped in outrage at the spriggan's boldness. Never would she let that creature touch her!

"I doona share what is mine, Cadman. Now tell me what you have overheard while watching us from your shadows?"

Keegan knew this rock faery?

The spriggan balked, taking a step back as if to run, but her guardian mate moved faster. Grabbing the spriggan behind the neck, he lifted the squirming rock faery so they were face to face.

"Nothing," the spriggan spat, trying to free himself.

"Doona lie to me, Cadman."

"Not friendly you."

"Nay, Cadman, I am not feeling particularly friendly at this moment."

The spriggan frowned at his large captor. "Talk like them, too."

A growl of impatient menace vibrated in the air from her guardian. Lana rubbed her arms, fighting back a shiver.

"Tell me, Cadman. I doona like hurting other fey borns."

"Heard nothing."

"I doona believe you. Try again." He gave the spriggan

a firm shake.

"Valor taken. Stolen you say."

Lana saw Keegan scowl darkly before setting the spriggan back on his bare feet.

With as much disdain as possible, Master Spriggan straightened his rock-encrusted coat. "Bad manners you," he snapped in that gravelly voice.

"Bad manners you, spying on a guardian," Keegan said tightly, mimicking the spriggan's inflection.

"Know what she be. Guardian like pretty. I like pretty. I know."

"Know what?" her guardian inquired with a touch of edginess.

The spriggan hopped forward. Before he could jab her in the stomach with his finger, Keegan shielded her with his body.

"Never touch, Cadman." He sliced the air in front of the spriggan's face with his hand. "Understand?"

Lana grabbed Keegan's powerful right arm and held on. The cold edge of dread spread inside her.

The spriggan stepped back slowly. "Pretty gold fleece. See her bathe in moonlight, see her in stream."

Her guardian muttered an oath under his breath, his body stiff with tension in front of her.

"See mark of sword on her flesh," the spriggan continued, walking backward. "She heads toward there." He stopped in a shaft of fading sunlight and pointed north with a dirty finger.

Lana swallowed down her fear. She did not trust this rock faery creature. There was something devious in his manner.

"Where?" Keegan growled, his patience all but gone.

"Knowth," Cadman said in satisfaction, showing pointy white teeth. "One of few sword hosts. One of very few." He twirled around, hands waving in the air. "Special she be," he chanted loudly to the sky. "Special she be. Feels Valor in her blood. Old, old legends be true."

"What is that creature talking about?" Lana whispered in her guardian's ear. "What legends, Keegan? What is Knowth?"

He turned away in response.

"Keegan?"

He would not answer her.

The spriggan stopped twirling with a shout. "I answer for guardian," he said. "You die, pretty. In the Otherworld below, the dark sword takes you. Die all over."

Not if I can help it, Keegan thought in defiance. Sitting with his back pressed against the trunk of the hawthorn tree, he glanced over at Lana while she slept on her side to his right.

Bracing his hand on his knee, he wondered how Cadman knew the dark sword was at Knowth, one of the great passage tombs of their ancestors. The spriggan let his deceit slip with that one, and then confirmed it when he mentioned their Otherworld, a fey born place below. How could the sword be in two places? He did not know which was the truth. He only knew he had found one of his enemies.

Sighing, he looked up at the sky. Night had fallen long ago and he ran a hand through his hair in mounting frustration. If Valor was in the Otherworld, finding the sword would be difficult. He was a creature of the earth, his senses tuned to this place, not the other. Never would he have sensed the dark sword there, at least not until the decaying body of her dead host became one with the iridescent cave pools.

His jaw tightened. He trusted Lana would guide him to the sword long before the foretold drowning.

Lana. He stared into the dying embers of the fire circle he built, and swallowed hard in disgust. Caring for her was rooting inside him, a living tempest. It amazed him he could feel so consumed with the idea of mating with her. He must find a way to protect both Valor and Lana, he thought furiously.

His thoughts immediately fastened on the false-hearted spriggan. He allowed Cadman to return to his underground home for the night, confident the creature was secure in his own deception. He had known Cadman for nearly five years now and always recoiled at the odor of the spriggan's flesh. Keegan rubbed his chin in ominous silence. If he had to put a name to his unease, he would say the spriggan's blood smelled wrong. It was almost as if man blood flowed with spriggan blood, but that could not be, he reasoned. Never had spriggans been able to conceive a babe outside of their fey born race. Shifting in discomfort, he pulled a small rock from under his hip and tossed it away. Most spriggans were truthful, despite their wayward ways. This one was not. Cadman played by a different set of rules and was therefore unworthy of trust. Soon, he would seek answers. For now, he would wait and see what other knowledge Master Spriggan might unknowingly betray.

He glanced right. The light from the half moon, joined with the bright stars above, bathed Lana where she lay. He could tell from her breathing she was feigning sleep. It was a warm spring night; moisture in the air and the scent of his mating claim on her was strong in his lungs, taunting him. Her back was to him, tresses cascading like golden waves down her back, the slender curves of her a constant lure. He looked away and resettled his arms on his bent knees.

For the first time in his long life, he felt desire and indecisiveness. Taking a deep breath, he closed his eyes and listened to the night, only to hear the soft sounds of her taking precedence above all others. He felt her in his innermost places. Hot and hungry she made him, like a mortal male with red blood streaming in his veins. He wanted to touch her, to bury his face in her hair, to taste her flesh. Here in the night with spriggan pillars on one end and trees on the other, he wanted to mate like a mortal and feel the hot sheath of her close around him.

"Am I going to die, Keegan?" she inquired softly, sensing his contemplation of her.

"I will not let you die."

She rolled over and faced him, her hair sweeping behind her. It made him ache.

"I would not have an untruth between us, my guardian mate."

"I will not let you die."

She sat up and shifted closer to him.

His stomach clenched.

"I believe you," she whispered, creating both ease and obligation inside him.

They sat looking at the yellow embers, their bodies awash in the gleam of the dwindling fire circle.

"Keegan, would you tell me of the legend Cadman spoke of?"

He did not want to do it, did not want to share the tale, did not want her this near to him where he could smell the very essence of her being.

"Please, I would like to know." She touched his forearm, her warm fingers golden compared to the cool paleness of his fey skin.

"The sword legend is old, Lana. Older than I know."

"I understand."

Her small hand remained on his arm.

"Valor is the name of a great sword spirit of the faeries. She chooses a female of strength to be her host. The current host has been with Valor since I can remember."

"One of strength?"

"Aye," he replied. "That is why I find it hard to believe you were chosen."

She nodded, pulling away and changing the subject. "Does the host not age?"

He shook his head. "She receives the gift of immortality from the sword spirit."

"If she is immortal, how can she drown?"

"The same as you or I," he replied softly.

"You can drown?" she said suddenly, her lovely brows arched in confusion and dismay.

"Aye, Lana. I can drown. Being fey born does not make me immortal."

"I thought fey borns were immortal."

He shook his head. "For some unknown reason, this false belief of faery immortality took hold among men and the fey have allowed it to continue. I am fey born. I live a longer life than mortals, but I do eventually die. I am not invincible," he said softly.

"But the host is immortal."

"In most ways. In life, there are always exceptions to any rule. Since this immortality is a gift from the sword spirit to the host, there are boundaries, subject to the claiming of the water or fire spirit. If the sword remains within water or fire for a time, the host will die."

"So the host is not completely immortal."

"Nay, she is not."

"What will happen to Valor should her host . . . drown?"

Silence welled up inside him. "Valor will need another host to survive."

She waited for him to explain and he looked away.

"In every generation, there are a wee few who are born bearing the mark of the sword. Most often . . ." He paused to form his words. "Most often they have some fey blood in their veins."

"The *claíomh hosts*?"

"Aye," he answered. "The *claíomh hosts*."

"Do I have any fey blood?"

He shook his head. "You doona, which I find strange, but then enchantment requires no explanation."

She seemed to think about that a moment. "Are the hosts always female, Keegan?"

His considered the gentle curve of her belly, where the birthmark lay hidden beneath the clothes. "Aye, the spirit of the sword is a sacred female."

"I thought the sword spirit would be male."

He shook his head. "Valor is the dark side of the true female."

"Dark side?"

"Taker of life, the opposite."

"I doona understand. I thought males are the opposite of females."

"The female and male have two sides. The light side of the female is the cradle and giver of life. Her dark side is the taker of life."

"And the male?"

"The light side of the male is the seed of life."

"Seed?"

He looked at her in utter bemusement. "His seed gives life to the womb."

She nodded, slightly flustered, then asked, "And his dark side?"

"The Destroyer. You doona want to know more than that."

"Do you have this dark side?"

"I am male. Both the light and dark side of the sacred male exist equally in me."

"As the light and dark sides of the sacred female exist equally in me?"

"Nay, Lana," he shook his head. "Because you bear the birthmark, you are more dark than light."

She pulled away from him and he could see the puzzlement and distress in her features.

"By the white moon, I am not evil, Keegan."

"I never said you were. Why do you equate darkness with evil? Is the night evil? Is the rich black soil evil?"

"Nay," she confirmed softly.

He could barely hear her response. "Life and death are equal. Light and dark are equal. That is the way of things."

She touched a trembling hand to her forehead. "Will I kill, Keegan?"

"Aye, if you become Valor's host, a protector of the lands, the fey, and your tribe you will." He thought she could live with that. "Valor does not take life indiscriminately, Lana, only if threatened."

"Have you?" she asked in a hushed tone.

"Have I what?"

"Have you taken a life, Keegan?"

He did not answer, for there was no need.

Silence hung in the air.

Lana found herself staring into eyes of dark passion and cruelty. The mortal grayness was shifting to fey amethyst. If the current female host of Valor should die, she could become the next host, and all that she had ever known in her life would change. She would become dark, a taker of life, and lose her body to the shadowy enchantment of immortality!

She scrambled to her feet, intent on fleeing, anywhere, somewhere, where all of this was just a nightmare.

A hand shot out, shackled her wrist, and yanked her back down.

She landed on a muscular chest, her forehead colliding with a firm chin.

"Let me go," she cried, her legs entangled with his longer ones.

He eased her back onto the ground and covered her body with his.

"You asked me to tell you," her fey guardian said tightly above her.

"Let me go. I would never kill."

"You kill to live, Lana."

She froze and stared up at him.

"Do you think the plants in the fields are not alive? Do you think the trees cut down to build your homes are not alive? Do you think the meat that fills your belly comes not from living and breathing animals?"

"Stop it," she gasped, shoving at his chest, not wanting to hear the truth.

He leaned on his elbows and took hold of her face, his large hands unyielding yet gentle. "One of our defenders is missing. We must find her so she can protect all that we hold precious."

She closed her eyes, hot tears squeezing out. She heard the wisdom of his words, yet her heart feared, feared she would not be good enough, and terrified she was.

"I canna ..." The dread came from deep within her and she opened her eyes to look up at him. The silver was changing, swirling, and becoming . . . total amethyst.

"The darkness is what gives us our strength. That strength overflows within you. Embrace it."

He moved above her. His tongue slid tenderly over her lips. "Why do you do this to me?" he said in agony, his large hands buried in the silken hair at her temples, holding her still. "Even before my mating mark you tempted me. Why? I doona like weakness," he growled, his embrace was almost frightening in its possession, as if he could not control the currents raging inside him.

She held her breath, unable to respond. His eyes were

shadows, both tender and dangerous.

"Kiss me, Lana. I want." And then his hot mouth settled over hers in a fevered kiss.

She clung to the strength of him. His mouth was firm and sensual with need, almost insatiable with hunger. He tasted of berries and of rain, but most of all he tasted of the forbidden.

He held her tightly, his body pressing her down into the soft ground, enveloping her.

Simple mortal.

Purebred fey.

Not allowed.

Never allowed.

She did not care.

Neither did he.

"Want you," her guardian whispered huskily against her swollen lips. His tongue swept across her face, pausing at his claiming mark on her jaw and then trailed wetness down her throat. "Want."

He suckled at the sensitive flesh under her ear, sending exquisite shivers down her spine. Lana arched her neck back, eyes closing, giving him better access to her throat. Her breasts ached against his hard chest.

He settled his lower body against hers and she felt the hard length of him rock against her softness.

A sigh of feminine surrender escaped her lips.

And then . . .

He buried his face in her shoulder, his body trembling.
An agonized moan vibrated against her throat.

She opened her eyes. "Keegan," she whispered in concern, turning to kiss his cheek. "What is wrong?"

"Not allowed," he said harshly.

"Please."

He launched himself away from her, into the air, into
darkness, and Lana thought she saw the silvery glint of wings
before the chill of the night enveloped her. Even her guardian mate did not want to lie with her. She could not know
she already belonged to the sword.

Lana turned and buried her face in her arms, her sobs
muffled and soft against the ground.

Behind one of the spriggan pillars, Cadman squatted low in
fury and resentment. He had seen all. So, the dominant
guardian wanted to rut with the sword host, he mused darkly
with inner vehemence. But then, so did he. He fancied her
greatly. Thinking of the golden fleece between her long white
legs, he played with himself until the little death came and
the torture of it drenched him in a thick sweat. When he finished, he hiked up his pants, feeling better.

His master made him promises of great treasure if he
stole Valor from the faery vaults of Tara. No one suspected
him, a mere spriggan. He grinned at the irony of it; he, a

mere spriggan. It has been almost as easy as stealing a farmer's babe. Now the powerful Valor lay imprisoned in water, guarded by the mirror fey, for all in the Otherworld wore but reflections of the above. And now he, Master Cadman Spriggan, was faced with the dilemma of another sword host.

He scratched his bearded chin, his tiny black eyes turning cold. By mentioning Knowth, he set the misdirection. An ambush already lay in wait. He needed to be rid of the repulsive guardian for what he had in mind, but it was more easily thought then done.

CHAPTER 8

THE DAMP MORNING CAME AND went, leaving behind warmth and a clear, blue sky.

Exhausted, Lana sat alone in the shade of the hawthorn tree, waiting for the return of her guardian mate. She slept little last night, troubling thoughts drifting between her guardian and trying to understand the light and dark within her. With her legs tucked under for balance and comfort she leaned back against the sturdy trunk of the tree, hair tumbling free about her shoulders. Beside her right thigh, Keegan's sword lay upon the ground in its worn leather scabbard. Her fingers absently traced the smooth surface, coming to rest on the hilt. She was destined to become this, she mused, afraid and slightly intrigued. It was something beyond her nature. *A bringer of death*, she thought, and wondered if the enchantment, which so secured her future knew of the flaw residing in her heart. *If it did, it made a poor choice.*

Ever so slowly, she pulled the sword out of its scabbard.

The handle was made of wood and flanked with a bronze guard. The blade had blood grooves in it, a mortal battle weapon carried by an enigmatic guardian. She had so many questions to ask Keegan. Would the magical transformation to a fey host hurt? How would it be done? Would she drink a magic potion and become light and mist? Would her heart be strong enough to survive it? She probably would not ask that question. Would she remember who she was? Would she still be Lana?

"Does it matter?" she said aloud into the silence, and slid the sword back into the scabbard. "Destiny has decreed this future before my birth," she whispered despondently, and then lifted her head. It must be for a good reason, she reasoned, trying to remain positive. Mayhap it was to benefit her people. She must trust that in time she would find her answers. For now, she must accept her destiny. *But how?* she wondered. *How?*

By following my instincts, she concluded, and felt calmer. *I will begin there and see where it takes me.*

She looked up at the cloudless blue sky, marking the sun's position. Morning became an early afternoon full of bird song and soft amber light.

Tucking a blond curl behind her ear, she watched a small badger hurry across the grassy path she had walked with Keegan the day before.

"Left you he has." Master Spriggan said, popping out from around one of the pillars.

Lana hid her surprise. "How long have you been watching me?"

Sitting down in front of her, he adjusted his blue, rock-crusted coat. "Always watch, pretty. Make sure you be safe."

"Did Keegan tell you to watch over me?" she asked with wariness.

The spriggan shook his big head. "Guardian stares at loch. Fury lives beneath his skin. Dangerous to speak to right now, so I stay away. Hungry?" In his hand, he held a golden slice of freckled bread out to her. "Spriggans make the best berry bread."

The bread smelled honey sweet, but Lana was cautious of the creature. She studied his small obsidian eyes, trying to judge the authenticity of his offering, and then declined with a murmured "thank you."

Shrugging, the creature bit into the offering he initially held out to her. Purposeful sounds of delight rumbled in his throat. Lana frowned, feeling the pull of her own hunger. Reaching for her small food bag, she dragged it across her lap and found it unexpectedly empty.

"Badgers," he offered in innocent explanation for the missing food. "A family of them came last night."

Climbing to her feet, she walked over to Keegan's larger food bag and kneeled in the grass. Peering inside his bag, she found it, too, was empty. "They must have raided this one as well. There are teeth marks along the edge of the opening."

"Aye, ate everything. Always hungry those creatures."

She looked up at the spriggan; his mouth was plump with berries and flakes of golden freckled crust.

"Wild animals doona approach humans unless desperate, and the land is full and bountiful with food this season."

"Must have been good food."

"Aye, it was." She looked around. "I was awake most of the night. Where did they come from?"

"Holes in the land. They dig."

"I know badgers dig." She shrugged and rose, resettling herself against the trunk of the tree.

"Hungry now?" He retrieved a second offering of bread from his deep jacket pocket. "I doona mind sharing." This slice was wrapped in thick green leaves and he held it out to her. "Eat. My bread be flavorsome. Even guardians have a liking for it."

If the guardians ate it, then it must be all right, she reasoned quietly. With only a slight hesitation, Lana took it and nodded her thanks. She settled herself once more against the tree trunk, still fighting indecision. The bread felt warm in her hands and smelled like honey. Purple berries littered its center. Holding it to her nose, she took a small whiff and then nipped at an end. Light spongy sweetness burst in her mouth. Never had she tasted anything like it before.

"Like?" the rock faery prompted knowingly, and smiled in satisfaction.

"Delicious." She finished her slice all too quickly.

"More?" He held out another offering, a thicker slice.

Lana accepted this offering, too, and bit into it. A furious rush of syrupy berries filled her mouth, making her light-headed.

When every last crumb was eaten, she licked her fingertips. Looking up, she found the spriggan watching her with a peculiar intensity. It unsettled her a wee bit, this sudden focus, as if she had grown horns.

"More?" he prompted.

She shook her head, feeling oddly warm in her stomach. "My thanks for the bread, Master Spriggan. I have never tasted that kind of sweetness before."

"Spriggan bread very tasty."

"Is there no other food left that you accept bread from our spriggan friend?" her guardian mate inquired with a touch of irritation.

Lana's heart jumped wildly in her breast. Shielding her eyes with her left hand, she looked up into the bright sun. A large shadow stood to the right of the hawthorn tree.

"I was hungry and our food bags are empty," she justified, trying to keep the quiver of relief out of her voice.

"Badgers," the spriggan interjected in quick explanation.

Silence.

Lana felt her guardian's ruthless assessment and wondered at his displeasure.

"Leave us, Master Spriggan," he growled.

Grunting in his haste, the spriggan rose quickly to his feet, bobbed his farewell, and disappeared behind one of his pillars. Just before he vanished, she thought she saw his body drop, as if stepping down into a hole in the ground.

Lana moistened her lips with the tip of her tongue and waited. She was very much aware of Keegan's disapproval, even though she could not fathom why.

Like the false breath of the Gods, a sudden white mist brushed across the tips of grasses and settled around her in a boundary of faint moisture. "Keegan?" Lana startled as a magnificent faery guardian knelt before her on one knee. His proud head was bowed in homage. Strands of brown hair shimmered, dancing in gold and red glints.

His body was lean and muscular, covered in the majesty of silvery gray. Every slope, ridge, and male definition of him was easily seen for her perusal. He was made of nature's excellence, a dangerous male sensuality making her cautious yet filling her with womanly excitement.

This was his true form, one of beauty and intimidation. Enormous wings glimmered, rising from his shoulder blades. They were spun from the laces of moonlight and black spider webs, the edges smooth and curved like a butterfly's wings. Her gaze dropped to the silver cuff on his right wrist. The sight of it steadied her nerves. He folded his right arm across his chest, his hand locked in a tight fist, a sign of tension.

"I ask forgiveness for touching you," he said.

"You dinna touch me." She sat up straighter, feeling the attraction of him and a sense of foreboding.

His long lashes lifted ever so slowly. He watched her

with a strange intensity and her body warmed in reaction, his dominion over her complete. Lana knew from that instant on, she would never be able to deny him anything.

Keegan's gaze narrowed. He knew what she saw when she looked at him.

The Gods formed him for the protection of the lands and waters. The Goddesses shaped him for a female's pleasure.

He stared at the quiver of her lower lip. She had power over him, his bride innocent. The mating claim he initiated with her was strong in his blood, a throwback to his once mortal ancestry. The handfasting tapped into the underlying wildness in him. He wanted to mate on the damp shores of a crystal loch, in the cool running streams that roamed the land; he wanted to lay his fey seed within her womb and ignore the punishment that would come after.

"I am not your true mate, Lana."

"We are handfasted," she stubbornly insisted, her eyes watching the sweeping movement of his wings. He forced his back muscles to relax.

"Lana, you were meant . . .

"Nay," she interrupted him. "I wish for us to mate, Keegan."

He sucked air into his lungs at her unaccustomed boldness. "We canna mate. We are different."

"Nay, we are not so different."

"I am Rain," he said forcefully between clenched teeth. "My true name, Lana. It is Rain." A slight mocking smile touched his lips. "I am fey."

"And I am not?" she shouted back at him, causing him to blink. "What is this then?" She pointed at the place of her birthmark. Her cheeks were flushed pink with life and temper.

He looked down at her flat stomach. "The sword's birthmark," he answered slowly, carefully.

" 'Tis a fey mark, is it not?"

He could not deny it. "It is fey."

"I am fey then," she stated decisively.

He grimaced.

"I am fey!" She did shout then, her eyes fever bright.

He had no choice but to nod in reluctant agreement.

"Well then," she said in triumph, "I am glad we have cleared that up."

"Have we?" He was not at all sure.

"Aye," she replied fiercely.

He saw scrutiny and judgment within the liquid depths of her eyes. *May the Gods and Goddesses help me, when she finds her true dark strength*, he thought. More temper was coming, and he braced for it.

"Where were you, Keegan?"

"Near," he answered, keeping his tone even.

"I was alone."

"Never. I sense you always."

"Why did you stay away so long?" He could hear the hurt in her voice.

A bitter half-smile touched his lips. "I needed time away from you. Needed time in the loch."

"You went for a swim?" she asked incredulously.

An ice-cold swim. He nodded.

"Why?"

Did she not know?

"Why, Keegan?" she asked softly after the silence came and stayed. "I was alone and fearful. I dinna know if you were coming back."

"I will always come back," he said firmly, noting the odd sweat on her brow. "I stayed away from you to cool the lust raging in my blood."

She swiped at her forehead and muttered something about a hot day.

He stretched out his wings to relieve some of the strain which formed there, and her eyes followed. "I am fey, Lana, but I am also male bred." He climbed to his feet to give emphasis to his body. A bitter resentfulness filled him.

This mutual attraction must end. He told himself she was not beautiful, told himself he did not want to hold her in his arms. Unfortunately, he knew exactly what he wanted.

Lana told herself she was under some lustful spell, a dream she could not awaken from. She felt hot and wanton, an ache in her woman's place like none other she ever felt before. Hysterical laughter gushed up and then stuck in her throat. She covered her mouth in mortification. What was wrong with her? Her guardian mate was studying her as well, probably wondering the same thing.

In the past, Keegan's fey form always made her distrustful. Now all she wanted to do was to crawl inside those resplendent webs and touch the firm warm male beneath. She climbed unsteadily to her feet with just that intent.

"How much of the spriggan's bread did you eat today?" His manner was one of peculiar attentiveness.

"I ate two slices."

"Only two?"

"Aye." She took a step forward and stumbled.

A large hand gripped her elbow to steady her. Looking down at the long blunt fingers wrapped around her, she stared at the silver webs crossing a thick wrist and felt a decadent urge. Bending down, she plastered her nose on the webs crossing his sinewy forearm. "You always smell so wonderful," she mumbled.

"You are spell cast," he countered gravely.

She lifted her head and looked up. "Why are you angry with me?"

"I am not angry."

"I can tell that you are," she retorted. "Your lips go all tight like this." She mimicked him.

"My lips doona do that."

"Aye, they do." She moved closer and he stepped back, his hand still locked around her elbow.

"Are you afraid of me, Keegan?"

"You talk of foolishness."

"Do I?" She motioned to the straining bulge between his legs. "Your words say one thing, your body says another.

Kiss me." She puckered up her lips.

" 'Tis a false lust you feel. You have been spell cast, Lana."

She huffed in disagreement and pressed her mouth to the silky webs covering his left nipple.

"By the goddess!" he hissed in surprise. His hand locked in her hair, pulling her off him. He tilted her head back and sniffed at her.

"Kiss me, Keegan," she said brashly, so unlike the Lana he knew. "I want to taste you in my mouth."

"I know." He inhaled the spriggan's sweet bread on her breath, a lust spell baked into food.

"Covet bread," he breathed out ruthlessly. The pupils of her eyes were unnaturally large for the brightness of the day, a marker of the lust fever to come.

"Spriggan mischief," he snarled. An exceedingly impudent spriggan, he thought with rising fury, to try to take a female he had marked in a mating claim.

She snagged a handful of his hair and tugged, trying to pull him down. He was not amused. "Lana," he said through clenched teeth, "let go of my hair." He covered her smaller hand with his. Sacrificing several strands of hair, he was able to pry the slender fingers loose.

"Why do you not kiss me?" she demanded, pursing her lips like a spoiled child.

"You have eaten a spriggan's covet bread."

She blinked, a thread of sanity returning, though briefly. "What is covet bread, Keegan?"

"You have been spell cast with a spriggan's lust, my brash one. It seems Master Cadman wishes to mate with you."

"Well, I doona wish to. I would rather mate with you."

"Therein lies the problem." Pulling her into his arms, he winked out.

Sweating profusely, Lana came back to awareness a few moments later. She must have passed out for a moment, she thought, rubbing her damp forehead. She lay beside a fallen tree, long dead, her body sweltering and throbbing. Up above, a twilight sky shone in deep mirror shades of lavenders and pinks, white clouds gliding effortlessly through the air.

The colors seemed muted here, indistinct against the horizon. Rolling over on her side, she found herself on an emerald green shore leading down to a large loch. In the blue waters, two white swans swam in silence, their beaks yellow and black in the faded light. She watched them, a mated pair, staying close to each other. Somewhere along the shore of the loch was their nest.

Pushing up on her elbows, she looked around at the silvery limestone cliffs and outcroppings of rock and ledge. Beyond the azure waters, emerald pastures and hills spread ever outward.

" 'Tis a fey place, Lana."

Startled, she looked behind her.

Keegan sat bare-chested, his back against an ancient oak, legs crossed at the ankles, his true form hidden once again.

She peered at his silver cuff, her talisman, her charm of safety. "Why did you bring me here?" she asked slowly.

"I doona wish to sate your lust fever in the front door of the spriggan's home."

"His home?"

"Aye. The pillars, which interested you, are the doorways to his underground dwelling. He is a rock faery, after all." A dangerous smile etched across his handsome mouth.

Lana sat up abruptly and buried her face in her trembling hands. Her pride was hurt, her body throbbing in hunger. A shimmering light appeared in the corner of her eye and she looked up.

Keegan was no longer behind her. Instead, he perched on the dead tree trunk next to her thigh. Like a hawk, he studied his prey with an appraising focus, left hand gripping the bark for balance, fingers digging into the decay.

"I know what you need," he said in a whisper of arrogant male confidence.

"What?" she snapped, a blending of temper and desire. "A guardian's *melding*?"

He smiled slowly, tilting his head to one side. "You know of our magical blood to blood mating."

"Nay." She knew only the word and nothing else of the dark mystery.

"Because that is exactly what I intend to do to you."

"I would much rather swim in a cold loch." She felt a need to fight him.

"I think not."

"I doona care what you think. If a cold swim in a loch is good enough for you, it should be good enough for me and my false lust."

"The waters will not give you ease." There was a warning in his voice.

"Why?"

" 'Tis a lust fever, and if not satisfied it will make you ill. It seems I must do something to aid you."

"By *melding* with me?"

"Aye, after I prepare you."

Drawing her legs close to her tender breasts, Lana wrapped her arms around her shins and shook her head. "Prepare me for what?"

"For my touch."

"You said you canna touch me," she murmured, her pride still hurt.

"I feel there is a need now."

She shifted a little away from him. "How convenient. Are all guardians so indecisive?"

"We are not indecisive. By the white moon, do you not understand what has happened here?"

"I understand. The spriggan gave me covet bread. What I doona understand is why."

"Child woman," he muttered under his breath.

"I am not a child."

"Pretty gold fleece." He imitated the spriggan's inflection perfectly. "Master Spriggan wished to convince you to mate with him. If you had eaten more of his bread, you probably would have done so."

"I would not have mated with him."

"You would have," he said with conviction.

She glared at him, giving way to the disturbance inside her. "Never would I have allowed that creature to touch me! Do you hear me?"

"I hear you well enough," he said severely. "There is no need to shout. 'Tis a dilemma for both of us. I must give your body ease from the lust fever, yet I canna find physical ease within you."

"What is *melding*?"

"It is the guardian's magical mating of blood to blood. It enhances the physical joining between a male and female."

"But we will not join physically?"

"Not that way."

Before she could ask what way, the urge to mate surged between her legs and she sucked in her breath from the shock of it.

"The lust fever has begun."

"Everything must pass," she said hoarsely with fervent hope.

"Not this."

Lana felt tears well in her eyes.

Slowly.

Ever so slowly.

As if every movement was for her benefit, he came down from the tree, muscles rippling, and edged up beside her.

"I will give you ease," he said in husky command. A strong hand snaked possessively around her nape. "Trust me. I will not hurt you."

She closed her eyes and gave herself willingly into his care.

Keegan pulled his willful bride into his arms. "It will not hurt for much longer." He lowered his mouth and kissed each of her eyelids tenderly. Sharp fingernails dug into the flesh of his shoulder.

His mouth skimmed across her jaw line and licked his mating mark, a reaffirming of false vows. In the back of his mind, he knew he should not be touching her this way, but he would not leave her to suffer.

Gathering her in his arms, he stood and strode down the grassy shores to the loch.

"Keegan, where are you taking me?" Slender arms locked around his neck, a nose pressed against his ear.

"To the loch. You stink of the spriggan's bread." He stepped down into the cool waters.

In answer, the smoothness of her tongue glided along the shell of his ear. He jerked his head away. He continued walking outward, the water reaching his shoulders, the bottom of the loch becoming uneven beneath his feet. Wet ardent kisses trailed down his throat.

He submerged, taking her with him. For a few precious heartbeats, he dragged her out deeper, wary of those flailing limbs. With a quick gesture of his hand, he magically removed her clothes and brought them both back to the surface. Bracing himself, he prepared to weather the coming storm of a young female tainted with spriggan lust bread.

Lana came up sputtering and found her clothes had mysteriously disappeared. Gasping for air, she found herself pressed against a hard male body.

"How dare you," she coughed angrily, and shoved wet hair out of her eyes.

"Now that the stink of the spriggan is gone, we can proceed. First, you must understand these be fey waters. Mortals are heavier here and you will drown." His arm tightened around her waist. "Do you understand me?"

"Why do you not kiss me?"

He arched a decadent brow. "Do you understand you must stay close to me?"

In answer, Lana clamped her mouth on to his with such force that teeth struck teeth.

He pulled back, his tongue skimming across a bloody bottom lip.

Their eyes met and locked.

"Forgive me, Lana. I have waited too long." His mouth lowered, slanting over hers in a welcomed possession. "Savor me," he murmured seductively against her lips.

She did, feeding on him. A throaty groan vibrated in his throat, spilling into her mouth. She could feel his passion, just out of reach. Her bare thighs slid against his, the sensation sending a wild yearning through her to join with him.

Shifting higher, she rubbed her woman's place against his thick man root, an unexpected jolt slamming through her.

It was nothing compared to the jolt of lightning spearing through Keegan's blood. He responded aggressively, deepening the kiss, and then caught himself. She was grinding against him, a like madness erupting between them. If he was not careful, she would impale herself through his breeches.

With every ounce of control, he struggled to tame his forceful nature.

He intensified the kiss, bringing her full focus back to what his mouth was doing, an erotic tease and play. She quickly responded and he had to tilt his head so he could breathe.

She was incapable of understanding what he truly was, what he had lived these long lonely years. The guardians were the oldest of the fey born, cunning, predatory, and lethal, if wronged. He lived a solitary existence, defending the waters, defending the fey, and took what he wanted without thought, without explanation. A barren life of power, he wanted it no more. Nothing had been left of interest to him until now, until *her*.

She was luscious, perfect, and innocent in his arms, despite the lust fever. His mouth softened, showing her how to taste him, how to stoke the liquid fires within. Her soft breasts pressed into his chest and he drank of her virgin passion. Slowly, he began to sense a secret, hidden deep.

His mouth stilled upon hers.

His senses tuned to the irregular beats of her heart.

He pulled back, breathing heavily in shock, passion waning.

Her eyes opened. "Keegan?"

He kissed her lips gently then, feeling the pulse of her heart in his mouth.

His hand moved to rest between soft breasts.

She immediately stiffened and grabbed his wrist, the power of her secret temporarily surpassing the lust spell in her blood.

"So now you know." Her gaze flashed with hurt.

"You have a weak heart, Lana."

"Aye." She tried to pull out of his arms. "Let me go. I doona wish to be rejected by you."

"I doona reject you," he gritted out, holding her close. Desire and passion wilted within him with the discovery of her weakness, but he would not leave her in discomfort. "You will take what I give you," he said with deliberation, and cupped her chin, turning her pale face back to him.

Tears streamed down her cheeks.

Lowering his mouth to hers, he kissed her, only to flinch back.

"You nipped me?" he said in disbelief, his tongue skimming over a bloody bottom lip.

"Let me go."

"I think not. Shall we fight more over this?" He knew her emotions were in turmoil; she was hurting inside and striking out.

"Care to draw more of my blood?" he challenged, and dragged her toward the shallows.

When the water reached his chest and he felt on sure footing, he turned to her. "It is time." Bracing his hands under her arms, he lifted her. A knee smacked him in the chest, but he refused to release her. Latching onto the dusky peak of a bare breast, he drew the straining tip into his mouth and began to draw her will to him.

Lana gasped, hands fisting in thick brown strands. She twisted in urgency and desperation, her body trembling. Large hands spanned her rib cage, holding her imprisoned while he suckled her, while that hot tongue flicked over the sensitive nipple with a heated exploration. Tears spilled down flushed cheeks with each pull of his lips. She strained against him in a wild agony only to have him latch onto her other breast with the same ferocity. Panting, Lana cried out in pleasure. His mouth was hot and moist, her body bathed in perspiration and anticipation.

Hands slid to her hips. He kissed the underside of her breast and his mouth began a slow, tantalizing journey down her quivering belly.

He dropped beneath the waters, brown hair spreading outward upon the surface and then he cupped her bottom as if she were some rare delicacy.

His face moved between her thighs, finding her moist heat. Lana cried out in astonishment. He kissed her there, where the hurt and desire burned. Gasping, she felt him settle in closer.

A firestorm raged between her thighs.

She bucked against his face.

His hands tightened, balancing her, fitting her more intimately to his mouth.

His tongue darted, flickered, an aggressive and heated exploration of her. Unearthly flames licked inside her womb.

Wheezing for air, she felt him tense.

His mouth pressed closer to her woman's place.

And he . . .

He . . . *melded*.

Lana screamed, her body shattering. Sheer pleasure fed to every pore of her being, drowning out the spriggan's false lust. Her eyes rolled back into her head, an inferno of wetness and blaze clenching in her womb, burning outward until only glowing embers were left of her spirit. It stole all that remained of her strength.

Sobbing uncontrollably, she went limp, falling back and below the surface of the waters, where her guardian mate cradled her and brought her back safely to the surface.

CHAPTER 9

THE NIGHT AIR OF THE mortal place felt cool on his heated flesh. He glanced down at his sleeping bride, feeling unexpectedly awkward.

She lay near the thick trunk of an oak tree, her pink lips parted slightly in exhausted slumber. Her slender body lay quiet, the lust fever gone, while his throbbed in unquenched desire. He fingered his bottom lip, still tender from her false boldness. Though he *melded* with her, the magical mating of *blood to blood* in the ways of the guardian, it had only been half a mating for him. The craving to join his body with hers remained, an untamed beast battling his hard won control.

He touched her hair, the blond strands soft between his fingers. Leaning down, he balanced on an elbow and brought the glossy strands to his nose. Closing his eyes, he inhaled the delicate fragrance of her. Slender white thighs flashed in his mind. Through the gift of the waters, he had tasted her virgin passion.

Made her quiver with his tongue.

Her body writhing above him.

The taste of her first ecstasy in his mouth.

His eyelids flung open.

Releasing her hair, he pushed up. "Stop this," he said tightly, angry with himself.

She murmured in her sleep, a response to his disquiet.

He raked a hand through his hair, his spirit entangled in obsession and idiocy. "It must end," he said with hushed vehemence. This fascination with his bride would only lead to pain and punishment for him. The fey were unforgiving of stupidity, and this infatuation was most definitely stupidity.

He scanned the area. They were not far from the pillars which first caught his fair one's interest. He returned here knowing she needed rest. Lana had not confirmed the sword lay at Knowth, and so he must wait for her to awaken. Wait for her heart to recover and rest. A few hours would not matter, he mused.

A small herd of goats grazed on the hill to the north. It was night again, the moon goddess high in the sky. A full four days had passed in the mortal world while he gave her pleasure in a fey place. Time moved differently there.

He inhaled deeply, the silence inside him lengthening.

This *claíomh host* has a weak heart. *Lana has a weak heart.*

The thought of it twisted his insides.

How could this be? he wondered. *How could Lana be a chosen host?*

The host must be strong, he reasoned. She must be able to defend the lands. Lana could hardly maintain her breath while walking up a small hill. Eyes narrowing at a familiar swift brilliance a few horse lengths away, he stiffened with recognition.

"Blodenwedd," he said softly, wearily, recognizing the flowery scent of the volatile territorial goddess.

She shimmered into view, wearing a white hooded cloak reflecting the moonlight.

Rising to his feet, he went to her and bowed respectfully. "Good eve, Goddess."

"BE THAT FRAIL CREATURE YOUR *CLAÍOMH HOST* BRIDE?" She ignored his greeting, her attention focused behind him.

"Aye," he said, regarding her steadily. "Why have you come?"

"CURIOUS."

"I doubt that," he grunted, but she heard. He met her glower with one of his own.

"YOU BE OF FOUL TEMPER THIS EVE, GUARDIAN. BODY NOT SATED?"

"Watching again, Goddess?" he asked with a slight mocking smile.

Her mouth snapped shut, her increased breathing showing her anger.

He waited, struggling for patience with her.

She lifted her face to him. "NEEDED TO FIND YOU."

"You have found me."

"WAITED UNTIL YOU FINISHED WITH HER."

"I am finished."

"BUT NOT SATED."

"Blodenwedd," he said between clenched teeth, "doona test my temper this eve. Why are you here?"

"INVADERS ARE COME."

He frowned. Many of the territorial goddesses had premonitions and the high king often sought their council. Blodenwedd's dreams, however, were never accurate concerning time so he always practiced caution around her.

"You have seen this?" he asked.

She shook her head. "OTHER TERRITORIAL GODDESSES."

"Go on."

"KING NUADA SENT ME TO YOU."

He nodded.

"BRESS MAC ELADAN RETURNED TO THE FORMORIANS."

"I know this." Bress was the youthful tyrant king who had ruled in Nuada's place before the just fey king returned with his new silver hand and reclaimed his fey throne.

"BRESS RAISES AN ARMY AGAINST EIRE AND THE TUATHA DÉ DANANN."

"These be the words of King Nuada?" he prompted firmly.

"AYE."

"Does he wish me to abandon my quest for Valor and return to Tara?"

"NAY." She shook her head and hesitated.

"Tell me, Blodenwedd." His jaw tightened. "What is

the king's wish?"

"RAIN, IN THE BATTLE TO COME THE KING BELIEVES . . .

"What?" he prompted.

". . . HE BELIEVES DEATH COMES UNLESS VALOR BE IN HIS HAND."

"How long do I have before our enemy arrives, Blodenwedd? When do the invaders come?"

"MAKE THE HOST TAKE YOU TO VALOR SOON."

"Lana will show me the way. When do they come?"

She shrugged. "A MONTH, MAYHAP LESS, THE OTHER GODDESSES SAY."

"A month," he muttered, looking away. *That is not much time*. When he turned back, the golden goddess had winked out, leaving him to the silence and torture of another long night.

He returned to his frail bride and looked down upon her delicate features. Not a defect could he see in her, but underneath the lovely pale skin, weakness lived.

"Keegan?" she said softly, not fully awake, yet sensing him.

"Here." He dropped down behind her. "Rest, Lana."

She sighed in her sleep.

He lay down on his back, careful not to touch her, a new sense of urgency blooming in his blood.

A month he had, mayhap less.

He willed his eyes shut, and allowed her a few more hours of rest.

❈ ❈ ❈

Lana awoke with a fully clothed fey guardian snuggled beside her, his nose pressed into her ear. Her first waking thought was that he had not rejected her.

"Ahem."

A spriggan stood near her hip.

"Sleeps," Cadman said quietly, pointing at her guardian.

Tensing a little, Lana wondered how the ugly rock faery had found them.

"Hungry?" He delved in his left pocket and held out more of his confounded covet bread.

"She is not," her guardian growled in answer, pushing up on his elbow. Power and threat vibrated in the warm air. "I will give you this warning only once, spriggan. She is mine. If you ever come near her or even think of touching her again, I will kill you."

Without a word of response, the spriggan wisely winked out.

Lana pushed up to her elbows, her heart warm and brimming with joy at his words. *She is mine,* he had said.

Icy silver turned toward her. A quick chill replaced the warmth which filled her but moments before.

"How do you feel this morning?" he asked in a strangely detached tone.

She blushed uncontrollably.

"I will take that as a good sign." He sat up and ran a

hand down his face, a mortal gesture she found endearing.

"Why did you not tell me about your heart, Lana?"

"I almost did," she whispered, sitting up.

"You could not be meant for the sword spirit," he said suddenly, and gestured to her chest. "Not with that flaw inside you."

His words hurt. She stiffened her spine, hands clenched in her lap. "You know the thinking and ways of the sword spirit?" she challenged impudently.

"Do you?"

"I bear the birthmark of the sword spirit. I must be good enough."

Climbing to her feet, she disappeared behind a bush to take care of her needs. It was a weak excuse to hide the turbulent emotions colliding inside her.

Keegan supposed she was indeed good enough, for who was he to question the spirit of the sword? A mere fey guardian. He stood and gathered their things. Moments later, she came stomping back, glaring and annoyed.

He regarded her with a raised brow. "Which way?" he asked.

Flinging her arm out, she pointed. "That way." And then stomped off in the same direction. He followed.

Hours later, they were walking north at a slow steady pace. Now that he knew she battled a weak heart, a new respect formed inside him. Thinking back, he remembered how she helped her family about the farm, how she cheerily performed chores for the druidess, and aided others of the village. Mayhap he underestimated her, he thought, rubbing his chin. Mayhap the strength of a great defender came from within self and spirit, and not physical strength alone.

Up ahead, she paused to capture her breath, her palm resting in the center of her breasts.

He hurried to her side, alarmed by her pallor. "Lana?"

"I am fine," she wheezed, her eyes closing, eyelashes splaying against cheeks gone suddenly pale, shutting him out. He could see her straining, laboring for each breath. He hated this feeling of helplessness, this inability to fix what was broken within her. Hands clenched at his sides, he stood beside her in silent support, waiting for her to regain her breath. The wait felt eternal to him, the wheezing sounds slowly ending, but not soon enough. He reached out to touch her back, to soothe away the tension of forcing air into her body.

Her eyes cracked open and he dropped his hand.

"Do you feel better?" he asked, studying her face.

She nodded shakily. "Aye, this one took me by surprise."

"You know when this thing, this weakness, happens?"

"Aye, sometimes my body gives me warning. The weakness comes upon me slowly and I can find a place to sit and rest. This time it came fast and unannounced."

"What does it. . .?" He stopped, realizing he should not be asking a question such as this.

"What does it feel like? Is that what you want to know?"

He nodded guiltily.

"I doona mind answering your questions, Keegan." She smiled brightly at him, her eyes glassy with fatigue. "My heart pounds rapidly in my chest, sometimes with pain arching in my left shoulder and down my arm. Sometimes there is no pain, only the stealing of my breath like being strangled by invisible hands around my throat. I am tired most of the time, but since I know no other way of living, I doona miss being in fine health. I used to resent the other girls in the village, wishing to be included in their friendships. It is not that they treated me poorly, only . . ." She paused to catch a breath. "They were so careful around me, afraid my weakness might spill onto them."

"That is why you were alone most often when I saw you."

She nodded. "I have my own friends though. Derina, Lightning, the sea, and the sky."

He looked over to the northern hills, concealing his resentment at her seclusion. "You have a brave spirit," he said grimly, and meant it.

"I am not brave, Keegan."

"More than you know." He cleared his throat, finding his chest tight with feelings for her. "Lana, do you head toward Knowth as the spriggan said?"

"What is Knowth?"

"A sacred passage tomb."

"I doona know my path, Keegan. I only know . . ." She shook her head in denial. "I doona really know where we go. There is a single thread inside me, pulling me north, yet I am unsure of even that. Why do you ask?"

"If it were Knowth, I could take us there now and save time. One of my fey kin has visited me. She gives warning invaders are coming to our shores. We must find Valor within a month's time." He turned back to her. The shadows under her night-hued eyes made her look even more fragile than before. The journey sapped what little strength she had to give him.

"Knowth," she said in slow thoughtfulness and then smiled. "Aye, Keegan, let us go there."

He moved close to her and rested his hands on her slender waist.

"Put your hands on my shoulders."

Reaching up, she linked her hands behind his neck. Her breasts pressed into his chest.

"Doona fear," he said softly.

"I doona fear, Keegan. We are together."

"Aye," he agreed, and closed his eyes.

Lana held on to him while a soft white light illuminated the air all around her.

A muted silence came to her ears and then a strange coolness . . .

She sucked in her breath. In the next instant, she stood near a great bend in a river.

Her guardian mate stepped back from her and said simply, "Knowth."

Shielding her eyes from the bright sunlight, Lana stared

at a large mound of earth.

"Knowth?" she murmured, filling her senses with the awe-inspiring sight.

The hill, or mound, as the land formations were sometimes called, was large and oval. Around its perimeter lay great carved stones, one after another, each decorated with scrolls and lines that seemed to link the mound to the sun and stars. Smaller mounds surrounded its perimeter and Lana counted seventeen in all.

"Is the sword here, Lana?"

"I am not sure."

"Is it below?"

She turned to her guardian mate. "Below what?"

"Knowth is a double passage tomb, Lana." He pointed to the mound. "There are entrances both east and west within her. The sunrises and sunsets of the land spill into those pathways, marking the ways to our Otherworld.

She had not considered that, had not considered the sword would be in a mysterious and magical place. The Otherworld, rarely accessible to mortals, belonged to the olden deities. It was a place of enchanted halls and beautiful hills and valleys, existing below the lands and seas. Those mortals allowed to enter through a magic tree or waterfall spoke of living in perfect harmony. She often wondered if the Otherworld was truly real. Now she knew.

"Lana, what do you sense?" her guardian mate asked, bringing her out of her ruminations.

She looked over her shoulder. Tall grasses swept before the shore of the river. It felt like they had come too far.

"Lana?"

She chewed her lip and looked up at him. "I doona know. The sword feels closer to me, but I am unsure."

"Let us enter Knowth then and see her pathways with our own eyes. I will not leave this place until I am sure." He took her hand and for the first time in their journey, he led the way.

Lana forced down a wave of apprehension. The soil rose up in front of them, marking a steep incline. The sun was bright in the sky, almost blinding. She held tightly to his hand, struggling to keep up with his pace.

They walked beyond a single limestone pillar standing outside the eastern passage and entered the dark coolness of Knowth. The light of day retreated behind them. Her guardian led her along a path of sod and clay and into shadows and dimness. An eerie purple light lit the way ahead of them, and there was an offensive smell to the air, as if something had died. The walls were beautifully decorated with spirals and faceted droplets and the stone ceilings were high above their heads.

"This path be a fey place, too?" she inquired, slightly in awe. After all, she had never walked down into the below depths of the land before.

"Aye."

She wrinkled her nose. "Do you smell that?"

" 'Tis the taint of fey spitefulness you smell. The faeries doona like mortals trespassing on what they consider theirs."

"Do we trespass here, Keegan?"

"We do, but I would see all of Knowth's ways, so I know that Valor is not here."

They walked a short while, ever downward, and came upon an empty cruciform chamber. Lana did not like the feel of the place.

"Wait here." Her guardian mate let go of her hand and approached a smooth flat stone embedded in the wall of the east corner.

She rubbed her arms to ward off the chill and followed.

A thin stream of water trickled from a crevice above the flat stone, followed by a seeping white mist. Upon closer inspection, she could see an etching of scrolls in its center.

"What is it?" she inquired, coming up beside him.

"A doorway to the Otherworld. The water marks its entrance. It is seen only by the fey born." He glanced at her. "Do you see it?"

"I see a flat gray stone with some sort of carvings, water, and mist."

"You see it then."

Her guardian mate turned back, a sudden tension stiffening his body.

"Lana, go back," he warned.

"Why?" she asked, taking a step back. Her gaze darted to the flat stone and trickle of water. She was not afraid to face danger.

"Go back now!" he roared.

Metamorphosing to his true form, Keegan took the brunt of the attack from the two white faeries emerging from the fey entry. He brought the fight into the air. They were as swift and strong as he was, their skin tinted the palest of white shades, marking a lineage to the oldest of the fey born.

Slamming into the ceiling of the chamber, he grunted and fought back. Wings battering, rocks cutting into his right shoulder, he smelled their hatred, their dark eyes pulsing with blood lust. He swung his right arm up and caught the smaller one in the neck, gaining a momentary reprieve.

"YOU DIE TODAY, GUARDIAN," the larger, white-haired one said, pulling out a Darkshade dagger. "HOLD HIM."

Twisting, Keegan blocked the thrust of the dagger to his mid-section and punched the smaller brown-haired faery full in the face. In the corner of his eye, he saw something move below, a shadow darting across the floor . . .

Without thought, his free hand came up, reaching for the mortal sword strapped between his wings. It left him open to attack.

White-hot pain slashed across his stomach where they cut him with the dagger. He struck out blindly, knocking the mystical dagger out of the faery's hand; it tumbled below.

His stomach awash with fire, he doubled over and pulled his wings in protectively. Dropping fast to the ground, he took the more aggressive white-haired faery with him. The pain made him angry. They landed hard on stone and sod. Freeing himself, he rolled and climbed quickly to his feet. In the next instant, the mortal sword was poised for battle in his hands.

"Lana!" he bellowed, searching for her.

"Here!"

He turned. Locked in the arms of a third faery, his bride fought for all she was worth. Her face set with fierce resolve, her right hand came up in a stinging slap, slicing a cut in the fey born's cheek as she once unintentionally did to him. It was a mark of her true dark destiny. Her captor reared back in surprise and she kneed him in the groin, gaining her release. She was free and running to him. "Keegan!"

Launching himself toward her, he scooped her up despite his stomach wound and headed back the way they had come.

"Hold on, Lana." He had to capture one of the faeries and question him. He would not wink out to safety and chance them not following. Instead, he would draw them out.

Lana did not understand why he did not wink them outside. "Keegan!" she cried, "they follow us."

"Good," he replied. "I want them to."

Powerful wings lifted and carried them through the tunnel. Heart pounding violently in her chest, the swish of air pummeling her face, Lana clung to him. She was dimly aware of the ground rising up, then sunlight kissed her face. "Let go, Lana."

Her guardian pulled her arms free and she dropped safely to the ground, rolling easily to her feet in the tall grasses.

The sound of wings and shrieks of rage broke the silence behind them. Shielding her eyes, she looked up and watched in horror as her guardian rose toward a pair of furious winged faeries. Locked in battle, they plunged like battling kestrels into the blue sky.

Sensing danger, Lana looked to the east entrance of the tomb. The third faery with the bloody cheek spotted her. Wings beating, he leaped in her direction. Jumping to her feet, Lana reached for the nearest weapon, a jagged hand-sized rock. With single-minded determination to bash the attacker in the head, she gripped the stone in her right hand.

"THINK THAT STOPS ME?" her white-skinned stalker taunted with a snarl.

If she were going to die, she would die fighting. The faery circled her, a smile of menace lighting its face.

"TIME TO DIE, SWORD HOST."

It lunged, big hands reaching for her throat.

Legs braced, wheezing faintly, Lana flung her rock at the faery's head, but it was all for naught.

To her stunned amazement, the point of a sword stuck out of her attacker's chest. The faery landed on his knees, wings scrunched up, dark eye's glazed with astonishment. She watched it shudder and then drop, face smashing into the ground in death.

She stared at Keegan's sword, at the sunbeams reflecting

off the blade. It stood upright out of the faery's back, wobbling slightly, having been flung from the reaches of the sky.

"Keegan," she said in sudden realization. He had no weapon.

Shaking off her fright, she ran over, grabbed the sword hilt and yanked it upward. The sword slid out of the fey flesh easily.

Adjusting her grip, she held the bloodstained blade out in front of her. It felt like an extension of her arms. It felt right in her hands, strong and able and deadly.

She should not be able to wield a weighty weapon made for a strong healthy male.

But she could.

She knew she could.

In the inner reaches of her mind and body, she tapped into what lay dormant within her and turned toward the battle raging above.

Her lungs no longer struggling for breath, she moved under the fight. Here on the ground, she became a true sword host, magical, courageous, resolute, a formidable fighter. Her focus intense and unflinching, she waited, fiercely determined to save her mate. When the fight in the sky moved toward the riverbanks, she followed at a dead run.

Head ringing from a punch to the jaw, Keegan swung out and tore at the fragile tissue of the left wing of the larger faery. The scream that followed nearly pierced his eardrums. Writhing in pain, the injured faery jerked off him and tumbled in upon itself, plunging toward the damp shores of the river below.

Without getting a moment's breath, Keegan turned to meet the remaining attacker and flinched when a dagger sliced his upper arm. The brown-haired one was quicker than he was and knew it. He was running out of strength, the deep gash in his stomach dripping blood down his loins to his thighs. He had to finish this one off quickly and then stop the white-haired one before it got to Lana. He pulled his wings in close and let the sudden weight of him pull them both down.

On the ground, Lana did not wait for the white-haired faery to rise to its feet. As its head and shoulders lifted from where it lay, she swung and chopped the head off at the neck with one swing.

Pivoting on her heel, she searched the sky. Out of the clouds, her guardian plummeted, twirling and locked in battle with their third attacker. They hit the edge of the riverbank hard, muddy water splashing in the air from their impact.

Tearing through the tall grasses, Lana held the deadly sword above her head.

She saw Keegan was badly hurt. The taste of bitter fury filled her mouth. Swinging with all the force within her, she decapitated the third faery, the severed head landing at her feet.

Lying on his back, Keegan froze, splattered in white blood. He blinked, trying to clear his vision.

The body of a headless faery lay atop him and his *claíomh host* bride stood above him holding his sword in a death grip. Her eyes were feral with the battle rage seen in the eyes of warrior men, and she was streaked in faery blood.

"Lana?" he said quietly, battling pain.

She was breathing heavily, her blond hair a mess about her shoulders. She did not seem to recognize him.

"Lana, put the sword down."

She held it as if she would take off his head, too.

"It is done. Put the sword down, Lana."

"Keegan?" she grated out, and he saw reason returning. She abandoned the sword near his shoulder.

"Aye, my trusty warrior." He grunted, and his head fell back into the sucking muck. "I wanted to question one of them about Valor."

Reaching over, he shoved the dead weight of the faery off him. The creature had retrieved the Darkshade dagger from Knowth and attempted to stab him with it. He tossed the deadly mystical dagger behind his head and into the moving river.

"The one chasing me on the ground called me a sword host."

Clenching his jaw, he stared down his blood stained body, trying to see the stomach wound. "They attacked us because they knew we sought Valor," he rasped. "But how?"

"Someone must have alerted them."

Those were his thoughts exactly. "Very few know of this quest." His head fell back. The faces of those who knew of the quest flashed in his mind. *The King, Lugh, Blodenwedd, Derina . . . the spriggan.*

"One of them," she murmured as if reading his thoughts.

"Aye, one of them." He trusted all except the spriggan.

"Keegan, how badly are you hurt?"

Bad. His vision began to fade. "Lana, you must listen to me." He felt himself sinking into cold darkness. "You must leave me. Avoid Cadman. He is not to be trusted. Find Valor and return her to the faery king."

"I will not leave you," she said stubbornly from some place far away.

He wanted to shake her into doing his bidding, but the wash of pain came again. It flowed into the pores of his flesh, stealing his strength. "Lana, find Valor." The all-consuming darkness covered him in the next breath and his eyes fluttered closed.

"Keegan?" Lana cried out in alarm. "Nay!"

She had to get help. Jumping to her feet in a panic, she wavered on the slippery incline of the riverbank and then fell to her side. Whatever courage and strength possessed her earlier fell away into nonexistence. Fighting weakly, she slid several man lengths down in the slick mud, the flowing river creeping over her ankles like icy manacles. Out of the corner of her eye, she saw an iridescent shine, a dragonfly hovering in watchful silence. Fighting for breath, she collapsed into muck and oblivion, fainting dead away near her gravely injured mate.

CHAPTER 10

SHE FELT UNEXPECTEDLY WARM AND comfortable, given the fact she was dead.

She was dead, was she not?

At least, she expected to be dead.

Licking dry lips, Lana peered up into a world of soft pink light and smooth rock formations. She wondered where the blue sky and puffy white clouds had gone. She blinked several times, her mind slowly focusing.

She was in a cave, she thought. Long needle-like aragonite and flowery white quartz crystals were high above her head. In a limestone recess to her right, a white spider waited in the center of a pale web, her gray legs nearly invisible among the cream and amber icicles.

"AWAKE NOW?" a soft female voice inquired tolerantly beside her.

Startled at the close proximity of the voice, Lana sat up abruptly. She found herself near the edge of the black rippling waters of a cave pool. The pale face regarding her belonged to a young girl of ten summers, yet there was an olden quality to the tilted blue eyes and flawless features. This was no mortal girl, she realized, but a small faery whose skin and hair wore the colors of a first snowfall.

"FEEL BETTER?" the girl faery asked. She stood in the shallows about two arm lengths from her.

Lana nodded, not yet able to find her voice. She could see no wings on this faery. Silvery green combs pulled sallow waves away from a face more angular than curved. Her nearly transparent clothes shimmered with soft lights, the same colors of the outside seas.

"Where am I?" Lana whispered hoarsely. "Who are you?" she sputtered to a stop, remembering what happened. "Where is Keegan?" She looked around in a panic. "Where is my guardian?"

"GUARDIAN BEHIND YOU."

Lana looked where the faery pointed and felt real fear. At the end of the pool, her guardian lay on his back on a narrow slab of gray stone. Water lapped at his body. He lay unmoving, wings outstretched and floating like decaying silvery leaves.

"Keegan," she cried out.

A tiny hand grabbed her wrist before she could scramble to her feet.

"NOT DEAD."

Lana looked at the girl faery. "Not dead?" she breathed

fiercely, the terror receding a wee bit. "Are you sure?"

The faery nodded her head, releasing her. "HURT ONLY," she said, and made a slashing motion across her stomach and left arm. "WATERS HELP HEAL HIM."

Lana sat back down, overcome with relief. Keegan lay there naked, green paste smeared on his wounds. The surface of the black pool stirred in undulating waves from some underground water current. She gave a weary sigh and rubbed her temple. Her chest ached and she took a moment to regain her composure. A slightly bitter scent tainted the moist air of the cavern. She lifted her face and sniffed.

"ELDER FLOWER AND FEY WHISPERS RENEW BODY," the girl faery explained.

Lana frowned. "Is that the green paste on him?"

"FLOWER," the faery repeated. "WHISPERS."

Lana nodded that she understood, though she did not. Her tribe used herbs for healing, not flowers, and she had no idea what whispers meant. She looked around to get her bearings. It was a large cave. She estimated it to be about the size of a small meadow, with one irregular and narrowly shaped black pool. Sheets of creamy white amber and gray streaks rippled and folded on the slanted rock walls.

"MOTHERSMILK," her small faery companion explained, gesturing at the fluid looking walls.

The walls did look like mother's milk, she thought in agreement. Round crystals lit the cave in a pink glow, brighter in some spots and softer in others.

"Where is this place?" she asked.

"A Safe Place."

"Is it part of Knowth?"

"Near."

"Otherworld?" Lana guessed.

The girl faery shook her head. "Water cave only. feeling better now?"

She nodded, looking down at herself. She had been cleaned up. Her trembling fingers brushed against a blond curl lying across her shoulder, no longer sticky with white blood.

"My thanks," Lana offered in all sincerity.

The faery nodded.

"I doona mean to be disrespectful, but who are you?" she asked.

"MacLir."

The girl faery had a lilting voice, one meant to soothe and comfort.

"Why are you helping us, MacLir?"

"Help guardian of the waters."

Lana glanced over her shoulder at Keegan to make sure he was still there, that this was not all a dark dream.

"Must go now," MacLir said directly, and took a step back. "You care for him."

"How?" she asked. She was not a healer.

"Time heals. Water heals. Smear new paste on him when old turns brown."

She could do that.

"Wrongly did they attack."

"You know who attacked us?"

"The fey followers of Lord Bress. Bad they be."

Lord Bress? Lana looked away, searching her memory. "The ousted fey king of the faeries?"

MacLir nodded. "Know him?"

"I know of him. He was a hero of the Fir Bog war and was named fey king when King Nuada was injured."

"Blemished Nuada became."

"He lost a hand," Lana clarified.

"Blemished."

Lana knew the faeries valued physical beauty above most things. "I heard stories that King Bress did not rule justly."

"Tyrant." MacLir barred her teeth in definite agreement.

"When Nuada returned with his new silver hand, he re-claimed his throne and threw Bress out." At least, that was what she understood.

"Nuada made whole by magic. Bress unfair and false. He fled."

Lana wondered if the young Bress, who fell from hero king to tyrant, stole Valor, had taken the great sword for his own. "Do you know where Bress has fled, MacLir?"

MacLir shrugged. "Back to his father's people. Hates us now."

Lana could see the girl faery did not want to talk anymore about Bress.

"I provided for you there." MacLir pointed and

Lana looked over her shoulder. Behind her were two small baskets of food, a pile of white pelts beside Keegan's sword, a small silver pail on its side and a silvery weave she guessed was fey cloth of some kind. In the center of all sat a large wicker basket of stinky, green paste.

"I am grateful to you, MacLir."

"GUARDIAN INDEBTED TO ME. MAKE SURE YOU TELL HIM."

"I will."

A distinctive male groan filled the cavern. "Lana?"

"I am here, Keegan." Lana climbed to her feet and hurried to the edge of pool. From the corner of her eye, she saw MacLir drop into the waters and dissolve.

"Where are we?" he rasped.

She picked her way around slippery black pebbles and pink pool spar crystals that were shaped in tiny clustered petals.

"We are safe and in a cave," she answered. Careful of her step, she waded into warm waters. As she approached, her guardian pulled his wings close to his side as if in pain.

"Keegan, are you hurting?" She came up to the narrow altar upon where he lay . . . naked.

"What cave?" her guardian mate demanded in a stronger voice, his right hand shielding his eyes.

"A cave near Knowth."

He looked at her sidewise, questioningly.

"MacLir brought us here," she explained, holding on to the edge of the altar, careful not to touch him. The waters rode high on her waist. "She has left food for us and some sort of green healing mixture I am to apply on your wounds."

"Ah," he said, holding up his left arm to inspect the paste. "So that is the stink I smell. Flower essences and healing fey whispers. MacLir has outdone herself this time."

"You know her?"

"Aye," he replied, offering nothing further. She studied the wound above his left elbow. The paste followed the jagged line of it, the length of a man's largest finger.

"Does it hurt?" she asked, suspecting it was a deep cut.

"Not as much as my pride." He looked down at himself and winced. "Where are my clothes?"

She kept her gaze on his face. "They appear to be gone, Keegan."

He glared at her and then plopped his head back on the slab, causing her to cringe.

"Interfering faeries," he mumbled, and tried to sit up. She slid her arm behind his shoulders, careful of his wings, and helped support him into a sitting position. Breathing heavily from the effort, he slid his left leg off the slab and faced her, his shin grazing her hip.

"You should rest, Keegan."

He shook his head. "We canna delay. We must find Valor."

"I think Bress took Valor, Keegan, or ordered the sword taken. MacLir said the faeries that attacked us were followers of Bress, and the one chasing me called me a sword host."

He looked at her through his lashes and his pain.

"It makes sense," she offered when he did not comment.

His head bowed. "Aye," he muttered. Nostrils flaring, he seemed to be gathering his strength for the next movement.

She rested her hand on the powerful slope of his shoulder and said, "You really need to rest."

He shook his head in denial of the injury.

She stared at his ear in fascination, a pink shell shape delicately rising to a point. His wet hair looked almost black in the pale rose light of the cavern. It lay upon him in dark ropes, covering his chest, shoulders, and back. Wrinkling her nose, she decided he did rather reek from the green paste.

Lana stroked his shoulder, offering reassurance and comfort, her fingertips grazing the firm, glossy edge of a wing. Turning slightly, she observed the commanding wings growing out of his shoulder blades. Never had she seen a faery's wings close up, seen the pulse of tiny veins and subtle connective tissue. The form and shape reminded her of enormous butterfly wings, but they seemed crafted of luminous silver webs and different shades of night. Reaching out, she touched the closest one, watching it stretch under her hand, a kind of mysterious and dangerous unveiling. Droplets of water fell from understated curves, creating tiny ringlets in the water.

Alluring smoothness.

Yielding, yet surprisingly warm and solid.

Enticingly beautiful.

Magnificent, she thought. Completely enthralled, she traced a gray vein with a fingertip and then heard . . . a venomous oath.

Lana turned back slowly, dreadfully aware of what she had been doing. "Doona touch a guardian's wings," she remembered the druidess's warning, "or dire things will happen."

And dire things were about to happen, she knew without a doubt.

His head was up, body vibrating. She realized alarmingly she had released something wild.

"Keegan?" She smiled weakly, holding onto his arm.

His face was harsh. From beneath narrowed lids, a strange, mesmerizing tempest watched her.

Lana swallowed down her uncertainty. Pulling her hand off him, she took a hesitant step back.

A low snarl rumbled in his chest, a warning not to move.

"I dinna mean to touch your wings. I just . . . just . . ." she stammered. "They are so beautiful."

He reached out and grabbed her nape, dragging her across a rigid lap.

Her nose collided hurtfully with a hard collarbone, sending shooting stars into her vision.

"Your wounds," she protested, tears welling in her eyes from smacking her nose.

He was not listening.

Fingers locked in her hair, dragging her head back. His mouth lowered and took hers in a centuries old kiss of possession.

Hard.

Domineering.

Passionate.

Pleasurable.

His tongue invaded her mouth and made her body hum with desire.

Then, just as unexpectedly, he pushed her gently away from him.

Lana stumbled back in the waters, panting for breath, her lips tingling from his touch.

He said something forcefully and then flung back his head, the veins in his neck popping, white teeth bared in misery. No sound did he make and Lana watched in horror as he collapsed backward into the waters.

With a startled cry, she rushed around his legs to the other side of the stone slab and pulled his head out of the water, cradling him in her arms.

"Nay, Keegan," she cried, not understanding. "What have I done? Please doona be hurt."

Never touch a male faery's wings or dire things will happen. The druidess's warning resounded in her mind.

Never touch.

"I am sorry." She gulped back tears.

Holding him to her, his face tucked into her breasts, she looked boldly down his length. He was still breathing, his stomach rising and falling. *Thank the white moon goddess!* She closed her eyes and took a recovering breath. When she looked at him again, his large man root was erect, rising from a dark nest.

"Does it remain that way even if they are unconscious?" she mumbled to herself.

"I am not unconscious."

Startled, she looked down.

"Smothered might be a better description," he said sardonically.

Embarrassed at her open perusal of his man root, she jumped back, releasing him. His head and shoulders sank below the surface once again.

With a cry, Lana grabbed a handful of silken hair and yanked, bringing him back up to the surface.

"Lana," her guardian mate said tightly, not even sputtering. "If you but let me fall into the healing waters, I would greatly appreciate it."

She blinked in bewilderment. "Now?"

"Now would be suitable."

Not knowing what else to do, she did as he bade. She released him and stepped back anxiously.

He dropped down, head and shoulders sinking into the darkness of the water. This time, the rest of him rolled off the stone slab, wings tucked close to his back, and disappeared out of sight.

She stood there, alone in the accompanying silence.

He did not surface.

Did not return.

Lana searched the waters around her. He was not mortal,

she reminded herself yet again. He was enchanted, a fey being of mystery and appeal and he had been under the fey waters a lot longer when he had given her pleasure.

Yet, the cavern seemed to expand with her dread.

Placing a hand above her heart, the familiar fluttering took hold.

"Please," she prayed aloud.

"Here."

Lana spun around.

Her fey guardian mate transformed back to his familiar, and, she had to admit, beloved, mortal shape. He stood there, hunched over, bare and glistening from the waist up, an arm pressed into the green paste smeared on his stomach.

"You . . ." Her mouth had gone dry.

A decadent brow arched at her. "Me?" He reached out to the edge of the stone for balance and support.

She stepped aside. "You could have drowned."

He shook his head slowly. "I can stay below the waters a lot longer than mortal males." He turned to her. "Do you not remember?"

She blushed profusely. "I remember." He had given her pleasure in the waters, his face between her thighs, his mouth . . .

"Doona touch my wings again, Lana."

Startled out of her sensual recollection, she looked up at him.

"I canna control . . ."

His head bowed low while she waited.

". . . certain impulses."

"Mindless rutting," she offered simply.

He gave her a quick look. "As you wish to call it."

She moved closer and saw him swallow hard.

"Doona touch me that way again, Lana."

A silence came to the cave and she stared up into his eyes. "I will not touch your wings unless you wish me to. You have my word, Keegan. Now let me help you."

Something dark and unsure flashed across his features and then was gone.

"Lean on me." She moved still closer, her arm snaking around his waist.

He stiffened, caught like a butterfly in a net.

"I can help you if you let me."

His sensual lips parted with breath and she had a curious sensation in the pit of her stomach.

"Keegan?"

After the smallest of hesitations, he said, "On the shore, be there a silvery weave?"

Puzzled by his question, she looked over her shoulder. She seemed to remember seeing it. "Aye."

"Please bring it to me."

"You want it now?" she prompted, not knowing what a small, square cloth might be used for.

"Now," he answered.

"Will you be all right?" she asked with concern.

"Aye."

Lana left him and retrieved the feathery light cloth. She waded back into the pool.

"Open it," he said.

Standing beside him, she held it open above the water.

"Press the folds against my chest."

The moment she held it against his bare chest, white light flashed in front of her eyes. She stumbled back and the next thing she knew Keegan wore a sleeveless gray tunic.

"Fey magic," she mused. "Are your lower parts covered, too?"

He grunted and then without looking at her, started toward shore. Indeed, a pair of gray breeches covered his lower body.

"Stubborn faery." She shook her head and followed close behind him.

CHAPTER 11

UNDER THE VAST BLUE SKY, a sea of tall grasses and yellow flowers rippled in the afternoon breeze.

Bathed in the shady sunlight, Keegan rested on his back under the branches of a lone oak tree. On either side of him, sprawling roots reached outward, some to the bank of the river at his right and others toward the high dry land. Covered by white pelts, he was naked again, suffering between sweltering and sickly chills brought on by the Darkshade poison in his system. A burning ache spread into his blood. His head felt thick and muffled under a black cloud of clinging mist. Bress's faeries used a Darkshade dagger on him, full of black conjuring and slow acting poison, a dagger meant to quell a guardian. There were few of these magical daggers in existence and still fewer who knew their true purpose. Having once reigned over the faery realm, Lord Bress would know.

He shifted again and pain sliced through his stomach.

His jaw clamped shut. Wounds from a Darkshade dagger tended to fester, claiming one's potency before the ultimate and final end.

I doona have the time for this. He knew the worst part of the poison was yet to come. He had to remain strong, had to find Valor. He could not leave Lana alone to finish the quest, a quest his king had given him.

"How do you feel?" his fair one asked, blessedly unaware of his inner battle.

He edged himself into a sitting position. The pelts slipped down, the fur stained by the green mush over his stomach wound. "I am well enough."

"I doubt it."

Her dark jewel eyes were level with his and he saw a new found boldness there, something intrinsic, the darker side of the sacred feminine. He looked away. She tapped into that strength and fierceness, confirming her true destiny, and for some reason it upset him greatly.

"Do you think I speak an untruth?" he prompted in annoyance.

"Regarding this, aye I do," she said firmly.

"What do you know about illness?" He struck out like a wounded beast. Resentment of his body's growing weakness unknowingly fueled the magical poison.

"I have lived on a farm and cared for animals all my life, Keegan. I am able to recognize fever, sweat, and chills, not to mention bloody wounds. Why are you so angry with me?"

"I am not angry with you," he ground out, pushing her hand away from his arm. "Why do you insist on caressing me?"

Her eyes shined with hurt. It tore him up inside. He did not know how to deal with these feelings, this caring and need for her.

"Even guardians can be injured," she said compassionately.

"It is ill-timed right now," he grumbled, and glared at the green paste in her small hand. "What are you planning to do with that?"

She motioned to his stomach. " 'Tis that time again. The green paste has turned brown."

He shook his head, not wanting the mushy stink on his hurting flesh, no matter its purpose.

A delicate brow arched in reproof. "I always thought our fey kin invincible; it seems they are not."

"It was a Darkshade dagger," he grumbled again, unable to help himself from being ornery and bad-tempered.

"What is a Darkshade dagger, Keegan?"

"It is a magical dagger meant to stop a guardian." He chose not to elaborate on the poisonous ridges of the short blade, the newborn pain in his joints and muscles, or the fever boiling his blood. "They knew we were coming, knew how to cut me. They were there to stop us."

She rested the back of her other hand on his forehead. He pulled back, glaring at her. *Why is she not listening to me?*

"You feel warm to me, Keegan," she said with a frown of worry.

"I am fine," he stated again, masking his wretchedness. To demonstrate his strength to her, he decided to stand. Holding the pelts to his hips, he attempted to climb to his feet and to his eternal shame, failed miserably.

"Aye, I can see how fine you are, you stubborn oaf."

Head sagging, overwhelmed by queasiness and blistering fever, he rasped, "Listen to me, Lana."

"I will not leave you, Keegan."

Cool fingertips caressed his cheek. He grabbed her wrist and held her with the last of his ebbing strength. "You must."

"We will find the sword together. Now let go of my hand."

He released her.

"I will not leave you like this," she insisted, "weak and unable to defend yourself."

"I am not weak." He felt his voice trailing off into oblivion where his being would soon follow. His eyelids were getting heavy. He turned away, the shame within spreading into full disgrace.

"Hold still while I change your dressing."

He felt her pull the pelts off him and closed his eyes. Gentle hands unwrapped the bandage around his stomach wound. She removed the old paste and smeared that monstrous green stink on him again. He would probably die from the reek of it, but he could not deny the false coolness it brought to his burning flesh and the ease and drowsiness that came after.

✳ ✳ ✳

Finally, he sleeps, Lana thought, shaking her head with concern. Her hands dropped to her lap. She stared at a brown lock of hair clinging to the sweaty slope of his shoulder and released a small sigh.

His manner confused her.

Sometimes, his eyes were cold, shutting her out. Other times, she caught him watching her, a smoldering gaze of promise, a yearning that reached into her dreams and shut out her loneliness. She felt more alive with his nearness than at any other time in her life. Yet, the moment she responded to his need, he erected a shield between them. There was a large part of her that wished to be held in Keegan's strong arms. She wondered if he sensed that, causing him to withdraw even more. What truly mattered to her lay within the spirit, not the body. Although, she had to admit, his body was extremely pleasing.

The most important thing right now was for him to get well. The other uncertainties she would deal with later.

She reached over and took his limp hand in hers, letting him know she was still there. "Rest now, Keegan. I will watch over you."

Into the night and the next day, Lana kept her vigil. He slumbered fitfully in silence, a fevered delirium taking hold. Poisons leaked from the ragged flesh, seeping into the green paste and turning it brown and crusty. She fought off the despair at his prolonged condition, keeping hope close to her heart. In her mind though, she knew he was getting worse and not better.

She cleaned the paste off every few hours, but even in the grip of oblivion he turned away, his jaw clenched in pain. When she carefully spread the healing paste liberally over his wounds, his nostrils flared, but never a sound did he make.

"I am sorry, Keegan," she said, holding him down when he tried to move away from her touch yet again. "MacLir said it must be done, and I believe her."

She stayed close beside him, tending to her own needs only when necessary. Often times she held his head in her lap, aware of the agony he suffered from those who had intentions to hurt them. His body shivered disjointedly, gone was the innate grace of movement, the vigor of his being. His head rolled from side to side, lashes splayed dark against fine cheeks turned hollow. Fear and anxiety nipped at her composure.

"Why are you not healing?" Her voice came out half-strangled in desolation. She leaned forward and touched her lips to his sweaty temple. "Keegan, my love, can you hear me?"

He did not answer and she rested her cheek upon his forehead.

It came upon her like a hot breeze, this insight, and sudden realization. "I love you," she murmured, amazed at the clarity of that one single thought. It did not matter what he was, a guardian, a being of magical embrace. "I love you," she whispered again, and straightened. "You must battle this dark illness." With his head in her lap, she reached for the small pail filled with water from the river. Cupping her hand, she sprinkled it onto his dry lips.

He did not respond.

She did it again. "Please, Keegan, you must drink."

The life sustaining droplets remained untouched, glimmering like clear jewels on his cracked lips.

Her throat tightened in despair and she lifted her face to the twilight sky. "Please," she implored, calling out to the Gods and Goddesses, "you must help him." Her vision blurred in anguish. "I doona know what to do. I love him." Her plea turned into a whimper. "Please, help him. I will do whatever you wish."

Night came and went, leaving only silence. Lana watched the sunrise in growing misery. Exhaustion and worry pulled at her. Keegan's sword lay close to her hip, the hilt near her hand. She studied her palm as if it belonged to someone else. She had the power to cut a fey born cheek with a slap, but she did not have the power to rid a guardian of the poison stealing his life. There was more of the sacred female's magical darkness in her than the light.

She eased Keegan's head from her lap and stood. "MacLir," she called out. Mayhap the water faery could help. "MacLir!"

"I be here."

Lana turned toward the river. In the shallow waters, MacLir stood expectantly. In each hand, she held a silver pail and cloth.

Lana climbed down to the river's edge and wrinkled her nose at the strong odors that assailed her senses. "I need your help."

"I KNOW." The girl faery held out the buckets to her.

"What are these?"

"HEALING FROM THE DRUIDESS."

The only druidess Lana knew was Derina. "Derina?"

"AYE, SOUGHT HER HELP WHEN GUARDIAN NOT HEAL."

Lana detected traces of garlic and comfrey root for wound healing and other healing scents she did not recognize. She glanced at the other pail. Purple bit, she thought, a remedy for fevers and poisons. Growing in the meadows, it was a plant of dark leaves with rounded heads of purple flowers. Mixed with honey and water, the druidess and tribe simplers often used it for pestilent fevers and poisons. They said it was an old remedy passed down from simpler to simpler.

MacLir handed her the pail with the strong scent of garlic. "CLEAN MY HEALING OFF HIM AND PUT THIS ON HIM NOW."

Lana looked down into it. This, too, looked like lumpy green paste. "Why did you go to Derina?"

"GUARDIAN NOT RECOVERED." MacLir frowned. "ME-THINKS DARKSHADE DAGGER CUT HIM."

"Aye, he said they used a Darkshade dagger on him."

The faery's jewel tone eyes widened. "WHY DID YOU NOT

SAY BEFORE? NEEDS DIFFERENT KIND OF FEY HELP."

"I dinna know it was important."

She huffed. "TRAVEL WITH GUARDIAN. SHOULD KNOW WEAKNESS AND STRENGTH OF HIM. DERINA KNOWS OLDEN WAYS. HER HEALING BEST."

Lana climbed back up the incline to dry land. She knelt beside Keegan and glanced over her shoulder. "MacLir, I need you to hold him for me. Sit by his head and doona let him pull away from my touch."

"CANNA LEAVE THE WATERS."

"What do you mean?"

The faery gestured in front of her. "POUR WATER FROM RIVER TO THE GUARDIAN. I COME THEN."

Without questioning the faery further, Lana took a half full pail of water and walked back to the edge of the river.

"POUR WATER." MacLir pointed impatiently in front of her.

Lana scooped more water from the river into the pail. As she walked back to Keegan, she tilted the pail and poured water in a thin stream to the ground.

MacLir followed, her small feet never leaving the trail of water.

Lana did not give the faery's odd behavior a second thought. She knelt down near Keegan's right hip. In a muddy pool at her guardian's head, MacLir knelt as well.

"Hold him, MacLir."

When the faery had done as she directed, she quickly cleaned Keegan's arm wound of the browning paste and slapped the new garlic paste on the wound, which was greeted with a low male hiss.

"HERE, WRAP WITH FEY CLOTH."

Lana took the silver cloth from MacLir and wrapped her guardian's arm. Steam rose from the arm wound and the strong smell of healing filled the air.

Next, she turned her attention to the much larger and ragged stomach wound.

"I HOLD HIM DOWN FOR YOU," MacLir said, her small hands locked on Keegan's shoulders. "DO IT NOW."

Lana did not think MacLir could hold Keegan, but there was no choice. She cleaned the wound quickly. Cupping a large amount of the warm mixture in her hand, and with a silent prayer on her lips, she smeared the new green mush generously over the stomach wound.

Keegan's jaw clamped shut.

He tried rolling away from the pain, but the faery held him down.

"STRONG STILL." MacLir strained, putting her knee on his shoulder. "WRAP WITH CLOTH. HURRY."

Lana took the other shimmering cloth MacLir held out to her. She eased it over the steaming wound, and almost immediately he calmed.

"DONE," MacLir said, breathing heavily. She sat back on her heels, her toes buried in the mud.

"What is in the cloth?" Lana asked, feeling reassured by his reaction.

"Serenity, a gift from the river." The faery stood, her shins and knees brown with mud. "I watch now. You must rest."

Lana started to protest.

"Rest," MacLir commanded sternly, holding up her hand. "No good to him ill."

Lana wiped her hands in the grass to clean them. She knew MacLir spoke the truth. She felt worn out, drained to the core of her being.

Reluctantly, and with one last look at Keegan who now rested peacefully, she lay down on her side and fell into a profound slumber.

Lana awoke immediately at the sound.

"Must find Valor," her guardian mumbled in a fey tone. "No time."

She bolted upright to a sitting position.

MacLir was gone.

Fading light brushed across the horizon, marking the return of twilight. She must have slept through the day. Edging closer to her guardian mate, she touched his shoulder tenderly. "Keegan?"

His skin felt cool.

He kicked the pelts off and Lana blushed at the sight of

his aroused state.

His head lolled languidly to the side. "NOT FAIR. DOONA BELIEVE IT."

His inflection had reverted to the ways of his fey brethren.

"SWORD HOST MUST BE STRONG," he rasped. "LANA FRAIL, CANNA BE TRUE."

Sitting back, Lana covered her mouth and listened intently.

"LANA," he groaned. His hands clenched and she choked back a sob at the desolation in his voice. "NEVER MINE."

He rambled on incoherently for a few minutes in a language she did not understand, and then turned away in silence.

With trembling hands, she changed the dressings and sat back, silently praying to the mother goddess for help. She lay down beside him once again and kept vigil through the night and next morning.

When the warm sunlight of afternoon filtered through the tree branches once more, Lana felt the worst of the Darkshade illness was over.

Cupping cool water in her hands, she brought it to his cracked lips. Most of it spilled down his chin and cheeks, but his tongue captured some.

Encouraged, she grabbed the pail filled with the honey water and purple bit and attempted to pour the syrupy liquid into him, but she got more on his chin than in his mouth. His tongue shot out again, seeking the moisture.

She brought the rim of the pail to her lips then and filled her mouth so that her cheeks puffed out. Leaning over him, she pressed her lips to his and carefully let the sweetly bitter, healing liquid trickle into his mouth.

He drank from her, ravenous in his need.

She alternated between the pail of cool water and the gooey healing liquid. Filling her mouth repeatedly, she pressed her lips to his, careful that every drop went into him. His famished mouth opened under hers, demanding in his body's thirst.

The final time, when nothing but water was left, she leaned on his chest. Holding his chin in her hand, she placed her lips over his and gave her last offering.

Dimly, she became aware of a hand cupping the back of her head and the lips that moved sensually under hers. She tried to pull back and was astonished at the strength which held her there.

He tasted of the slight bitterness of the healing herb. The dryness within him rapidly disappeared and a satiny tongue thrust into her mouth. It seemed as if he could not get enough of her taste, as if she ended the drought within him. Her world careened into his insistence, and she felt devoured.

Arms tightening around her, he twisted and rolled over.

Lana found herself on her back, caught in a guardian's spell.

Reality ceased.

Dark magic and desire rose sharply.

His large hands moved downward. A bright, magical heat flashed between them and then she became as naked as he was. His body fluid and supple against hers, he molded the fullness of her breast with his left hand, sending darts of fire across her skin.

Warm kisses licked at her collarbone, the center of her chest and then captured her nipple. She gasped and he suckled her, taking his time, moving from one breast to the other until she could bear it no longer. Hands fisted in his hair, she moved against him, her legs entwining with the hard columns of his.

His mouth returned to her neck, teeth scraping against the mating bite on her jaw. A large knee coaxed her legs apart.

His body poised above hers in mystery and danger.

And then . . .

Lean hips lowered.

A sudden hardness pressed into her dewy softness.

Teasing at first, seeking entrance.

Slipping away only to return.

Testing her response.

Pushing.

Harder.

A sharp burning ache surged through her womb followed by an empowering fullness that lodged within her.

Lana cried out more in surprise than in pain. His mouth came down, smothering her distress, drinking in her discomfort. His breath and tongue caressed her, a kind of gentling, a preparation for what was to come next.

Slowly, his hips began to move.

Sliding out.

And back in.

Enticing her with long, liquid strokes meant to tame her. He murmured to her, soft endearments against her cheek.

Lana's world narrowed to him, to the throbbing wetness centered between her legs.

A deep rhythm . . .

A reaching within her female being.

He licked at her jaw, the place of his mating claim, a re-affirmation.

Hands guided her knees up, giving him better access to her.

He drove himself deeper, giving her pleasure.

His weakened body, soaked with a new sweat, answered her body's siren call.

She strained against him, her thighs opening wider, seeking release from the growing conflagration within.

And he answered.

His forehead lowered to hers and he *melded* with her in the way of the guardians.

Lightning jolted through her womb and through her limbs, pouring hot flowing fire into her bloodstream. Lana shuddered uncontrollably. Gasping against his lips, bright lights exploded behind her eyelids like a thousand glorious stars only to fall like tears down her flushed cheeks.

Keegan drank deeply of the nectar of her ecstasy, feeding the insatiable hunger which drove him to claim her for his own.

Releasing her sweet mouth, he licked at a salty tear. Throwing back his head, her breath in his lungs, her body clenching around him, he gave into the demands of his body. His root swelled. Blood boiled with lust, hunger, and need. He took her over the edge. Spewing his seed into her womb, he pumped until there was nothing left to give her. Only then . . . only then did he collapse in exhaustion. Along with the sensual sweat of his body, the Darkshade poison evaporated from the pores of his skin.

Lana lay breathless. She felt like she floated on air, except her guardian mate lay atop her. His nose pressed to her temple. She never knew her body could react that way. She felt calm and wonderful, a slight sticky throb between her thighs.

"Keegan?"

He grunted in her ear, having fallen into a healing sleep.

Very slowly and, with some difficulty, she wiggled out from under him. First, her shoulders, waist, and hips, then she succeeded in freeing her legs. He did not move, but lay still as stone sleeping on his stomach. His back glistened with sweat; tangled strands of brown hair clung to his shoulder blades. Struggling, she managed to gently roll him over on to his back. Removing the stomach bandage, she inspected the wound and found it nearly healed. Only a thin red line remained of the previously slashed flesh. She did a quick check of his wounded arm and found it nearly healed as well. The druidess's paste must include a magic spell, she concluded with relief.

Covering him with the white pelts so he would not catch a chill, Lana walked down the grassy path to the flowing river. Kneeling at the edge, she began to wash. The waters felt cool upon her sensitive flesh and she experienced a little shiver. For a few moments, her mind drifted on the touch, feel, and taste of her guardian mate, but then her thoughts moved back to Valor. They must find the sword, return it to the king, fight the battle to come, and win. She had no doubt of victory. Only then could she allow herself to think of settling down with Keegan on a farm, or wherever her guardian mate wished.

Lana splashed water on her arm and caught sight of a dragonfly hovering to her right. She turned toward it. Cradled among stalks of tall yellow flowers lay a gown of unusual hues, the blue green colors of the sea. Her gaze lifted to the dragonfly and she smiled. "Are you a messenger for MacLir, little one?"

The dragonfly darted away in answer and Lana's gaze settled atop a flat gray rock where there were beaded combs for her hair. They were in the same likeness as the girl faery had worn. She had no doubt then who had left the gifts.

"My thanks, MacLir," she whispered, and stepped down into the cleansing caress of the river.

* * *

Waking slowly from a dream of vivid pleasure, Keegan breathed deeply of the sweet air. He felt surprisingly well rested for one who battled the poison of a Darkshade dagger. He became aware of soft fingers stroking his right hand and tracing the silver cuff at his wrist.

He glanced down his chest.

She caressed him again, inspecting his fingers and pale nails. He watched, too dazed to move. A single finger traced the smoothness of his palm, following the long line there, awakening all parts of his body with the searing memory of her.

By the white moon!

He remembered the mating and closed his eyes in misery.

He had taken her, in greed and passion, his body straining to give her pleasure. And when those delicious female cries had subsided, she took his seed into her womb. If the sword spirit claimed her, the repercussions of this act were too horrific to consider. His eyelids cracked open and he tugged his hand free.

Lovely long lashes lifted, stealing his heart. She gave him a strange smile, kindling the liquid blaze once more.

His traitorous body hardened despite suffering the after effects of poison and physical weakness. He lifted a leg to mask his ardor. It started out as a dream, a joining he secretly craved, an unwilling desire, an idiotic infatuation he dare not act upon. She was forbidden, but now, having drank of her, he wanted more. She was becoming an obsession, one he dare not ever acknowledge, for both of their sakes.

If at the end of all this, the sword spirit's judgment proved unyielding, he silently vowed to take full responsibility for taking her virgin sheath, and endure whatever punishment was deemed. He would make sure to take full blame for this act of lunacy.

"Keegan?"

He blinked at her.

"Thirsty?" she inquired.

He nodded, suddenly mesmerized as she took a sip of water from a silver pail. *What is she doing?* He soon had his answer.

Leaning over him, he found silken lips pressing upon his, a gentle request to open. Cool fresh water rushed into his mouth. He did not remember ever being fed like this and swallowed reflexively, only to have her lean over and perform the service again.

She sat back, that golden mane of hair framing her shoulders, dark eyes alert and watchful. He felt his will seeping away, losing a piece of himself within her gaze.

He sat up abruptly and reached for the pail of water.

Before drinking, however, he quickly inspected its contents.

"What are you doing, Keegan?"

"Checking the water." *To make sure it is clear of fey born.* One never knew where a water faery like MacLir would pop up. *Undines* could show up in ponds, mud puddles, or even in raindrops if they so choose.

"I can get more water from the river," she reassured, not understanding his need to check the pail. "You should drink all of it, Keegan."

He intended to do so and drank, quenching the dryness lingering within him, and set the pail down at his hip. They needed to get moving.

"You should finish this, too."

In both hands, she held out another, smaller pail to him.

The scent of honey and ancient healing herbs wafted into his nose, taunting him. He sniffed at the remotely familiar scents. No water faery would ever reside in there, he knew. "What is this?"

He took the pail and sniffed again, his tongue grazing the cool rim. *Garlic and numerous other herbs*, he mused.

"Derina sent it," his fair one explained, seeing his hesitancy.

"Derina?"

"MacLir went to the ancient for help. You were not responding to her healing flower essences."

"What did she do, pop up in the druidess's pail of water outside her entrance?"

"I doona understand."

He shook his head. "Not important."

"MacLir is different from you, is she not?"

He hesitated before answering, his attention suddenly riveted to her disturbingly sheer clothes. Crafted for mystery and allure, he immediately recognized the fey weave. The glimmering blue green shades, used exclusively by water faeries, appeared nearly translucent in this light. No mortal had ever worn clothes such as these, spun from cave crystals and seashells.

The bodice was secured over her creamy breasts and small waist with tiny blue ribbons formed from sea grasses. Shirred folds, cast from the gauzy waves of the sea, fell down her hips and long shapely legs to her bare feet. His gaze lifted from her lovely pink toes and locked on the silver dragonfly cuffs gracing her upper arms. Fey cast and fey polished with swirling filigree, they were a gift of high approval from the water fey.

"Keegan?"

He could not look away from the delicacy of the metalworking. With this rare gift, the water fey sanctioned his mating with her. He swallowed hard.

She leaned forward. "Keegan?" Crystal beads of the palest blue glittered in the combs pulling sun-kissed plaits away from her oval face.

The fey clothes moved lithely with her, showing every slender curve.

"Keegan, is MacLir a water faery?"

"Aye," he replied huskily, and cleared his throat. He had never known the water faeries to endorse any mortal for a mate. He found their preference extremely unsettling.

"MacLir is an *Undine*," he explained, regaining some of his composure. "She is an elemental water faery and can only be where there is water."

"Not on dry land?"

"Not ever."

A delicate brow furrowed. "Keegan, why did you not tell me the true purpose of the Darkshade dagger?"

He tipped the pail to his lips and finished the contents in several swallows. "There was nothing you could do. The blade cut me. The battle was my own."

"Foolishness." She pulled the pail out of his hands and set it aside.

He shrugged lightly at her glower, and breathed in the sugariness of berries somewhere near.

"Hungry?" she inquired all too sweetly, adjusting the dragonfly cuff on her right arm.

He nodded, unable to keep his stomach from grumbling.

"It seems you are." She reached behind her and brought a white cloth to her lap. Untying it, she revealed a mound of blackberries, his favorite.

Cupping a small handful, she put them in a cracked clay bowl the druidess must have sent, and proceeded to grind them up with some leaves.

Scooping the squashed berries with three fingers, she leaned forward and pinched his nose. His mouth automatically opened and in went the berries.

Releasing his nose, she sat back.

Keegan closed his mouth reflexively and stared at her in disbelief.

"Chew," she commanded.

He was not a child.

"Chew."

He chewed. The sweet berries in his mouth gifted him with life's renewal and the flavorful scent of her.

"More?" she prompted, head tilting, eyes flashing, proving her point well enough.

He would not have survived without her tending. Nodding, he swallowed down the squashed berries.

"Can you eat these berries without me squishing them?"

He touched his nose. "Aye. I doona think my nose can take continual pinching."

"I dinna pinch it that hard."

She handed him the cloth containing the remainder of the fruit. He finished it in thoughtful silence, his gaze straying unerringly to the dragonfly cuffs.

"Derina has sent some tripe, but I have not unwrapped it yet. Do you feel up to eating it? The slices are thin."

He shook his head. "I doona want sheep stomach in my stomach, ever."

"I gather then you doona like tripe."

"Not ever," he said, considering the directness of her gaze. She was waiting for him to acknowledge their joining. "You tended me, Lana?" he inquired with slow deliberation.

"Aye. I tended to all your needs."

It would be best for both of them if he let that remark pass.

"It seems I am indebted to you."

The color of her cheeks deepened to a rosy hue.

He felt her nearness with every fiber of his being, the soft heat of ivory flesh in his hands, the scent of woman laced with berries and heather . . . His gaze dropped to the white column of her throat and he saw the pulse quicken there. His body clenched with remembrance and desire. He imagined her under him once again, her slender thighs opening to receive his thrusts. He could almost feel . . .

He reached for the silvery cloth near her hip and pressed it to his chest. Immediately, the cool press of a sleeveless tunic with laces up the side and front covered his chest. Long breeches of fey grayness slid down his legs and stretched painfully over his erect manhood.

The tunic and breeches were not as finely crafted as her new fey clothes, but they served his purpose, covering his responsive flesh.

She sat in silence, watching.

"You are well?" he inquired into the ongoing silence.

"I am well."

He nodded and looked away, searching for his sword and boots.

"Your sword lies behind you, Keegan."

He found it, his hand sliding over the familiar hilt.

"Do you feel free of the illness now?" she asked.

He turned back to her. "I am not adapted to illness and suspect I made it difficult for you."

"A little."

He chuckled at her response. "I doubt that."

She smiled. "True."

"How long have I been down, Lana?"

"Days."

"How many days?" He demanded, feeling the loss of even one day was too much.

"Four days."

Muttering an oath under his breath, he tossed the pelts off, and stood abruptly. Unfortunately, his weakened body was not yet ready to charge off to do his bidding. The land shifted into wavering mist and he tilted to one side, losing consciousness.

"Keegan!" Lana cried out in warning, reaching out to catch him.

He fell on top of her, knocking her to the ground. His face mashed into her chest plate.

Gasping for air, Lana took a moment to recover, which was difficult with a heavy guardian sprawled on top of her. Her right hip and elbow throbbed from the impact with the ground.

"Keegan?" She grabbed a handful of thick brown hair and tugged.

No response.

He was unconscious.

"Stubborn, thick-headed . . ." she muttered, wiggling out from under him and sitting up. He dinna even remember their mating!

"Dagger not cut deep enough."

Lana turned at the sound of the familiar voice. "Cadman?"

Pain exploded in the back of her head.

CHAPTER 12

DROPPING HIS ROCK, MASTER CADMAN Spriggan stared down at the *claíomh host* lying motionless on the ground. Had he hit her too hard? he wondered. That had not been his intention. Leaning down, he stuck his ear in her face and listened. She breathed still, her small breasts rising and falling beneath his hand. She moaned in pain. *Mine now*, he thought with gleeful satisfaction. He traced the silver dragonfly cuff on her slender arm and straightened. The water faeries had sanctioned her. *How strange*, he thought, scratching his bearded chin. She was not destined to become the mate of a water guardian. For that matter, no guardian had ever taken a mortal bride. It was forbidden to dilute the olden fey line.

Out of the corner of his eye, Cadman saw the guardian roll to his stomach. He flinched in fear, turning to flee, and then stopped. The guardian lay still after that, locked in the throes of the dagger's poison. Cadman smiled, baring his teeth.

He hated them, the aloof guardians, hated their beauty and innate grace, hated their strength and absolute fierceness when threatened. Yet, most of all, he detested the way all females responded to their virile allure, spreading their legs in wanton abandonment. Why should he not be as the guardians? He had vigor and potency. He could ride a female for long hours and take his pleasure from her. And when Lord Bress returned to retake the land, not only would he be rewarded with a great treasure for stealing Valor, but he would be given the spriggan kingdom to rule. He looked down at the unconscious host, so lovely, so delicate. He would need a mate, a special female to carry on his unique bloodline.

Kneeling beside her, he took her in his arms and stood to his full height. No longer would he keep his father's squat shape. He was a half-blood. His spriggan father had taken a fancy to a young human female on a farm as he had taken a fancy to this one. His father tricked the female into eating spriggan's covet bread and then rode her hard, not knowing her mate had already given his seed into her womb just hours before. Spriggan seed and human seed joined within the female's womb, something that had never happened before. Blood that had always been incompatible and unsuited coupled, and nine months later she died giving birth to twins.

His brother was born with a large spriggan head. Covered in the wet blood of birth, he died at the hands of his mother's enraged mate. He, however, escaped the mate's fury as he was human formed. During the first tender week of his life, his true spriggan father had come and carried him off, a great prize — to all others, an abomination. The spriggans reviled him. The humans loathed him.

His father kept him separate from all others. Taught him the spriggan ways, taught him to shape change to his father's short, bearded form. He even showed him how to structure a remembered place in his mind and then how to wink in using light and air. Unlike guardians, spriggans did not need wings to wink in and out of place. They were better than guardians were.

It was not until he learned all he could from his spriggan father that he had killed him. A quick slash across the throat with a dagger and it was over. He felt no remorse for the supposedly heinous act, only blissful satisfaction. For all he endured, his father was to blame.

Turning now, Cadman sneered down at the guardian. He thought of bashing him over the head with a rock, but a rock would never stop a guardian, and he had other things planned.

He winked out instead, taking his lovely prize with him.

Out of the cool dark shadows of unconsciousness and an approaching night, Keegan awoke slowly. He lay on his stomach, a sense of unease washing over him. Shifting his good arm in front of him, he raised his head with difficulty, feeling the dull achy pull at his healing stomach. In his clearing vision, gray mist became green fields of tall grasses and darkening skies of purple. He swatted at the few tufts of grass in his face.

"Lana?" he called.

No answer.

He lifted his head higher. Nostrils flaring, he quickly pushed up from the ground, his sharp eyes sweeping over the rolling landscape.

Warm winds moved through the rich green blades of grass.

The decaying scent of a wrongful death stained the air.

The river.

Apprehension settled heavily in his blood. Despite his body's weakness, muscles flexed, and he launched into the air, taking to his true form, wings beating furiously.

He knew immediately he was too late. In the next moment he leaped down to the land, crashing through the tall grass and stalks of yellow and purple flowers, dropping down to his knees.

Keegan stared down at the sight of the crumpled *Undine.*

"MacLir?"

The water faery did not move.

Reaching out with trembling fingers, he caressed her pale cold cheek and felt the presence of a premature death. His hand balled into a fist. She lay on her side, curled up like a child, the shimmering of her life force gone. The back of her small head was caked in white blood.

His jaw flexed, the bite of anger cutting, deepening. He cupped her head gently and lifted her in his arms, holding her broken body close to his heart.

Whoever did this to her had to have been fey born.

Whoever did this had taken Lana.

Whoever did this was going to die.

He looked down upon MacLir for long moments, feeling the loss of her and of Lana. The *Undine* had been dragged roughly out of the river, judging from the bruises on her wrists. Her body showed the signs of the painful wilting which happened to water faeries who dared walk on dry land. "Vengeance, I promise you, little one," he said vehemently.

He lifted MacLir in his arms and climbed to his feet, the hum of the river calling, begging for her return. Striding through the dense grasses, he came to a narrow path leading to the river. He entered the moving waters, letting the cool currents guide him to the proper place.

Standing shoulder deep near the river's center, he held her below the surface, her white hair fanning across his arm in a farewell embrace.

He pressed his lips to her cheek, and with a quiet word to her, he bowed his head in grief, his eyes closed in sorrow. Silently he beseeched the waters to reclaim her and began the whispered chant of respect for a fallen friend.

The river surged around him.

Reclaiming . . .

Recovering . . .

Repossessing . . . fey flesh.

A dark seething built inside him.

An all-consuming rage.

For who had done this.

For those who had taken Lana.

There would be no compassion, no mercy . . . not ever.

Hatred flowed and shriveled the noble part of him until all he felt was a need for retribution.

And as MacLir's small body dissolved back into the tender care of the blue waters of the river, he flung back his head and roared his fury.

The cruel resonance of it covered the land like a smothering blanket.

And all the waters grieved.

Lana struggled her way back to consciousness. She lay on her right side in a smear of strange purple shades. She stared at a wall of flattened rocks with swirling etchings that looked like thin black snakes curling into circles. Her excessive imagination again, she thought distractedly. *Snakes on walls.* Lashes drifted down at the wave of sudden wooziness. Her tongue darted out over dry lips. Disoriented, she took a shaky breath at the knifelike ache throbbing at the back of her head. The reeking smell of rot assailed her sensitive nose and she felt her stomach lurch. Bracing herself, she carefully pushed up to a sitting position.

With a trembling hand, she wiped her watery eyes.

"Hurts?" a male voice asked.

Lana brought Cadman's face into focus, except it did not look like the Cadman she knew at all.

"Feeling better?" he asked.

She swallowed hard and shook her head, which only made her eyes cross in pain.

"Mayhap you should not do that just yet." He gave her a gentle smile. "Here, press this to the back of your head. It will make it feel better."

He spoke differently too, she thought.

"Take it." He held out a white cloth to her.

"What is it?"

He looked at the cloth. "Nothing fey, I assure you. Just a plain woolen cloth dipped in cool water."

Taking the damp cloth, Lana pressed it to the tenderness at the back of her head and winced.

"What happened?" she asked when she felt she could speak. "Where is Keegan?"

"I am afraid some angry faeries attacked. I could barely save you."

"Where is Keegan?"

"They have captured him, Lana. May I call you Lana? "

She did not care what he called her. Obstinately silent, she climbed to her feet and stumbled, falling to one knee.

"There now."

He reached out to help her

Lana crouched back against the rocky wall. "Who or what are you?"

He smiled tolerantly, though his jaw tensed. "I am Cadman."

"You are not he."

"But I am, Lana. 'Tis my mortal form."

She looked at him questioningly. "Spriggans doona have mortal forms. You look like a man."

"Aye," came the self-satisfied reply.

She did not like the sound of that.

"It may seem strange to you, but I am a half-blood." He tugged at his short brown beard. "My mother was a farm girl, my father a spriggan."

She scoffed at that. No child could ever be born of a spriggan rape.

" 'Tis true. I have been unjustly condemned for their deed, made to pay for their love and devotion to each other."

She could not imagine any girl who would willingly lay with a rock faery.

"Neither the lands of spriggan nor of men could accept their joining," Cadman continued despite her mistrust. "They were banished and raised me on the outskirts of the fey woodlands. You must believe me, Lana."

She was not sure what she believed anymore. "You gave me your covet bread, full of lust and aching," she accused.

He smiled and sighed. "Doona condemn me for that. I find you beautiful and could not help myself. It will never happen again, unless you will it."

Never would she will it.

"You stare at me with those night eyes, Lana. Am I so ugly?"

She shook her head. "Nay, 'tis only that you look so different from the Cadman I know."

"Mayhap you can grow accustomed to me as you have grown accustomed to the guardian?"

His words held an undercurrent that made her uneasy.

"Can you?" He sounded irritable, almost impatient.

She shrugged.

"We will start with that." Taking her arm, he helped her stand. Lana found he was now as tall as she was.

"First we must get you well," he said. "Then we will rescue the guardian. Then we will find Valor."

"Keegan, you know where he is?"

He shook his head. "I have an idea where they took him. Doona worry, they will not harm him."

"How do you know?"

He looked at her with a smug grin. "They were after you, my sweet. They will use the poisoned guardian to draw you out."

Poisoned? How did Cadman know Keegan battled Darkshade poison? She kept the thought to herself. "Do you know where they hold Valor?" she asked.

"I know as much as you know."

She made an effort to appear calm. "Where are we?"

"Do you not recognize a feypath when you see one?"

A feypath? Derina had taken her through one of the underground passages long ago. Carved out of rock and stone, the feypaths were ancient, shrouded in dark incantation and foreboding. They were sacred to the fey and were never meant for mortal trespass.

She wrinkled her nose at the remembered foulness.

"You smell the taint of faery spitefulness," Cadman explained. "My kin doona like encroachment. After a while, the smell will seem like a wild flower's fragrance to you."

"I think not," she retorted, finding the stench offensive.

He laughed low. "Mayhap. Come, I know of a place to rest up ahead."

Lana allowed him to support her as they walked. "Cadman, I doona wish to rest. We must find Keegan and Valor."

"We will, but you must be able to walk on your own, Lana. How do you expect to rescue the guardian and the enchanted sword when you canna stand without my assistance?"

Despite the painful pounding in her head, she recognized the truth of his words, to her chagrin.

"Now walk with me. Place one foot in front of the other. One of my homes is near."

She gave a consenting nod and leaned on him heavily. The back of her head throbbed, as if she had fallen on a rock, but her thoughts became less foggy. Though she did not like Cadman's hands on her, she expressed her gratitude, and walked beside him, her steps surer with each passing moment, his easy words of reassurance an ongoing hum in her ears.

They walked along the feypath for a long time; at least, it felt like a long time to her. On either side of the rocky walls, gray vines grew.

At last, he guided her around a sharp bend and stopped before a smooth slab of stone shaped in an arch. Sculptured stone faces surrounded the arch, marking a doorway to another place.

"My home," he said, and pushed the slab aside as if it weighed nothing.

Lana entered a large cavern with several wooden pillars. From holes in the low ceiling, light-refracting crystals hung suspended on clear threads. Ledges jutted out, holding pots and vessels with handles. Gleaming piles of finger rings and bracelets, bronze and silver torcs, and women's combs were everywhere. *Stolen treasures*, she mused, a spriggan's craft. Folded neatly to her right were colorful woolen cloths. All dyed from the labors of a mortal hand, no doubt. The deep blue purple probably came from the spiderwort plant, the red one from madder root, and there were other shades too numerous to mention. It took a long time to plant and grow a dye garden and to care and shear the sheep. The wool had to be presoaked, a pot of water had to set to boil beneath a sturdy flame, flowers picked and petals dropped in for the desired hue. Then the wool was added. After tinting, it must be dried in the sun, spun into yarn, and then woven into cloth.

It took only seconds to steal it.

"Come, Lana. You can rest here for a while."

He guided her to a space beside the wall where a bed of sheepskins were piled.

She knelt in the soft bedding, feeling a little bit better. As she rolled to her hip, a hand tenderly caressed her cheek and Lana fought back a cringe of revulsion.

He sat across from her, his steely eyes locked on her face.

Silence gripped the cavern. The air felt thick in her lungs, making her heart flutter.

"Do you like my treasures?" he asked in all seriousness.

She raised her head and looked around. "You have many."

"Aye," he said proudly. "More comes."

She nodded, waiting for him to continue.

His hand swept the chamber. "I have been promised incredible treasure from the Formorian."

He had her at a disadvantage. "The Formorian?" she asked warily.

"Beyond the northwest tip of the land, he and they shall return. The sea raiders of the long noble legs and single hands, the black forces shall slip through and retake what belongs to them," he ranted, making no sense to her. "The rushing wave of death . . ."

"Bress?" she interjected, guessing the name of the "he," and effectively silencing him.

He smiled and nodded. "Lord Bress returns with his father's warriors to retake the fey throne."

She shook her head. "The throne belongs to the Faery King Nuada."

"Nuada is blemished," he replied with a touch of resentment, gesturing irritably. "The throne belongs to Lord Bress, the Formorian. Do you know the bard's song of the Fir Bog battle, Lana?" he asked.

All in her tribe did.

He began the familiar chant, mimicking the soothing voice of a bard and changing the words.

ભ ભ ભ

Emerging from the white mist, a great war came. The
Fey King, Nuada, a powerful lord, lost a hand in the
confrontation. Considered blemished, he gave up his
sovereignty willingly to Bress, a hero of the battle.
Born of a Formorian lord and a Tuatha woman, the
fair Bress ruled for a few years. He was ousted from
the throne and in his place returned the blemished
Nuada, who now had a new hand of silver . . .

ભ ભ ભ

"I doona remember it that way." Lana knew he altered the verses, leaving out many important parts. *Nuada, a just and fair king. The vain Bress ruling for seven years, sacrificing the welfare of his subjects for his father's kin . . .*

"History is a matter of interpretation, is it not?" he commented quietly.

"History canna be changed to suit one's whim."

"Mayhap." He gave her a strange twisted smile. "You will be safe here, Lana. No harm shall come to you. I will see to it."

She ignored his assurances. "When does Bress return, Cadman?"

"Soon."

"How soon?"

He grinned in answer and took her hand.

She yanked free. "You are a betrayer to your people," she said through her teeth.

He peered at her, all gentle manner gone. "Not I." He snatched her hand back, his thick fingers digging into her flesh, daring her.

"Do you know why the guardian needs you, Lana? I do. Do you want to hear?"

She glared at him.

"You were never meant to return, Lana. Your guardian would do anything to save Valor, anything, even sacrifice you."

The coldness of his gaze startled her for a moment.

"I speak the truth to you, whereas your guardian, like all of his kind, speak only mistruths."

"Keegan would never lie to me."

"Guardian's lie? Never," he agreed. "They imply, suggest, speak only partial truths to mislead and misinform. They are fey born, Lana."

"You are fey born," she rejoined.

He shook his head. "I am born of a mortal woman." His thumb stroked her wrist. "I am more like you than like them."

Coldness crept into her blood, into her very existence.

The smile returned to his lips, a smooth, fey falsity. He released her and stood. "Rest for a little while," he said more calmly. "I will prepare for our journey to rescue your guardian."

"Why would you do that?"

"Because I am honorable. What makes you think I would attack your guardian?"

"You side with Bress," she accused. "And it is his faeries that attacked us."

"Lana, Lord Bress is honorable. He would never condone faeries attacking you and your guardian with a Darkshade dagger. Those faeries must be acting on their own for reasons unknown to us. Mayhap they search for Valor as well. The great sword would be a worthy prize for any fey born."

You are commanding them, she thought. *I never mentioned a Darkshade dagger.*

"I have a few things I must prepare for our journey. It would be wise to take the time to rest now. You look weary. I will return soon." He strode away without a backward glance, disappearing into one of the shadowy rooms of the cavern.

Lana clutched at her wrist. Bruises already formed on her flesh from Cadman's cruel grip. Heart quivering, she placed a palm over her breast, wondering what to believe. She felt languid and slow, and eased her head down upon the soft skins. Her heart hurt, a deep draining ache, something new and terribly unfamiliar.

Just for a moment she would rest, she thought to herself. Her eyes fluttered closed and she slipped into oblivion.

CHAPTER 13

He stood in the dark meadow without expression, nostrils flaring, dragging in the scents of the warm night. There was a perfect and dangerous quality to him, the mark of a rightful fey guardian. He sought movement in the meadow, sought prey. He lifted his face to the northeast breeze and took a deep breath. No fey marker did he detect. The air and land smelled clean.

The swirling of unfamiliar emotions tightened like ropes across his chest and he bared white teeth, his silvery wings stretching out and retracting.

He dropped down to one knee, sinewy muscles rippling beneath fey webs. Long, blunt fingers dug into the black soil, searching for scent sign. Retribution flowed in his blood-stream, fueling a primordial and elemental rage. He knew fey born ways.

No mortal ever glimpsed a faery unless the faery wished it. And MacLir never wished it, except for Lana.

This left only the fey born.

One of his fey kin was a *dúnmharfóir*, a black-hearted murderer.

And the *dúnmharfóir* had taken Lana.

Fey born perceived the residual presence of other fey born, yet he detected nothing, no shimmering shards and no lingering scent.

He blinked once, a slow closing and opening containing the fury within.

Inhaling deeply, he refocused.

A sinister light flashed in his eyes at the thought of MacLir being dragged from the river to dry ground. The murderer had smashed her head in.

His menacing snarl rent the air.

The *dúnmharfóir* dared to take Lana.

Dared!

He jammed the fingers of his left hand deeper into the moist soil, seeking her scent.

He was Rain.

First Guardian of the Waters.

Protector.

Defender.

Warrior.

His eyes shut, leaving the weaknesses of his mortal inclination behind.

The muscles in his left arm strained.

He focused on the scents beneath land, those retrieved

through his sensitive fingertips. The guardians belonged to a long ago time. They were the warrior fey, beholden to the land, air, and waters. In return, gifts of extraordinary uniqueness had been given to them.

His face became harsh with concentration. He had to go beyond the typical underground scents before he could locate her distinctive fragrance.

He focused. First came the foulness of plant and animal decay, death returning to the dark soil. Always death, he sensed first.

Next came the pleasant essence of plant and animal life, affirmation of existence.

He tilted his head, brown hair falling down one shoulder.

Somewhere near, the coppery odor of womb blood marked an animal's birth.

Then there were the bodily wastes, a part of the land, and forever felt.

His fingers strained, seeking the scents at the lower depths of the land. He could distinguish the fresh underground streams now, the crystals, and the minerals.

Beyond that lay the feypath's taint. He detected faint traces of heather mixing with the fey stain of his spiteful kin.

Raw violence shuddered through him.

The delicate floral fragrance of heather combined uniquely with Lana's sweet flesh. He would know her scent anywhere. A growl rumbled in his throat.

He had found her.

She had been brought through the underground fey-paths. He jammed his fingers deeper into the earth, seeking what he needed. "Show me where," he demanded in a low snarl. "I want."

The sharp pain in her heart lessened to breathable dullness. Lana lay quietly on the soft sheepskins, deliberately peering through her eyelashes and faking sleep. In the outlying chambers, she could hear voices arguing, a mixture of fey and mortal accents rising in agitation. The thought of believing anything Cadman said sent uneasiness through her. She had to rely on her instincts and find a way to get out of here. She had absolutely no idea which way to go, but knew only she must leave the underground chambers. She would rather take her chances in the feypaths than remain in Cadman's lair.

Looking through her eyelashes, she let her breath out slowly. Carefully, she looked about to make sure no others watched her.

The chamber appeared empty.

Rolling to her side, she attempted to climb to her feet only to find her ankles bound together.

"Not go," a craggy voice commanded from above her.

Startled, Lana looked up, searching for the owner of the voice.

"Tied your ankles together."

On a jutting ledge several feet above, a creature with a big head looked down upon her. Lana could see dull white hair falling in limp strands over large ears. He had a dirty white beard that came to a point over a bulging stomach barely contained by a straining, rock-encrusted gray coat.

"Promised to watch you for Cadman."

Keeping a wary eye on her spriggan guard, she leaned forward, and reached for the white bindings around her ankles. They seemed loosely tied, yet she could not free her feet.

Her frustrated groan initiated a chuckle from the creature above.

She kicked out. "Release me."

He shook his head. "Fey ties unbreakable."

"Enough," Cadman said, strolling back into the chamber, followed by as many as twenty faeries, mortal men, and an odd assortment of short spriggans.

"KILL HER," one of the faeries said, and knelt in front of her, peering with the white eyes of a killer. "I DO IT."

Lana pressed back against the stone wall, a strange calm dissolving into her blood. She did not know why, but she did not fear these creatures.

"Guardian be enraged," a spriggan with red hair said hotly, causing a murmur among them.

They fear Keegan, Lana thought, seeing alarm wash over their faces. All of them do, she observed, and felt a great reassurance in that.

The spriggan with the red hair stepped forward and gestured toward the feypath. "Guardian coming."

"He will not find us here," Cadman responded confidently. "I was careful to leave no trace of my presence when I winked out."

"Foolish," another faery snarled with hard, black eyes. "Follows her scent, not yours."

A frown crossed Cadman's face for a moment. It was evident he had not thought of that. "It does not matter." He waved their concern away. "Traps are in place, the guardian will never get this far, and our plans proceed as expected." He looked at all of them. "Already Lord Bress, our true fey king, directs his Formorian ships nearer to our shores. When he lands and reclaims his throne, those loyal to him will be richly rewarded."

The creature kneeling in front of her asked, "Another sword host not dangerous?"

Lana watched as Cadman moved in front of her, forcing the white-eyed faery to rise to his feet and step back.

"I claim her as part of my reward," Cadman said firmly. "I took the greatest risk and stole Valor from the vaults of Tara. None of you would do it. I brought Valor to the Faery Mound of Darkness. It was my idea to place her in the black waters there. Where would you be without me?" he demanded, and then gave the answer. "Under the suffocating hand of a blemished fey king. Now go. Our time of victory draws near and we must be prepared."

No one moved. Instead, they spoke in hushed whispers among themselves in direct conflict with their half-blood leader's commands.

Lana took full note of their divergence. Mayhap they did not like taking orders from a half-spriggan being. The tall, willowy faeries had the same shades of whiteness as those who attacked them earlier. The hairy spriggans, in their rock-encrusted coats, all had big, ugly heads and beady eyes. The mortal men stood apart, probably outcasts of their own tribes. These were Lord Bress's followers.

"I grow impatient," Cadman remarked with irritation.

They were all edgy, she mused, all surly and ill-mannered, with loyalty and credit given only to themselves. An army ready to fall apart. She could not fathom any other outcome with this insolent behavior.

Cadman took a single step to his right, his back to her, his hands clenched in anger. He wore the sleeveless green tunic and breeches of the men of her tribe. His white arms were long and slender, almost feminine in shape, nothing compared to the muscular slope and contours of her guardian's strong arms.

She fervently wished Keegan were here. She had to tell him Valor's location, a place called the Faery Mound of Darkness. *Wherever that might be.* The name sounded familiar, something Derina once said long ago, but she could not recall it. This mound of darkness had to be a fey place, she reasoned. Mayhap a hill or cavern, or another passage tomb like Knowth.

"The longer I wait, the less treasure you will be granted," Cadman said angrily, hands on his hips.

For a moment, Lana did not think they would respond. She saw wavering and hesitation in some faces, and resentment and antagonism in others.

"The guardian comes," she remarked, adding to discord. Cadman pivoted and glared at her in warning, but she ignored him. "This guardian is among the most ancient and powerful purebreds, a great and menacing first guardian of the waters. He will not take your participation in my abduction lightly."

"Not *Báisteach*!" a spriggan sputtered, his face going deathly pale.

Lana's brows drew together. *Báisteach* meant Rain in the olden language. Rain was Keegan's fey name. She looked at Cadman, seeking to promote the growing discord among her weak-minded kidnappers. "Cadman, you did not tell them it is Rain who tracks them? Rain," she emphasized her guardian's name, "the most dominant, most intolerant, and most powerful guardian of them all."

"It matters not," Cadman interjected quickly.

"IF IT BE *BÁISTEACH*," the faery with the white eyes snarled, "NOT EVER WILL HE STOP."

"He will not make it beyond my traps," Cadman snapped back. "He will not find us here. I have thought of everything. Now do as I say and return to the Faery Mound of

Darkness. Remain there until I summon you. I want our properly weakened Valor watched until Lord Bress is ready to claim her. Now go!" Cadman bellowed, pointing with his right hand.

The fey born creatures shimmered, winking out, leaving silver shards behind them. The men left by another chamber, taking their sweat and stink with them.

Lana wondered if the Faery Mound of Darkness was near. She looked around, seeing shadowy tunnels leading to other chambers. She had to find a way out and get word to Keegan. He would know this Faery Mound of Darkness.

Lana looked up and suddenly found herself alone with Cadman.

A sharp crack of pain shot through her right cheek.

Her head reeled back from the blow, bottom lip split and bleeding. She landed hard on her right forearm, stunned. Through her stinging and watery eyes, she saw Cadman's flushed and furious face.

"Never speak, Lana, unless I give you permission. Do you understand? Never contradict what I have said. It is time for you to forget what you left behind. You are my slave now, and will do my bidding."

She wiped her mouth with the back of her hand. "I am not a slave. I am freeborn."

"You were never freeborn. The sword spirit claimed you in your mother's womb."

Lana could not argue that.

"I see you agree with me." He crouched down in front of her, the tension in him simmering just below the surface. "I have saved you from a dreadful destiny, Lana. Should the current host die, the sword spirit will lay her claim upon you. Your lovely white flesh will reform into the cruel slash of a magical blade, a bringer of death and oblivion. Never would you experience pleasure again, smell the scents of the salty sea in the morning, bask in the warmth of an afternoon sun, enjoy the company of friends and family, or feel the warmth of food in your belly." A devious smile curved his lips. "Never will you ever again run your fingers through the silken mane of that old stallion you are so fond of. What is his name? Lightning, I believe. You should be grateful to me, very grateful."

He mocked her fears, trying to turn her into a terrified female. It made her furious.

"Where is the Faery Mound of Darkness?" she demanded.

He struck her again, just as violently, and Lana fell backward again, hitting the hard rocky ground. A thousand white lights flashed into her vision and the coppery taste of blood pooled in her mouth.

"I dinna give you permission to speak, Lana. You have an impressive spirit for a female, but I suggest you learn to diminish it or I will do it for you."

She pulled herself up. "You beggarly creature," she sneered, her heart pounding. "Do you think snatching Valor will make you great? You are nothing but a weakling, an expendable pawn of the tyrant Bress."

His eyes narrowed. "You know nothing of what you speak. I am his great high commander. Without me, he is nothing."

"Why does Bress need Valor?"

He tilted his head, one eye squinting down at her. "It seems I am going to have to teach you obedience, but for now I will answer your questions because it pleases me to do so. You are mistaken if you think Lord Bress needs anything. He wants Valor. The enchanted sword brings greatness to its owner."

"Valor belongs to the High Faery King, Nuada."

"Valor belongs to the hand that wields her. She is not faithful."

"That canna be true." She wiped blood from her mouth.

"Why? Doona give loyalty to a fey talisman, Lana. The fey doona abide by the rules of men. Has your guardian not explained the dark side of the female to you?" He gestured with his hand. "Valor is the bringer of death, Lana. There is no goodness in her, no mercy, no compassion. She is a killer."

"Valor is a great defender of our lands," Lana said with indignation.

"Defender?" He stroked his chin and laughed acidly. "She is no great defender, no honorable spirit. Do you want to know what she is? Very few do."

Lana nodded that she did, even though she knew she could not trust his words.

"It is an old myth that fey blood flows in the veins of a *claíomh host*. It is not fey blood that flows there."

Lana listened intently despite her mistrust.

"It is the bloodline of a sorceress."

"A sorceress?" she echoed in surprise.

"Aye," he breathed, "a very powerful sorceress. During an ancient time of peril and war, a withered old sorceress cut a white branch from a sacred oak tree, angering the Gods and Goddesses. Under the amber light of a full moon, she conjured up a dark enchantment from the bowels of the land turning the oak branch into a gleaming sword unlike any the world has ever seen. A living sword spirit, so potent the Gods and Goddess, already angered by her act, became enraged. In retribution, they cast the sword spirit into the flesh of the sorceress's first granddaughter, and Valor was born."

"So the current sword host . . ."

He did not let her finish. "The current sword host has always been Glenna, the sorceress's first granddaughter," he answered. "There has never been another sword host."

"How do you know this?"

"Spriggans once served the ancient sorceress. They vowed silence when the Gods and Goddess threatened punishment, and so none have ever spoken of it."

"The sword spirit gave Glenna immortality?"

He sat back on his heels. "Aye, she did."

"If that be true," Lana asked suspiciously, "why do I bear the mark of the sword spirit? Why does Valor need another sword host?"

A calculating look came to his eyes. "Valor is not entirely invincible, Lana. Fire and water can destroy her. I am sure the guardian could not have been entirely lax in his duties. He must have at least told you this."

Keegan had explained it to her, but she would not admit it to Cadman.

Her tormentor looked away for a moment. "Generations have come and gone, and always there has been a sword host born, sometimes one, sometimes more than one."

He looked at her, a smug smile on his lips.

Lana understood immediately, the certainty of it jarring her. Her voice came out barely a whisper. "The sorceress had another granddaughter."

He leaned back and smirked with importance. "Aye, she did."

"I am a descendant of the sorceress." A shiver of cold ran down her spine.

"Aye." He gave her a leering grin. "The Gods and Goddesses doona like to be threatened. They cursed the sorceress's entire female line. There were two granddaughters. You are a descendant of the youngest, Erin."

Lana looked away and stared blankly at the ground. She fought the sense of gloom, the sense that her life had never been her own.

" 'Tis a curse, Lana. Not a privilege, but I will overlook it."

"Why would you do that?"

"Because you are beautiful and I want the sorceress's bloodline flowing in my offspring."

Lana fought back her revulsion. "Why?"

"To some it is a curse, but not to me. Dark power lives in you and I want it for my heirs. I will be a great king someday; I must have great heirs."

"What of your Lord Bress?"

He gave a small chuckle. "His rule will be short."

Lana studied her captor closely. "You have no intention of giving Valor to Bress, do you?"

He shook his head with obvious relish. "I will keep up the pretense while it suits me, but she is mine as you are mine."

She could not believe what she was hearing. With a slender hand, she pushed tangled curls out of her eyes.

"You have lovely hair, a rich golden fire that tempts me. I look forward to mating with you," he said.

"I will not lie with you."

He raised his hand to strike her again.

Lana glared at him. She did not flinch, did not cower.

"You bruise too easily," he murmured, and dropped his hand. "I will have to be more careful in my discipline of you. I canna have my mate's snow white skin a blanket of purple bruises."

"I am not your mate, not ever. Keegan has already claimed me."

Her captor's face hardened, his gaze lingering on her jaw.

"I can smell the taint of the guardian's mating claim on you." A scowl furrowed his brow as if he just realized what that meant.

He held up a hand. "Bah, 'tis nothing," he growled.

Lana smiled quietly.

He did not like her show of defiance. "You are mine and will do what I say."

She shook her head slowly.

"There are ways to break your spirit without breaking that beautiful body."

"I am a descendant of the sorceress, as you said. Even the Gods and Goddesses feared her conjuring. Do you think a mere spriggan half-blood worries me?"

"You are defiant now." He stood and stared down at her. "But I wonder if you realize how truly dark your destiny would be without me."

"My destiny will not be dark."

"With me, you will live in light, warmth, and comfort. With the guardian . . ." He shook his head. "He will give you to the sword spirit and you will live in eternal night and bloodshed." Pivoting on his heels, he walked away. Lana stared after him, listening to the silence of the chambers.

Her hands were shaking. With a fierce kick, she again attempted to free her bound ankles. Whatever she was, whatever her true destiny, two things remained perfectly clear in her mind.

Keegan would never give her willingly to the sword spirit.

And invaders were coming to her lands.

She would do everything in her power to protect her tribe. Above her head, a distant rumble of thunder echoed through the chambers, followed by a swift crack of lightning. Soon after, the violent patter of rain drenched the land.

Her guardian was coming.

CHAPTER 14

THE PURPLE SHADES OF TWO primordial feypaths lay before him, a beguiling and malevolent crossing from which he must choose his way.

The underground passages of his fey kin were unexpectedly beautiful to him, pale pink crystals and gems in surrounding rock faces, faded colors in shadows, swift breezes carrying the scent of fey taint and spitefulness only to disperse into nothingness and easy breath.

The feypaths always evoked envy and fear among men, something unknown just beyond the reach of understanding. They had, and always would, belong to the *Daoine Sidhe*, the faery folk. They were passages crafted in long ago times, sparse of life and full of glows.

These glows disintegrated now through the crimson haze of his anger and urgency. His gaze moved over the three dead faeries and what was left of the two men. The fury within made him more aggressive, more violent, and more destructive in his reactions, especially to those stupid enough to seek his death. He felt no remorse for his response to their ambush. Crouching low, his hand rested on churned soil from the fight. His wings moved back and forth in agitation, the sword scabbard on his back of little hindrance to muscle and sinew.

He bared his teeth in silence, a brutal wildness humming through his blood. An uncontrollable deluge of hatred flowed within, where there should be only deadly calm.

Calm.

He reached for it. He must be calculating and composed to rescue Lana and Valor.

No battle had ever been won by joining unmanageable rage with stupidity, and he had fought many to know. He scanned the crossroads that lay before him, identical shadows and glimmerings. He reached for the discipline and patience that had seen him through many a trying time and examined his choices. In the serpentine descent, he could not stand to his full height. Carved out of rock and stone, both jagged and smooth, the narrow fork awaited his decision.

He lifted his head and inhaled slowly.

The foul taint was cast into the air by a long ago faery king to dissuade the interest of men from entering the underground passages. Beneath the taint, he detected a faint trace of heather, confirming his tracking of Lana to this place. He looked down at his bloodstained hands.

The faeries and men who thought to attack him from

behind were no more, as the form of Keegan was no more. He preferred to remain in his true shape now, the one of deadly strength and intolerance. Something once safely contained was now dangerously released.

Emotions.

Passions.

Wants.

Craving vengeance.

They had taken Lana.

Stolen Valor.

Murdered MacLir.

His hands fisted. They threatened the fey, his lands, and his waters.

Flinging his head back, he bellowed out his challenge, the rampant echo traveling through the dark shining feypaths of his kin.

He wanted those who took Lana to know a fey guardian hunted them.

He wanted them to know what they had let loose.

His nostrils flared once again; the faint scent of heather lingered in both passages. Her captors were trying to assist him in making a wrong choice.

His eyes narrowed into gleaming slits. He could hear the flow of the river, a muffled melody, just to the right of his position.

What lay ahead were the ancient passage tombs of Knowth and Dowth.

He had already been to Knowth.

Dowth was located north of the river and had two entrances.

Dowth North and Dowth South would take him to two different locations within the great faery mound.

He studied the smooth stone feypath at his right. This one would lead him to Dowth North, a long passage, about twenty strides in length, ending in a cruciform chamber. He had been to Dowth North only once in his lifetime, but remembered it well. At the end of the cruciform chamber lay two more entranceways. Both of them led deeper into the faery mound. The first dark passage, seen only by fey born, led to the chamber of cave pools, a sacred place. The second passage had a corbelled roof and led nowhere. He dismissed it immediately from his mind.

He focused on the jagged walled feypath at his left. This one would lead him to Dowth South. A shorter passage of about five strides, Dowth South ended in a circular chamber. Within the circular chamber lay two more entranceways as well. One was a single recess to the right, and the other seen only by fey born. The ancient builders of Dowth South aligned the passages to the setting sun of the winter solstice. On that one special day, sunlight spilled down into Dowth South's darkness.

He had a choice to make.

Valor lay imprisoned in water.

When he found Valor, he would find Lana.

His hands fisted.

Dowth North had a chamber of sacred pools.

He launched himself into the confined space, choosing Dowth North, and became a deadly hunter seeking prey in the sacred Faery Mound of Darkness.

"Walk, Lana," Cadman growled, shoving her forward.

They were in the feypaths once again. Dwindling light flickered across her skin in violet shades. The eerie hues slithered along the feypath's rocky walls with an intimidating radiance. Yet, majesty existed here, something untamed and admirable. Beneath her bare feet, black pebbles littered the uneven dirt floor. She had the sensation of moving downward, the pressure in her ears varying. The sea-hued gown she wore kept her in comfort, no matter the swift changes in temperature from the periodic winds. She glanced at one of the dragonfly cuffs adorning her upper arms, a reminder and reassurance of Keegan. He would come.

Wrists bound with the same fey threads once tying her ankles together, Lana covered her mouth with both her hands and coughed. The rotting smell that permeated the dank air felt like a living entity, tainting her breath. It drifted through the underground passages, a mourning wind of stink and regret, not like the salty breezes of the calming seashore. She wondered if she would ever see the foamy waves of the sea again, and thought probably not.

She walked slightly ahead of Cadman, the pain in her chest sharpening and waning, a constant companion in these last few hours. She remained calm, keeping the discomfort hidden as best she could, fighting the tidal wave of fear that her damaged heart had had enough of this life.

A growing feebleness in her limbs sought to steal her perseverance and slow her stride. She fought it, concentrating on the winding feypath ahead instead of herself.

With a bend to the left, a growth of sickly brown vines sprouted from the stone walls. Branches growing thick upon themselves, they appeared to be strangling each other in their zeal for life.

On the opposite wall of the long purple-lit passage, concentric circles and small and large spirals swept the gray stone. She ran a hand along the etchings that looked to be ancient symbols of a long ago moonset and moonrise.

"Stop touching the walls and move," her captor growled from behind her.

"Where are you taking me, Cadman?" Lana looked over her shoulder.

"We go to Dowth."

Dowth was the name the druidess once called the Faery Mound of Darkness. She remembered the reference now. Dowth meant darkness.

"Is Valor at Dowth?" she prompted.

"You ask too many questions."

She stopped and faced him, unwilling to be put off. "Is Valor at Dowth, Cadman?"

"Aye, Valor is at Dowth," he mimicked sarcastically, grabbing her upper arm hurtfully. He propelled her forward. "I should have left you tied up back in my home, but unfortunately I doona trust you would wait for me."

She coughed again and felt a jolt of pain in her chest. It was gone in the next shaky breath. With her right hand, she held on to her left wrist, a small security that kept her spirit from splintering into ruin and despair.

"Cadman," she said, keeping her tone even, for he eyed her suspiciously now. "Why do you not wink us there to Dowth?"

"Wink to Dowth?" He frowned as if just remembering he had the power to bring them there in an instant.

"You are fey, Cadman. Would it not be faster to wink us to Dowth instead of trudging through these stink filled paths?"

"It would be," he agreed, and then sneered, "but then your lovely scent will not be in the feypaths, and I want the guardian to come this way."

Anger replaced her weariness and fear. "You have set a trap for Keegan?"

"I have set many traps," he retorted. "The first few needed to be stronger, that is all."

She smiled knowingly. "Your other traps dinna stop my guardian. What makes you think these will?"

He glared at her and then looked over his shoulder, a

general disquiet marking his features. "These will stop him. They must."

"My guardian is fiercer than the rest. He will not be stopped." She let her tone show her pleasure. "Never."

He looked back at her.

"You canna win, Cadman."

"I have Valor."

"For now," she admitted, giving him that.

He continued to stare at her, his features scrunched in observation. "What is wrong with you? You look all white and sweaty."

"Nothing," she rebuffed. "I am tired only. You dinna allow me any food or drink."

"You deny too quickly." He stepped forward, pushing her roughly against the wall, his hand a hot brand upon her chest.

Leaning forward, he sniffed at her jawline. Lana turned her face away at the sour scent of his breath.

"The guardian has taken you," he said with low fury, pulling back. "You are no longer unbled." He slid his open hand down her body, coming to rest on her stomach.

"Stop it, Cadman."

"Hold still." His fingers dug hurtfully into her tender flesh. "But no babe grows in your womb."

He grabbed her chin, forcing her to look into his eyes.

"A claiming and a mating of *a claíomh host* is forbidden, Lana. What spell did you cast upon him? A fey guardian would never breech a vow."

"I cast no spell," she replied indignantly.

He searched her eyes for truth and then released her. "They will punish him, you know."

"Who will punish him? Why?"

A beastly smile crossed his features. "When I am fey king I will make sure of it."

Her heart pounded in her breast.

"You must also be made to pay for this lack of discretion. You look pale, my lovely. Doona fear. I will be lenient with you. When Valor submits to my hand, I will ride you in celebration every night thereafter, and you will drop many of my sons."

"I will not surrender to you. Neither will Valor."

He smiled. "Both of you will learn."

Suddenly, a fearsome howl rent the air.

Cadman balked, covering his ears and flinching in pain.

Lana turned toward the reverberation, searching the purple shadows beyond. The sound did not hurt her ears. "Keegan," she guessed aloud in triumph, and then bolted toward the sound.

"Stop."

A foot shot out and tripped her.

She fell forward, sprawling on her stomach. Her bound hands were unable to break her fall.

"Keegan," she cried, her chin cut and bleeding from impacting on a jagged rock. "Valor is at Dowth!"

"Shut up!" her captor said loudly, arms locked around

her waist from behind.

Lana rolled over and kicked out, missing him. "Valor is at DOWTH!" she yelled, determined her guardian mate hear her.

Cadman grabbed her bound hands and yanked her to her feet. She did not have the physical strength to fight him, but it did not stop her.

"Let go of me!" she shouted, twisting in his arms. "You have no right to hold me!"

"Stop fighting me, Lana." He easily stilled her efforts, his thin body pressing into her back.

"Nay!" Hot tears streamed down her cheeks. "Keegan, Valor is at . . ."

A cold hand plastered across her face, blocking her air.

"Silence," he hissed in her ear, and then a piercing white light burst before her eyes. She flinched in surprise. He was winking them to Dowth.

A terrible silence roared in her ears.

Cold air slid along her skin.

In the next instant, she lay prone on the edge of a ledge.

CHAPTER 15

LANA LIFTED HER HEAD AND looked down upon the timeless, serrated ridges of a double shore. Dotted crystal prisms refracted light and color in the underground chamber.

Two dazzling black water pools held dominion here, one spilling into the other amid a shawl of white mist. Fingerlike wisps of mist crept insidiously outward from the waterfall to the triple boulders flecked with pink gems. A small, shallow valley of stunted, white-barked trees stood in the northern corner. Never had she seen tree branches twisted and bent as these, growing downward into rock and soil instead of upward to the scarce light. They seemed forlorn, etched in dimness and shadow, an unforgettable solitude and wildness clinging to them.

Uncomfortable with their white presence, she looked away taking a shaky breath. The air was crisp and cool, every breath clean and sweet.

"Welcome to the Faery Mound of Darkness, Lana."

Lana glanced over her shoulder at Cadman. Her captor sat perched on a small ridge behind her, streaks of refracted light spilling across his thin face.

"Is it not beautiful?" he asked, his black beady eyes watchful of her every response, her every emotion.

Aye, it is beautiful . . . in a distressing way, she thought, and nodded in answer. This was a place of whiteness and shadow, of treachery and deceit, but also of regal grandeur and olden sacredness. She searched the magnificent pools for the enchanted sword, Valor. Sitting up to see better, the inside of her right knee scraped against a bulging stone she barely noticed. Her attention focused below, she saw three men standing at an entranceway to the pool cavern. In each hand they carried a short sword and dagger. The men were guards, she reasoned quickly, the same as the six faeries who stood near the flowing waterfall, more of Lord Bress's loyal and misguided followers.

Then a glint in the water caught her eye. She looked again, sitting up straighter. Hung from the ceiling on a thick rope was a cage made of branches. Partially submerged in the farthest pool, she could see the hilt of a sword peeking above the surface of the rippling waters.

"That is Valor," Cadman said proudly.

"How long has she been in the water?" Lana glanced over her shoulder.

"Long enough," he replied smugly. He leaned forward, his eyes bright with expectation. "Have you ever seen Valor, Lana?"

She shook her head.

"There is none other like her in all the lands. She was conjured from the branch of a sacred tree whose roots fell to the deepest hollows of the most forgotten places. Her blade is made of an unknown metal, but her most important and unique feature is her hilt. The place where her master holds her is crafted of spiral-cut bone. She is lighter, swifter, and longer than any other sword ever seen."

Lana thought only of the sorceress's first granddaughter, Glenna. Locked in the enchantment of the sword spirit for all these years, she wondered if anything was left of the young woman.

"Valor is a fearsome sword which will smite her master's enemies, but it is not what makes her great. Do you know what makes her great, Lana?" her captor prompted excitedly.

"Nay," she whispered, sickened by the sweaty flush on his face.

Savoring the moment, his voice came to her barely above a whisper, imparting his great secret to her. "It is said Valor is the only blade that can stop *Freagarthach*."

Lana quickly searched her mind for the translation of the olden word. "The Answerer?" she prompted in alarm, "the great sword defender belonging to the High King of the Faeries?"

"Aye." Cadman leaned back, pleased by her intelligence. "Answerer is one of the four talismans of the fey. I see you know your mythic legacy."

She knew very little about legacies, mythic or otherwise, and shoved a blond curl out of her eyes.

"*Freagarthach* is Answerer's olden name," her captor explained. "The great Answerer inflicts only mortal wounds when drawn and *only* the dark enchanted blade, Valor, can defeat him."

"Him?"

"Answerer was crafted for a male hand, Lana. Therefore, the sword must be male."

"You stole Valor to destroy Answerer," she stated, knowing the truth.

"Aye, what better way to destroy a powerful magical sword than with another powerful sword crafted from dark conjuring?" He grinned.

"You have no guarantee Valor can destroy Answerer," Lana argued.

"She will," he said confidently. "Valor is crafted of the dominant dark side of the sacred female, the taker of life. Taking life is much easier than giving life. Dark always wins over light, whether male or female."

Lana strongly disagreed.

He leaned forward again, his face flushed and earnest. "Do you want to see Valor? Do you want to see the darkness I am protecting you from?"

"I want to see her," Lana said, but not for the reasons he stated.

"Come then, my lovely." Jumping down, he walked over

to her and reached for her arm, pulling her roughly to her feet.

Lana pulled her arm free, not liking his touch.

"You will be grateful to me." His gaze slid down her body with vile intent. "Very grateful," he murmured.

"I want to see her now, Cadman."

"So you will." He gestured behind her.

About two horse lengths from where they stood, a narrow stone stairway curved down the wall to the pools below. "Shall we?" He placed a hand on her arm and pushed her forward.

"The steps leading down to the pools become very narrow, so I will lead." He walked in front of her. "In case you trip and fall, I will be there to catch you."

"How noble," she muttered under her breath.

He turned his back and started down the steps.

Lana reacted on impulse. Had she taken the time to contemplate her tackling maneuver, she probably would have proceeded more cautiously, but all she could think about was rescuing Valor. She jumped and landed on his back. Snaking her arms over her captor's head, she pulled the binding on her wrists snug under his pointed chin.

Cursing, he clawed at her wrists and bindings, trying to free himself.

With all her strength, Lana held on. She pulled back hard, wanting to choke the life out of him.

He slipped on the third step, falling forward and taking

her with him.

They tumbled down the rest of the twenty or so narrow stone steps in a struggle of flailing limbs, and hit the bottom stone slab with a loud thud.

Lana lay in shock, her body hurting, breathing heavily.

The spriggan half-blood landed on top of her, knocking her nearly unconscious.

"Foolish female, you will be punished for this." He pushed off her in a rage and climbed to his feet. "I have treated you well, but you will soon learn the meaning of my anger."

Lana barely heard him. She felt the bruises already forming on her back, right arm, and hip. She tried to steady her breathing, but the clutching pain in her chest sent a wave of cold dread into her bloodstream.

"GUARDIAN COMES," one of the faeries warned loudly from the other side of the pool.

In a blur, Lana lifted her head, wiping the burning tears from her eyes.

For a single breath, silver shards of light formed above the pool closest to her, a glowing power of deliverance.

"Drop the net!" Cadman snapped, gesturing wildly with his hands.

A black net of fey webs fell from the ceiling in a soundless whoosh.

Keegan.

"Nay!" she screamed, but it was too late.

The net closed around him. Her mind reeled back at the

sight of him, suspended above the pool in front of her, ensnared, caught like a fly in a deadly spider's web. Except, he was Rain now. His true form made him look bigger, more threatening than she remembered.

His beautiful head lifted. Amethyst fire glinted at her and Lana swallowed down her fear. She realized instantly he wanted to be caught. He turned away and focused on her captor, eyes widening slightly at the sight of the spriggan half-blood.

Cadman chuckled and slapped his thigh in triumph. "Welcome, Great Guardian of the Waters. You may wink in but the dark enchantment of the webworking will not allow you to wink out." He bowed and swept his arm out in feigned respect. "I see you have followed Lana's sweet scent. And I, rather brilliantly, entrapped you. Who is the greater fey warrior here?" He flashed her a grin and Lana realized the display of power was meant for her benefit and her benefit alone.

Cadman stepped closer to the net. "Do you wonder why you and the water fey could not sense Valor, Great Guardian?"

"I am sure you will tell me," Keegan replied, shifting subtly.

Cadman rocked back on his heels, secure in his own genius and skill. "So simple, if you but think of it. Do you know?" he prompted self-righteously. "Valor was born here." He pointed to the trees of white bark in the corner. "See the largest white tree over there, the one bowing in everlasting sorrow? That is where the sorceress did her dark conjuring.

She cut down a perfect branch and so created her own misbegotten fate."

Lana looked at the grouping of trees in the northern corner. *So this is where Valor was born*, she thought. The tree's tangled branches seemed to flow one into the other, cascading down an incline of notched rocks.

Cadman continued with his explanation. "For tempting the sorceress with their beauty, the Gods and Goddesses sent the sacred hollow of white bark trees into the below, away from the world of light, temptation, and bad intention."

"It is unfair," Lana objected softly, feeling regret for the trees, and twinges of anger at such an unjust punishment. The trees belonged in highland meadows beneath a pristine blue sky, not here in shade and grayness because of a sorceress's wrongful choice.

"True enough, but then the fey are not known for their fairness. Now, shall we talk of you, Great Guardian?" Cadman gave a wave of dismissal to the trees. "You still wear the sword and scabbard down your back, I see. Do you think that inconsequential mortal blade can slash magical webs conjured from bog and fire?" He laughed throatily, hands on his hips. "How does it feel to be powerless? How does it feel to be held at another's whim?"

"What makes you think I am powerless, Master Spriggan?"

"Keegan," Lana said loudly, calling her guardian mate's attention to her. "Valor is in the cage in the high pool near the waterfall."

"Shut up, Lana," Cadman sneered, moving back to her and raising a hand as if to strike her.

A growl of warning vibrated in the air.

It lingered there, fierce and primal, a menace of echo and silence.

Lana saw a momentary flash of alarm cross her captor's features, then he dropped his hand and faced her guardian mate once again.

"Doona worry, Great Guardian," he said in quick recovery. "I will not mar that lovely flesh." He snickered to himself. "Well, mayhap a wee bit in bed play." He tilted his head, waiting for a response to his taunting words. "You watch me with that unblinking stare, Great Guardian." Cadman held up his arms and turned, as if showing off a new tunic to a friend. "Wonder what I am?" He placed his hands on his hips once more and puffed out his thin chest.

"I know what you are," Keegan said with soft threat.

"You do? Tell me then."

"Besides being an abomination, an idiot."

"Cadman is a half-blood," Lana said quickly, giving her guardian as much information as she thought he would need.

"I can see that," her beloved said.

"His spriggan father raped his mother."

Cadman struck her full in the face with the back of his hand. "He dinna rape my mother. I told you that."

Holding her stinging cheek, Lana glared at Cadman. Her captor was completely unaware of the rage emanating from the powerful guardian he thought he had dominion over.

"He serves Lord Bress," Lana continued in defiance.

"Does he now?" Keegan replied, his mouth edged with cruelty. Lean muscles shifted again, preparing.

"True, a fey king to replace a blemished one. Nuada does not deserve to rule the fey realm," Cadman said, turning back to Keegan.

Lana felt a shifting in the air, a wave of relentless and overwhelming power. She stared at Keegan. She could not believe Cadman did not note it, and quickly added, "Cadman plans on betraying Lord Bress and keeping Valor and the fey throne for himself."

"Why am I not surprised?" Her guardian mate was not looking at her. His full attention remained on the strutting Cadman.

"True again, my lovely, but I suspect the great and magnificent guardian has figured all that out himself."

"Aye, he has," Keegan interjected and then winked out, materializing beside Valor's cage in the water.

"How did he . . .?" Cadman said in stunned surprise, and then barked, "Stop him!" He jumped up and down. "KILL HIM! He must not take the magical sword!" The half-blood spriggan began to rant in a fit of temper. "Kill him, Kill him . . ."

Instantly, the six faeries standing near the waterfall dove into the pool after Keegan, their wings tight against their backs.

Lana scrambled to her feet.

"See, Lana," Cadman pointed in confident glee, "the guardian cares not for you and seeks only to rescue Valor. You are nothing to him. Nothing."

Using all her remaining strength, Lana hauled back and punched him in the face with her bound fists. Taken by surprise, he fell down on his back. Both hands covering his bloody nose, he moaned loudly, rolling back and forth in pain.

Having lost her balance, Lana had fallen back too, landing on her hip. As she tried to scramble once again to her feet, bloody fingers dug into her forearm.

Cadman sneered at her. "Foolish female!" He brought them both to their feet. "Your guardian may have survived the previous attacks, but my faeries will end it here. Valor shall be mine as you shall be mine."

"Never!" she rasped. And then the dormant strength that had risen to the surface once before came to her aid again.

The erratic beat of her heart steadied.

The strain of each breath eased.

The weakness in her limbs turned to strength and certainty.

Fighting his grip, she sunk her teeth into his right hand. He let out a blood-curdling howl and released her. Lana hauled back again, her fists connecting with his pointy chin. He stumbled back and she dashed away, running around the serrated edge of the smaller pool. Her health had somehow magically been restored. She did not know how long the strength would remain with her, but she intended to make the most of it. The men who kept guard at the one entrance-way had cowardly abandoned their posts when the guardian arrived. Good, there were less of Lord Bress's followers to fight, she thought.

She could see Valor's partially submerged cage hanging in the spray of the waterfall, surrounded by the whiteness of the mist.

In the center of the pool, a fearsome battle raged below the surface between the six faeries and one guardian. The water undulated into a frenzied whirlpool.

She could not see Keegan.

She could not see the faeries who sought her guardian mate's death.

But she could reach Valor.

With a quick glance over her shoulder, she saw Cadman had staggered to his feet, and then a deluge of water blinded her. Lana tripped and fell to her knees, drenched in an icy chill of wetness.

A geyser of water shot upward and Keegan burst from the black waters with four faeries in pursuit. Two floated to the surface, dead.

Pushing wet hair out of her eyes, she scrambled quickly to her feet. Squeezing between two small boulders, she hurried through the twisted tangle of white bark trees. All the while, she tried unsuccessfully to free her hands from the fey bindings. The waterfall was only a few strides ahead.

Above her, Keegan was locked in a fierce battle with the

four angry faeries. A sudden ear-piercing screech and a faery with a bleeding face dropped, his body tangling with the rope that held Valor's cage.

Lana stopped short.

Furious and blinded by blood, the faery cut the rope with his dagger. In the next instant, Keegan's sword pierced the creature's side. The faery died instantly, tumbling limply into the pool.

Lana looked back to Valor's cage.

She stared aghast at the empty space. "Valor!" she cried out in a panic.

The cage and Valor plummeted beneath the surface of the waters.

In that one defining moment, her world slowed to a stop.

It was up to her now.

No choice but one.

Her face lifted.

From across the pool, she met her guardian mate's unhappy gaze.

Lana gave him her most bright and reassuring smile. *I will always love you*, she thought despondently, *even if you canna love me.*

"Nay, Lana!" her guardian mate called out explosively, trying to reach her, but his three remaining attackers would not let him.

Her lashes swept low.

She stepped closer to the swirling waters.

"It is all right, Keegan," she whispered, knowing he would win the battle. She felt confident of that. Only she could save Valor.

She blinked, staring into the white mist.

She was terrified.

Yet, Valor needed her, valued her as no one ever had, except mayhap for Keegan.

The memories of her uneventful life faded away, leaving only the sounds of the spray and waterfall.

Taking a deep breath, she dove into the mist, hands outstretched and bound in front of her.

Wet, bone-chilling waters engulfed her in crystal clear darkness.

She forced her eyes to remain open, descending rapidly in the fey waters, her mortal body heavy there.

There was an amber shimmering down below. *Valor.*

If only she could hold her breath long enough to reach the cage.

It seemed to take forever. She kicked out with her feet, propelling her forward.

Her bound hands reached outward.

Her mind called to the sword spirit. "Valor!"

"HERE," came the musical female reply.

Heart pounding, lungs bursting, Lana reached the cage. Pushing her hands between sturdy branches, her fingers wrapped around spiral-cut bone and grabbed the hilt of the enchanted sword.

✴ ✴ ✴

"Kill him!" Cadman screamed in maddened rage, foaming at the mouth. "KILL HIM NOW!"

Keegan caught a glimpse of the spriggan abomination before the three remaining faeries renewed their attack. The abomination ran back and forth along the opposite side of the pool's crystal shore, locked in a spriggan frenzy, yanking on his hair, and waving his arms about. It was a common response for a spriggan overcome with frustration, as he knew well.

"Lana," the thing kept calling. "Doona touch the sword."

Lana. Fury surged in his blood; he had been unable to prevent this day. In the deepest reaches of his fey heart, he knew what he lost. *Lana*, he thought, *my beloved*.

The realization of what he felt for her came as an excruciating awakening. With renewed strength, he clawed the face of one of his attackers and grabbed a dagger out of the faery's right hand. At least it was not a Darkshade dagger. The remaining and unhurt attackers backed away, giving him the advantage, and he launched himself at the larger one who was unprepared for the abruptness of the attack. Keegan thrust the dagger into the creature's cold heart, killing him instantly. Two left. Wings tucked close, he whirled to his right and slashed at the chests of the others, cutting through muscles.

The two remaining faeries were hurt, bleeding profusely, their pain turning them vicious and careless. They rushed him, as he knew they would, expecting him to launch into the air. Instead, he ducked low, wings held tight to his back, coming up behind them. They swiveled too late, and he slashed their necks on one final move.

Falling to their knees, they stared at him in shock, their wings crinkling. White blood pumping out of their wounds, they died snarling at him.

Keegan looked across the pool. It had taken him a short time to eliminate his attackers. They were no match for a guardian driven by revenge and lethal calm. In the blink of an eye, he crossed the distance over the waters, catching the spriggan thing by surprise.

"Save her!" Cadman screamed at him wearing a mortal's face. "Doona you care? The sword will take her."

Save her, echoed inside him, a litany of pain and horrific yearning. *Save her.* Every fiber of his being wanted to jump in the waters and wrench her free from the sword spirit.

But he could not.

Could not!

He was forced to make a choice, saving the dark enchanted sword of the fey, or his heart's desire. Lana made that choice for him.

"Save her, guardian!" Cadman screamed at him.

The spriggan's cry brought him back from the brink. Keegan refocused on the abomination.

"You are going to let the sword take her!"

Aye, he thought miserably. The thing backed away from

him. "Valor will not let her die, Cadman."

"Fool, doona you know what will happen to her?" The abomination pulled out a Darkshade dagger from beneath his tunic.

"I know," Keegan said, and dropped his own dagger. He wanted to feel this one's death in his hands.

The spriggan's lips curved, thinking he could win.

Behind him, Keegan heard the feminine rush of breath and the ominous silvery sound of a blade being pulled from the waters to the shore. He knew to the depths of his fey spirit what awaited behind him.

The abomination lunged at him, aiming the mystical dagger at his heart, but he was no match for the swiftness of a guardian. Keegan shackled Cadman's wrist and locked his other hand around a thin neck.

"Let me go!"

Keegan struggled not to give in to his fury, his need to snap Cadman's neck. He needed to know Bress's plans of attack.

"Let go of the dagger." He squeezed down onto the bony wrist until he heard a crack of bone. The spriggan thing cried out in pain and dropped the dagger.

"Stop!" Cadman choked, trying to save himself. "I will tell you all."

Keegan kicked the mystical dagger into the pool. "Where is Bress?"

"Bress arrives soon. I know his plans for attack," Cadman rasped.

"How soon?" Keegan asked.

"Days, mayhap hours. I am not sure."

"Where does he land?"

The spriggan abomination shook his head. "I am dizzy. Release me and give me a moment to think. I will tell you all I know."

Keegan set Cadman back on his feet.

The abomination stepped back, rubbing his bruised neck. "I dinna mean to kill the water faery, you know. She attacked me and I had to defend myself."

For that you will die, Keegan promised silently. The small faery had been a healer of life, not a destroyer of life.

"You can have Valor. I'll take the other one."

Keegan could see confidence growing in the thing before him. "What other one?" he asked, already knowing the answer.

"I dinna really want Lana," Cadman dared to cajole. "She is pretty but really much too sickly for my seed to take root. I will take the other sword host for my mate."

The brazen insinuation of the abomination sickened him. The thought of Cadman mating with Lana drove him over the edge. Reaching out, Keegan snapped the spriggan thing's neck, killing him instantly.

"For MacLir," he whispered, and tossed the limp body into the pool. "Let the waters take their vengeance."

It was over.

He closed his eyes and exhaled, his heart locked in a

tangle of wretchedness.

Slowly and with infinite desolation, he turned around, unwilling to look.

Dropping down to one knee, he offered his respect. He did not even know how to deal with the feelings tearing his insides apart, constant waves of longing and despair.

He bowed his head in forced reverence.

Eyes cracking open, he stared at the ground.

He placed a fisted hand across his chest, battling the tightness there.

In a ragged whisper, he said, "Valor, I honor thee."

CHAPTER 16

"Keegan." A soft and familiar voice called his name.

He lifted his head.

She was incredibly beautiful, kneeling in unsurpassed radiance beside the glimmering form of the enchanted sword. His bride was fey now, a magical being of allure and secrets wearing a sea green gown.

Blond tresses fell about lovely bare shoulders. She inhaled quietly, the gentle swell of her breasts rising and falling above the bodice without strain.

The silver dragonfly cuffs shone on her upper arms, a gift from MacLir. They were a mark of the water fey's approval. They made his heart ache for what he lost, but never truly held.

The delicate fragrance of heather reached out to caress his lungs, a fey scent of longing wounding his blood.

"Are you injured?" she asked.

He shook his head.

"I am glad, Keegan. Valor has allowed me this moment to speak with you." She gestured behind her. "Valor asks that you care for her beloved host. She is gravely weak."

Keegan looked to the unconscious woman lying behind Lana. She had blond hair too, but of a shorter length.

"Her name is Glenna, Keegan. She is the sorceress's first granddaughter. I ask that you watch over her for me. She has been in the water too long and needs much rest."

Unsure of his voice, he nodded that he would take care of her.

"Valor tells me I am the last descendant of the sorceress's second granddaughter, Erin."

"Rianon?" he asked, referring to her older sister.

Lana shook her head. "It seems Rianon and I share the bloodline of my mother only. We have different fathers." She bowed her head slightly. "My father and sister must never know, Keegan."

"I will not tell them, Lana."

Melancholy shadowed her features. "Tell them I died of my weak heart and you buried me under an ancient rowan. That will give ease to their sorrow."

"I will tell them."

She tilted her head questioningly. "You wish to ask me something?"

He did. "Does your heart still give you pain?" He needed to know.

Her right palm moved to rest above her heart. "Nay,

Keegan. Doona concern yourself. Valor has seen to it."

"It is my concern," he said tightly. He felt himself drowning in her dark eyes.

"Has it been your concern?" she inquired, her tone gracious. "I dinna know."

"Aye," he ground out, wanting to say so much more, but the words lodged in his throat.

She looked away when he did not continue.

Was unable to continue.

"Valor wishes to return to the High King Nuada immediately. She senses the threat and the selfishness that comes."

"I will deliver her to the High King," he promised, regaining his composure.

"My thanks, Keegan." Her lashes lowered. "You are most honorable."

He stared at her trembling lips, feeling his insides rip apart.

She started to fade.

"Stop, Lana. Stay with me!"

She looked up, barely there, a filmy presence only.

His body shuddered, the surge of love for her nearly devastating in its intensity.

"Lana," he said hoarsely, unable to say what he truly felt. *I love you.*

She searched his face. "Keegan." Tears formed in her eyes, raining down her cheeks like tiny crystals.

With a trembling hand, she reached out to him.

He leaned toward her, hungry for the feel of her fingertips on his face one last time.

Passion rekindled, arcing like lightning between them.

Yearning.

Wanting.

So desperately . . .

Then she dropped her hand and turned away, stiffening.

Keegan stared at her lovely profile. How had he allowed it to end this way?

She turned slightly to him, her brow creased in worry.

"Lana, what is it?"

She blinked, her face set in distress.

"Lana, what is it?" he demanded. "Tell me."

She shook her head. Her eyes wide, tears spilling down her cheeks like a waterfall, he heard her cry out in his mind, and then only silence.

She dissolved, merely the whisper of her sweet breath lingering to taunt him.

She was gone.

He sat back, his gaze dropping. Lying beside the enchanted sword were two dragonfly cuffs, the swirling filigree stunningly silver against the backdrop of black stone.

Valor had not even allowed her to keep the gifts of the water fey.

He flung his head back and roared, the anguish inside him venting so all the lands knew of his grief.

He fell forward on his arms, his head bent, his hair a brown shroud about him.

The pain of loss rose in his chest. He moaned, his hands fisting in front of him.

Gone.

As if she never walked the land.

Never breathed the air.

Never lay by his side.

He breathed raggedly for a time and then lifted his head with effort.

The dark sword Valor waited for him, perfect in its hardness and cutting luminosity.

He blinked once to clear his vision and took in a struggling breath, not looking at the dragonfly cuffs, all traces of sorrow and loss forced deep inside.

Pushing up, he straightened.

He was a guardian of the waters, he reminded himself, a great, powerful, and unemotional being.

He reached for the sword's hilt.

He must do what he had promised to do.

As his fair one had done.

Fingers wrapped around the grip of spiral-cut bone.

Immediately, he felt a physically powerful presence and immeasurable strength enter his arm. The blade was longer and lighter than other blades, able to reach the enemy quicker, he surmised. Holding the sword up, he peered into the sheen of the blade, hoping to see his beloved's face. Forged of a metal he had never seen before, it reflected nothing, not even his own countenance. The diamond cross-section did not even have a blood groove.

With a single thrust upward, he sheathed it into the scabbard on his back.

Disquiet, emanating from the sword, clung to his flesh. It was a dark conjuring barely contained, and within it he felt *her* presence.

With the back of his left hand, he wiped the tears from his cheek, amazed to find his face damp. He had no right to love her, no right to love that which the sword spirit claimed at birth.

He looked at the unconscious young woman lying on her side. Lana said her name was Glenna.

A blue gown draped her slender form; her face was turned away. He knelt near her shoulder. Tiny gold and silver beads, woven into thick blond hair, fell across her cheek and nose, hiding her features.

"Glenna?"

Gently, he lifted a thick curl from the young woman's face and froze. Glenna was a like image of Lana, the same pale skin, the same oval shape of the face, the same light brown lashes.

"Glenna," he said tenderly, "I am going to take you somewhere safe."

Not a sound did she make to acknowledge him, this innocent who had suffered so much because of another's whim.

She looked hollow and vacant, her very life essence drained out of her.

He scooped her up in his arms and stood. She was feather-light, her head rolling listlessly to the side. The bronze bracelets on her wrists and ankles chimed softly. With a bitter detachment, he observed the carnage he had wrought.

Valor.

Lana.

He had succeeded in saving only one.

Nay, he thought. His fair one succeeded.

Now he must do his part.

With a lingering glance at Lana's dragonfly cuffs, he closed his eyes and envisioned the druidess's small cottage. He winked out, leaving only the shimmering shards of his fey presence behind to settle and disperse upon her cuffs.

✳ ✳ ✳

Night and peril approached the lands of the *Tuatha Dé Danann* and Keegan knew he had little time left to deliver Valor to his king. Transforming to his mortal self, he walked out of the waning shadows of the moon and stood in front of the entranceway of the druidess's cottage.

Gazing down at the pail of water, he called her name quietly. "Derina?"

"Here, guardian," she replied from somewhere within. "Come in. I have been expecting you. What have you brought me?"

Shifting sideways so as not to bump Glenna's head, he

walked into the warm candlelit glow of the cottage.

"Lana?" the druidess asked, wearing brown druidess's robes. She peered up at him, her white hair a tumbled mess of beads and dried rosemary.

He shook his head and her empty eye sockets crinkled in a frown.

"Lay the girl there then," she directed, pointing to the bed in the back.

With the ancient following in her shuffling gait, Keegan walked to the back of the round house and gently eased his burden onto a bed of white and brown pelts. Streaks of amber moonlight fell across the girl's waist from the open shutters behind him.

He moved back to make room for the druidess.

"Who be this woman-child, guardian?"

"Her name is Glenna," he replied. "She is the first *claíomh host* and I must ask you to care for her, Derina."

The druidess continued to scrutinize the young woman. "The first sword host, do you say?" She scratched her cheek. "She doona look fey to me."

"She is no longer fey. Valor freed her. She is the first granddaughter of the sorceress."

Derina nodded in understanding. "So that olden tale of the host being not of faery blood be true then."

"So it seems," he said softly.

She pulled a large brown pelt over the young woman, tucking her bare feet under. "Wait for me in the other room, guardian." She gestured for him to leave.

Confident of the druidess's caring, he returned to the main room. Stepping around the center fire, he walked back toward the doorway and leaned a weary shoulder against the sturdy doorframe. Folding his arms across his chest, he waited, impatient to be on his way.

The druidess soon joined him, no doubt sensing his urgency.

"How is she?" he asked.

"Verra weak. Let us see what rest and my food will do."

"Will she die?"

The druidess tugged at her hair, trying to establish some order with the strands. "Methinks it be too early to say. I will do my best."

"Call the simpler if you need help. This girl is entrusted into my care."

She waved a hand in his face. "As you wish. Tell me where be our Lana?"

Keegan looked away, unable to answer, silence falling like a heavy rain about him.

"Be that Valor you carry on your back then?" the ancient asked after a time, touching his arm.

He nodded.

"Valor has taken Lana?"

"Aye," he replied.

"I am sorry for both of you."

He looked back at her. "You knew that I would love her?"

"Aye, you had but to open your eyes to see it."

He turned away once more. "You said you were expecting me."

"Has your grief blocked all your fey senses, guardian?" she inquired with an edge to her tone.

Frowning, he pushed away from the doorframe.

"Look west," she directed, "and tell me what you feel?"

He looked outside to the clear bright night and luminous white stars.

By the white moon! The battle between his king and the invader had already begun.

Reaching for Valor, he winked out.

CHAPTER 17

WITHIN THE GLOW OF A newborn sun, a long and bloody battle raged, the stink of death simmering in the air from the night before.

Hours earlier, Keegan winked into the fray gripping Valor's hilt in both hands. Immediately he transformed to his mortal self, the fey wings an encumbrance in the closely fought battle. He began hacking and slashing violently through swords, daggers, spears, and flesh, all the while searching for his king.

The Formorians lived mainly on the sea. They were a horde of sea raiders, an ugly race from the offshore islands who wished to lay claim upon Eire. Led by the vain Bress, they came from beyond the extreme northwest to invade and plunder. Forces of cruelty and oppression, they ruled over their conquests with a tyrannical hand, demanding tributes and taxes.

They were a flood of darkness and they would not rule here.

Never would they rule while he still had breath in his body.

He had to find his king and was increasingly alarmed that he could not sense him.

Valor's fierce strength radiated into his hands and up his arms and shoulders. The boundaries between enchantment, fey, and mortal physicality waned. He became a bringer of death, a weapon of utter destruction. For many hours, he fought without mercy against greater odds until at last he saw the fey warrior Lugh wielding Answerer, the great faery talisman. Surrounded by the enemy, Lugh stood in mortal form, draped in the color of red blood over their fallen king, Nuada. Keegan pushed his way through, a grave torment setting in. Had he arrived too late?

"He be dead, Rain," Lugh called out. "Take Valor and force these invaders back to the sea."

Keegan did not hesitate. Emotions gone into nothingness inside him, he slashed and cut his way to triumph until finally the battle was over.

A sun of fading crimson hung low in the sky, leaving behind ribbons of scarlet light on the last day of the foul invasion. The *Tuatha Dé Danann* had defended Eire with perseverance and won.

Keegan felt no joy, no satisfaction. He stood beside their mortal brethren because he must. It was as simple as that. Whatever emotions, whatever passions he once yearned for were gone.

It was better not to feel, he thought, his right hand tightening around Valor's grip. He looked around. Death was everywhere, the blood of diminishing lives returning to the black soil. Bodies twitched here and there, a clinging to the misery of life before death's final claim. Pockets of flies gathered, and he turned away.

Men walked around him, faces showing the exhaustion of a hard won victory. The tribe of the *Tuatha Dé Danann* had fought courageously under their chieftain. The fey fought daringly as well, except they no longer had a high king to serve. Nuada died at the edge of the enemy's blade before he had been able to reach him. Keegan ran a hand through his hair. He had failed.

He felt the dull edges of shame grind into him and looked down at Valor. Not a drop of blood stained the enchanted blade. It shined as if never encountering flesh, bone, or sinew, but he knew better.

He heard footfalls come up behind him and glanced over his shoulder.

"Rain."

Keegan nodded to the warrior faery. "Lugh."

They stood together, shoulder to shoulder, drinking in the brief silence. Both were half-clothed and barefoot. Torn breeches clung to their muscular legs. Straps crossed their bare chests, holding scabbards on their broad backs. Both held a magical fey sword in their right hands.

"Sooner you should have come, Rain."

"I should have," he agreed.

"Where did you find Valor?" Lugh asked.

"Dowth."

"Who took her?"

"Cadman, a half-blood spriggan-mortal."

The warrior faery looked at him in doubt. "Never have I heard of a creature such as this."

"Nor will you ever again. Bress promised the spriggan abomination treasures if he stole Valor. There were other followers; they are no more."

The warrior faery understood. "Blodenwedd said you found a *claíomh host* in the village."

"Aye," Keegan agreed.

"She dinna guide you fast enough," the warrior faery said in blunt criticism.

"My failing, not hers," he replied tersely.

"As you wish."

"Did my king die bravely?" Keegan questioned.

"Quickly and bravely."

"A brave death is preferable to a sick or weak life." Immediately, he regretted his words and felt the untruth of such an intolerable statement. Once he thought the physically weak worthless, but no longer. Lana taught him the right of it. She had been born with a weak heart and an unwell body, but her unconquerable and resolute spirit belonged to that of a highborn faery queen. He could hold her in no higher regard and respect. She was his fey queen and always would be. Her inner strength had surprised him. Sometimes even the weakest were stronger inside their spirit than even the most physically strong, if given a chance to prove themselves. She taught him that. Never again would he judge a being only by the outward appearance.

Black crows flew across the battlefield. All those still whole and living looked up to watch their eerie passage.

" 'TIS OVER," Lugh said after a while.

"Not yet," Keegan rumbled in a low voice of objection.

"WE FIND BRESS SOON," his fey warrior companion promised, and moved away to continue his inspection. Keegan suspected he had just spoken with the next high king of the faeries.

He remained where he was, in the center of the battlefield.

He had discarded his tunic long ago and wiped the caked blood from his right forearm across his hip.

His fingers tightened around Valor's hilt, his flesh almost one with the enchanted blade. He did not want to let go, did not want to release her.

He felt Lana's essence and Valor's strength and power.

Valor.

Lana.

Valor.

Lana.

They were one and the same now. He must learn to respect that. His lips twisted. In all the years left to him, he would forever remember the beautiful dark eyes of his beloved.

It came as a smothering wave of grief upon him, sudden and uncontrollable. His left hand clutched at his heart and his breath came out harshly.

"Lana," he groaned. "Forgive me." He had loved, a brief and wondrous passing he had been too dull-witted to acknowledge.

He closed his eyes, battling for control.

He missed her.

Lashes lifting, he shied away from the overwhelming pang of loss. He had fought for many days, his mind and heart locked in blankness. He wished for the blankness again.

The enemy had fallen. The few who remained fled back to their boats, but the one he most wanted was not among them.

He wanted Bress.

He wanted to squeeze the life out of him with his bare hands and make him suffer.

He inhaled the scent of the newly dead, strands of brown hair fluttering across his cheek. Out of the corner of his eye, he detected movement, a glint of metal behind an ancient tree in the low meadows near the loch.

He stilled, giving no clue he noticed.

There, it came again.

Silver and movement.

He bolted toward it, careful to stay in mortal form and not bring attention to his feyness. Dodging around several men of the *Tuatha Dé Danann*, he came upon the thick trunked oak, her green leaves fluttering in the end of day breeze.

Nothing.

He looked toward the shining waters of the loch and saw a man with long blond hair running across the low meadows beyond.

His lips pulled back in a predatory sneer. He set out after him at a dead run.

It did not take him long to reach the coward. With a quick swipe of the sword, he sliced open the man's right thigh. His prey yelped in surprise and pain, tumbling down upon himself in the slippery grasses.

When the man rolled to a stop on his back, Keegan walked up to him. He was surprised at the youthfulness of the face staring up at him in horror. He remembered the deceitful tyrant as being older.

The young man's eyes darted to Valor in fearful recognition.

Keegan slowly smiled and held the sword up for his enemy's benefit.

"Valor," he said in icy menace. "I believe you wanted her."

The young man's breath hitched in terror and he scrambled back on all fours, leaving his sword and dagger behind.

Keegan bared his teeth, fey amethyst replacing the silver gray in his eyes.

"Nay!" his enemy bawled, holding up his right hand in front of his face as if bone would deflect Valor.

Slicing his head off would be too easy. In the next breath, Keegan flipped Valor into the scabbard across his back. Instantly, the strength that had radiated up his arm permeated into his back and shoulders, but he was too engaged to notice.

Seeing Valor no longer threatened him, the coward scrambled backward again, promising all kinds of treasures for his life and freedom.

Keegan ignored his words and continued stalking his prey.

"Bress," he snarled.

"I am not he."

"You are he. Do you not recognize one of the fey guardians you once ruled and had dominion over? For seven years you sat on the high fey throne and all you could think of was yourself."

"I brought treasures to the throne."

So, he abandoned his denial. "To yourself only," Keegan replied. Leaning forward, his right hand shot out and locked around Bress's neck.

"Nay!" the young man choked, hands futilely pulling at Keegan's wrist.

The coward was no match for his superior guardian strength. He lifted the man's weight easily, feeling the rapid pulse of life beneath his fingers, and wishing to end it.

"You should not have tried to reclaim the fey throne."

Staring into Bress's rolling eyes, he continued to slowly squeeze.

"Rain, release him!" Lugh commanded from somewhere to his left.

Keegan held on to his flailing quarry. He felt nothing. The young man's eyes were bulging out, blue lips locked in a silent scream, feeble hands scraping at his wrist, trying to wrestle free.

A large hand settled upon his left shoulder, fingers digging in. The glint of Answerer wavered before his face.

"RELEASE HIM, RAIN."

"Why?"

"THE GODS OF THE LAND WISH IT," Lugh answered simply, unemotionally.

"I doona wish it," he snarled in reply. *Let him use Answerer*, he thought defiantly, *I have Valor*.

"THE GODS WISH IT, RAIN. CONTROL YOUR HATRED AND RELEASE HIM."

The fey warrior's recognition of his uncharacteristic show of feelings tempered his rage.

He was a guardian of the waters and emotions did not rule him. His fingers eased their deadly hold. He released the nearly unconscious enemy and watched him crumple to his knees before him.

Stepping back Keegan made way, allowing others to pull the gasping Bress back to his feet.

"Doona kill me," he croaked, begging for his life. "I can ensure the cows of Eire always give milk!"

Keegan arched a brow in disbelief. Even the fey could not do that.

"I can teach to you how to harvest four times a year,"

Bress shot back, seeing no one believed him.

"ONE TIME SUFFICES," Lugh replied coldly.

Keegan studied the warrior faery. Was this the reason the Gods ordered Bress spared?

"I can teach you when to plow, sow, and reap for the most crops!"

The coward continued promising to share knowledge of farming and increase crop yields, if only they would release him.

Disgusted, Keegan strode a few paces away and took up a stance near a large boulder. Folding his arms across his chest, he stared off into the twilight. He remembered a long ago day when Lana had come into her father's fields, offering goat cheese and a shy, bright smile. She had suggested placing a knife on the plough to lessen the workload. He glanced over his shoulder at the receding backs of the men who dragged Bress away. It was the kind of knowledge the coward only wished he possessed to trade for his miserly life.

"RAIN."

Keegan turned to Lugh.

"YOU HAVE FOUGHT BRAVELY," the warrior faery said.

Grief, vengeance, and retribution possessed him, not bravery.

"BUT EMOTIONS RULE YOU NOW, A DANGEROUS THING FOR A GUARDIAN."

Keegan did not reply. Instead, he found himself studying the great sword Answerer in Lugh's hand. Would the warrior faery have used it on him?

Back at Dowth, before he foolishly attempted to save both Lana and Valor, he overheard Cadman's boastful speech. He wondered if it were true, if Valor could destroy the great fey talisman Answerer, the one blade that inflicted only mortal wounds.

"YOU WISH TO SPEAK?" Lugh inquired, sheathing Answerer in the scabbard at his back.

Keegan shook his head. He did not want to know if Valor could destroy Answerer. Some things were best left unanswered.

"YOU HAVE CHANGED, RAIN."

Keegan glanced at the ground, a momentary acknowledgement, and then looked once more to the sanctuary of twilight.

"WHEN THE MOON HAS RISEN FOR FIVE DAYS HENCE, BRING VALOR TO ME AT TARA. WE TALK THEN."

Keegan nodded. "I will be there."

Lugh left him standing alone on the meadow in silence.

Slowly, he became aware of a sense of dread radiating into him from the enchanted sword. Something felt wrong between the great sword spirit and the willful *claíomh host*. Keegan suspected he was the cause of the rift and felt secretly gladdened by it, a selfish notion.

His thoughts turned inward to a promise he made to Lana. He would check on Glenna before going to meet his punishment at Tara.

✦ ✦ ✦

"Derina?" Keegan called softly from outside the druidess's cottage. It was early morning, the sunrise peeking over the horizon in shades of gold.

The ancient appeared in her doorway smelling of mead.

"Morn to you, guardian" she grumbled in greeting. Empty eye sockets peered up at him while she shoved pieces of bread in her mouth.

"Hungry?" she inquired, and held a crumbly piece of bread out to him.

He shook his head. "Not this morn, Derina. My thanks."

"I am hungry all the time. Besides, I canna sleep. The fey keep winking into my home. First Blodenwedd," she ticked off a list, "then you, then a water faery in my pail of water here," she pointed to her pail, "and now you again. How be MacLir?"

"Dead."

"Oh." That stopped her tirade.

"I dinna wink into your home."

She frowned at him. "Same thing. I am up and not asleep."

He could see that. "How is she?" he inquired about Glenna.

"The *claíomh host* sleeps."

"Has she awakened at all?" It had been five days since he left her here in the druidess's care.

"Aye, she has been up and has eaten, too."

He felt better. "She will live then."

"If she chooses to."

He eyed her with disquiet. "What do you mean?"

The druidess did not answer. She walked past him to stand quietly in the waning darkness of the new morning. "I doona know what I mean, guardian." She brushed the crumbs from her hands and tucked them into her brown robe. "This one be filled with sadness and loss."

"Is she not happy to be free of the sword spirit, Valor?"

She shrugged. "It be too early to tell what she feels." The ancient glanced back at him. "Where be Valor now?"

"She is safe. I am to deliver her to Tara this day."

"To the new king?"

"Aye, the fey have chosen Lugh."

"A fine and fair king he will make."

"Aye," Keegan agreed.

He removed his wrist cuff. "Derina, will you give this to Glenna?" He placed his mother's gift in her withered hand.

"Why do you wish this?" She looked up at him with white brows arched in a grave frown.

"I give it to Glenna because I canna give it to Lana."

The ancient's fingers curved around the sea-etched cuff protectively. "I will give it to her, guardian."

He took one last look at the silver cuff, the only thing left of his mother's memory, and turned away. He would not need it at Tara. "My thanks, Derina. I must go now."

"I wish you good morn then. There be still time. Do

you not wish to break your fast with me before you leave?"

He smiled and declined once more. "My new king awaits. I bid you good morn, too, Derina." He turned to leave, but found he could not. Glancing over his shoulder, he stared into her lined face. "What color are her eyes, ancient?"

She did not pretend to misunderstand and he was grateful to her for that. "Glenna's eyes are blue."

"Blue," he repeated and turned away. They were not black, not the color of the darkest night, not the color of his beloved's. He took comfort in that and winked out, returning to Valor.

CHAPTER 18

With Valor secured in the scabbard at his back, Keegan returned to *Temair na Rig*, the place known as Tara of the Kings. A wind-swept grassy hill, it stood tall above the surrounding land, a place of great prospect and of banks, mounds, ditches, and stones. The unknowing found it unremarkable, lacking grandeur, certainly not a dwelling for the fey born, or an entrance to the Otherworld. *How little they know*, he mused in silent contemplation.

He walked between two standing stones, one taller than the other, and took in the lush surrounding countryside. The grass curled between his bare toes. The smell of life was strong in the air and in his lungs, the scent of blood and battlefield fading into memory. Tara was the forever hill, a sacred and revered place of the above and below. Five roadways led to it, if one knew where to look, and he knew where to look. He exhaled, finding the openness regal and strangely comforting.

He wondered if Lana could see the clear blueness of the

wide sky. Could she smell the meadow's colorful flowers still? Could she see the blackbirds with their orange-yellow beaks and eye rings from within the enchantment? Did she miss the rocky land and long stone walls across the hills? Did she grieve for home and the people of her village, the sounds of the drums and the winds off the sea? Did she yearn for him as much as he yearned for her? These questions would remain unanswered.

His lashes lowered. Through the closeness of the enchanted sword's scabbard against his green tunic, he felt an exquisite and magical intimacy, a connection to his beloved's presence. Along with the cherished link, however, he sensed an underlying fury emanating from the sword spirit. He had taken Lana's virgin sheath, claimed her for his own when he had no right. No right, except for the love in his foolish heart.

He no longer cared about the punishment he would face this day. Lana was gone. He missed the way her nose wrinkled when she laughed. Missed the way her eyes brightened when she smiled. Missed the gentleness of her spirit and the way she made him feel so passionately alive.

He knew the time for the sword spirit's retribution drew near. Dwelling on it would only weaken his resolve.

Closing his eyes, he took a deep breath. "I miss you, my fair bride." He tilted his face toward the sun, feeling its warmth and wishing to stand this way forever in quietness.

But he could not. The sun crested over the horizon, an orange fireball in the sky.

It was time.

He could delay no longer.

He dropped down on one knee in the dew-drenched grass and transferred to his true form. Tunic and breeches receded into silvery, moon-kissed webs, a familiar feyness over flesh and muscle. Stretching out his wings, he bowed his head and envisioned the main hall of the below. Folding his right hand across his chest, he dissolved into silver light and vapor.

In the next instant, he appeared in the main hall of Tara. In front of him was the glacier white dais where the king's rock-crystal throne resided. It was empty.

He stared at the flat stone pavers and the tiny fissures where the green mosses lived, and waited for his arrival to be announced to the new fey king.

The air felt cool against his flesh, seasons and time suspended here. He could hear the trickle of water coming out of the cracks in the stone walls surrounding him, a natural refuge and residence for the water faeries.

He shifted his weight, still kneeling on one knee. The Good People gathered behind him, standing beside stunted trees draped with shaggy mosses. The spriggans had come too, tugging on their rock-encrusted coats. The pixies whispered among themselves while sitting astride their white snails. Others of his kin came as well, silent in their observation of him. They had all come, waiting to see the fair judgment of their new king.

To his right, a path led through a garden of pink flowers.

It is from there he heard footfalls approach.

The king had come.

He continued to kneel, his head bowed respectfully.

He heard the king step up on the dais. "RAIN."

"My king, I have come as you bade," Keegan replied.

"SHOW ME YOUR EYES, GUARDIAN."

Keegan looked up.

The High King Lugh sat on a throne chair crafted of rock crystals, onyx, amethysts, and bronze. He wore the colors of the clouds, his tunic and breeches finely crafted of fey born weave. Diamonds shone in the woven plaits of his long brown hair. To his right, the territorial goddess Blodenwedd stood in a gown of white webs, her eyes unreadable.

"BE THAT VALOR?" The king gestured to the sword.

"Aye," Keegan confirmed. Standing, he swiftly unsheathed the enchanted sword from the scabbard.

A hush descended on the hall.

"THREATEN ME, RAIN?"

Frowning, Keegan looked down at his hands. He gripped the white bone hilt, the tip of the sword pointing at his king.

"Nay, my king." He knelt down again on one knee, confused by his actions. It was almost as if Valor had directed his body. Flipping the sword to rest horizontally on his open palms, he held Valor out in offering.

"RESPONDS TO YOU," the king said observantly. Keegan could not deny it.

"She responds to her wielder, my king."

"ALWAYS YOU DEFENDED OUR SACRED WATERS, OUR REALM, AND OUR MORTAL BRETHREN. NOW 'TIS TIME TO RETURN VALOR TO THE FEY THRONE."

Keegan nodded, fighting the urge to return Valor to his scabbard.

The king rose from the throne chair and descended the two white steps of the dais. "WILLINGLY GIVE UP VALOR, RAIN?" the king asked, standing before him in royal splendor, a just king, a fair king.

Confirmation locked in his throat. Keegan gave a quick nod of his head and extended his arms.

He stared at the teardrop guard, at the pommel carved of an unknown wood, and finally at the spiral-cut bone grip that translated the sword spirit's strength into her master's arms.

From beneath lowered lids, he watched the king reach for Valor's hilt.

The blade began to glow . . . red.

The king pulled back his hand and frowned. "WHAT BE THIS, RAIN?" he demanded.

Keegan stared at Valor, unable to answer. His heart pounding, he felt Lana struggling within the enchantment, her unconquerable spirit battling the hard will of the ancient sword.

He felt her alarm and panic . . . for him. A strong impression of peril radiated into his flesh from the sword. Lana was trying to warn him, her impressions strong in his mind.

The High King of the Faeries must never hold Valor.

"RAIN, WHAT BE THIS GLOW?"

Keegan looked up into the sullen face of his king. "I canna explain, my king."

"VALOR SPEAKS TO YOU?"

"Not Valor." He hesitated.

"EXPLAIN."

"The sword host speaks to me, my king."

"SWORD HOST?" the king echoed in mistrust, showing his displeasure. "SINCE WHEN DOES A HOST BE SPEAKING TO A GUARDIAN?"

Keegan remained silent beneath the suspicious scrutiny.

"ANSWER ME, RAIN."

"I have no answer, my king."

"VALOR CHOOSES A MASTER? CHOICE NOT HERS TO MAKE. SHE BELONGS TO THE FEY THRONE."

"I know."

"I WILLNA HAVE HER PARTED FROM OUR GREAT TALISMAN, ANSWERER. BOTH DEFENDERS BELONG HERE."

Keegan knew the words were right and truthful, yet his heart did not agree. Valor did not belong with him, but Lana did. *Lana did!*

The king's right hand shot out, long fingers expertly wrapping about the sword's hilt. With a muttered hiss of pain, he lifted it.

Immediately, the connection Keegan felt with Lana dissolved into nothingness, leaving him hollow inside.

Climbing slowly to his feet, he stepped back, wings moving in silent protest. He stood with clenched fists, battling the urge to retake her.

"INTERFERE, RAIN?" the king asked, sensing his intent.

Keegan shook his head in denial.

"VALOR BE FIGHTING ME. YET, I WIN."

Slowly, the crimson shade of the blade faded to silver and with it, his heart.

"THAT BE BETTER," his king soothed. He held the sword up for inspection and Keegan never realized how beautiful a blade could be.

"NOT TRUE," the king whispered in open denial, and then turned and scowled darkly at him. "WHAT BE THIS, RAIN?"

Keegan waited for what he knew was to come.

"VALOR BE CLAIMING THE RIGHT OF PUNISHMENT. EXPLAIN."

"I took the virgin sheath of the sword host. Lana belongs to me."

"FORBIDDEN," the king said, affronted.

"Aye," Keegan agreed, "but I would take her in my arms again, if given a second chance."

"TAKE THE GUARDIAN OUTSIDE TO THE CREST OF TARA," the king commanded. "VALOR WISHES TO SPEAK WITH ME."

Keegan did not fight when they led him outside.

He did not fight when they bound him between two standing stones on the grassy mound of Tara, a naked and sacrificial offering to the indignant rage of the sword spirit.

He did not fight when they forced him to his knees, cloudy fey webs wrapped around his wrists and forearms and around his thighs. The webs stretched his limbs hurtfully as he prepared to wait for the coming of twilight, the time of all fey punishment.

In the distance, he saw a pair of hares romping about, their white ears easily followed. He focused on the small animals, willing his body to remain calm. It was bad luck to hunt hares, he remembered; killing one immediately turned it into the corpse of a bleeding hag. Not that he had ever seen that happen. He shifted aching muscles. The hours felt endless until his king came and stood in front of him.

"Rain, Tell me Why?" his king directed, unwilling to mete out the sword spirit's punishment.

Keegan stared straight ahead. Shooting sunbeams sent lavender light across the sky and land. Punishment would be met at the onslaught of twilight. He had but a few remaining moments of wholeness left to him.

"Answer me." His new king faced him, his features set in rigid angles.

Slowly, Keegan's eyelids lifted. "I never intended Valor to claim Lana. I only needed her to guide me to where the enchanted sword was held. I meant no disrespect to the sword spirit."

"Knew Lana be sword host?"

"Aye, the old druidess told me."

"Why handfast? Take her instead, as be our fey

RIGHT."

"I lived among our mortal brethren and chose to follow their ways. I intended to return her to her tribe once I rescued Valor. I wished her a normal and happy life. If I had taken her *as be my fey right*," he echoed the king's words, "her life would have been different."

"YOUR INTENTIONS BE DIFFERENT, METHINKS."

Keegan shrugged. "Mayhap. Lana always fascinated me."

"THIS BE THE FRAIL LANA OF THE VILLAGE?"

"She is not frail," he said in defense. "She has the strongest spirit I have ever encountered in my lifetime."

The king looked away, disgusted. "YOU LEAVE ME NO CHOICE."

"Aye, let us end it. I grow weary of the delay."

Keegan watched the king pace in front of him, trying to find a way out of the dilemma of obligation and duty.

"Lugh," Keegan said. "I have found you a just warrior. Doona change your heart now that you are king. I have made a mistake, one I would willingly make again. In all the years I have lived, only Lana has . . . fascinated me." He refused to say, *I have loved,* in front of his new king. "I would claim her again no matter the cost."

The king stopped his pacing and turned to him, his face harsh and regretful.

"AS YOU WISH IT, RAIN." He sighed heavily, a great burden forming within him. "WE BEGIN PUNISHMENT. KNEW LANA A SWORD HOST?"

"Aye."

"KNEW THIS AND MATED WITH HER?"

"Aye," Keegan answered.

"KNEW HER FORBIDDEN?"

"Aye."

"TOOK HER STILL, IN DEFIANCE?"

"Not defiance. Wanted and craved her touch," he said, casting out his grief, "held her in my arms and then . . . wanted her in my heart."

The king shook his head in disdain and moved out of his line of sight.

Keegan stared at the purple light sweeping the sky, his body tensing.

Here it comes.

"FIRST GUARDIAN OF THE WATERS," the king began from somewhere behind him. "DISHONOR VALOR, YOU DID. MUST BE PUNISHED." He paused. "GRIEVES ME TO DO THIS. GRIEVES ME," he mumbled.

From behind, small hands stretched out his wings until the muscles in his back strained.

His hands clenched around the bindings that held him fast.

"YOUR NAME BE CAST FROM OUR HISTORY, FROM OUR LANDS, AND FROM OUR WATERS. THAT BE VALOR'S WISH. NO REMEMBRANCE OF YOU SHALL BE."

"Valor will remember me," Keegan said in bold rebellion. "Lana will see to it."

"CLIP HIM."

A tidal wave of pain sliced into his back.

Screams of soundless agony locked in his throat and then hurtling darkness washed over him, carrying him away in its numbing embrace. His head sagged from bloody shoulders. Trembling eyelashes fluttered closed.

They severed his wings, stealing away the magical part of him.

He did not know how long he hung there in the crawling darkness of the eternal night, bathed in pain and the light of a hurtful moon. For him, it was evermore. His existence slowly dwindled. White blood spilled from two open and ragged wounds, soaking his back, running down his legs, and into the land. His head rolled listlessly from side to side. Not a groan or whimper did he make. His mind floated, wandering in and out of consciousness.

Slowly, his thoughts drifted back to Dowth, memories washing over him.

It had been at Dowth that a faery's wings entangled in the ropes holding Valor's cage above the water. Blinded by blood and frenzy, the faery cut the ropes, sending the cage and enchanted blade falling to the bottom of the pool. It was in that instant his life abruptly changed. From across the pool, Lana looked at him, a sad smile spreading across her lovely face.

And he knew, before she dove into the black waters.

He knew what his foolish arrogance cost him.

A love exceedingly precious and rare was gone before it

ever bloomed.

He lost her to a greater destiny.

A cool wind caressed his cheek, dragging him unwillingly back to the present and the overwhelming pain. He licked dry lips and stared unblinkingly at the ground, mulling over thoughts of death. He preferred not to go on living without her, knowing her locked in a forevermore enchantment of a fey defender.

He felt the draining of his life, the ending of a guardian, and embraced it.

"FOOLISHNESS," a female voice shrieked at him.

His head slowly came up. "Lana?" he rasped.

"BLODENWEDD!" a goddess screamed, causing him to recoil. White hands made quick work of his fey bindings. "THERE," she said firmly.

The bindings slithered away from his flesh. He fell forward, a limp rag, smashing his face into grass and soil.

"STUPID GUARDIAN."

He got one eye open and peered at a white knee, kneeling in the grass beside his nose.

"DIM-WITTED, MINDLESS GOAT, STUBBORN IDIOT . . ." she ranted at him as she lifted and cradled him in her lap. Gentle hands pulled hair out of his eyes while a dank grayness swirled in around him. For a moment, he thought he felt a goddess's cool tears splashing on his cheek. *That canna be,* he mused in a sea of spinning blackness. *Goddesses doona cry.*

He lost consciousness.

✳ ✳ ✳

A fortnight later Keegan stood on the rain-slashed cliffs, staring outward to the sea, arms folded across his chest, warm winds lifting the hair from his shoulders.

His goddess rescuer brought him to this remote haven, the farthest west end of land where he regained some of his strength over the fourteen days that had come and gone.

"CONNEMARA," she said softly in the lilting voice of one who cared, and then called him "STUPID GUARDIAN," yet again. Never had he thought so selfish a creature as Blodenwedd would risk a king's displeasure by saving a condemned guardian. He was as judgmental of her as he had once been of Lana.

Standing on the windy ledge, wrapped in bandages and ill-fitting clothes, he looked outward upon the early morning brightness. He remained always in his mortal form now, the other no longer possible without severe pain. His ruined back continued to throb as it mended. His heart was locked in ice; his mind remained engulfed in grateful numbness.

To his left, dark mountains rose within rings of mist, offering glimpses of a herd of wild goats standing on the ridge, their horns perfectly formed. Their white coats were long and majestic in so barren a place, and he felt one with their isolation and solitude.

"GUARDIAN."

He looked over his shoulder. "Blodenwedd, I am no longer a guardian."

"To me, you be always a stubborn guardian." She wore a cloak of gold webs matching the color of her hair. He stared at a golden curl resting on her breast and then his gaze fell away without further comment.

On the ledge below, a single jackdaw was building a nest. The small, black-faced crow lived on the sea cliffs, a new companion of his. The bird tended to steal things. He noticed earlier one of his clean bandages poked out of the bird's nest.

"Rain."

Sighing, he once again turned to her.

"You canna be my consort."

He nodded, not really hearing her.

"You canna be my consort for you be blemished now."

A brow arched at her fixation. "I understand," he said politely. "Being clipped was not one of my finest moments."

"I canna come back here anymore," she murmured with a slight edge to her tone.

"I understand."

"The king suspects I saved you."

He nodded. "I am grateful to you for my life."

"You doona show it."

"I have never been one to grovel, nor show adoration, even for you."

"Nay," she said, "still bold and rebellious you be."

He smiled and she gave him a sad smile back.

He looked back to the sea, refusing to feel the loss and disgrace of his existence. *Blemished*. There was nothing worse to the fey, who valued superficial beauty above all things. Shifting his arms, he felt the twinges of tenderness in his disfigured back muscles.

"Rain."

"Blodenwedd," he echoed her consoling tone.

"What will you do?"

He supposed she had the right to ask, given she saved his life. He gave her question some thought. "I will diminish beside some loch, I suspect."

"I dinna risk myself to save you for diminishing!" It was not a scolding, but close to it.

"Blodenwedd," he said quietly, "Go home. You have done all you can here."

She stomped in front of him, her beautiful face set in an unemotional mask. She stared at him with cold goddess eyes.

He stared back, refusing to bow down.

"I can compel you to live," she said softly.

He gave her a mocking smile. "I doubt it."

Then, rising on tiptoes, she did something that utterly surprised him. She kissed him gently on the lips, a gift of comfort and of friendship.

Stepping aside, she pulled up her hood, covering her long tresses. "Choose life, stupid guardian," she said, and then winked out, leaving him to his solitude once again.

Keegan looked out to the sea, the small crow his only remaining companion.

CHAPTER 19

DERINA STOOD IN THE HIGH meadow, leaning on her hazel walking stick. With empty eye sockets, she watched Glenna mingle with the horses of the tribe. The guardian's silver cuff rested against her hip, secured to her favorite rope belt.

"Did she like horses, too?" the woman-child asked, referring to Lana. All of Glenna's questions seemed strangely centered around Lana.

"Aye, she did. The one over there with the scars on his chest be her favorite."

"I heard one of the men call that horse Lightning."

Derina shrugged. "I doona recall his name, only his temper."

The girl smiled. "Methinks he is sweet-tempered."

"If you offer him food," Derina said, studying the girl.

Standing there in a blue cloak with a bronze brooch under her chin, the girl reminded her so much of Lana they seemed almost like twins. But whereas Lana had a physical frailness about her, this one emitted a deep grieving, an acute loss seeping from within.

"Did he come here, too?" Glenna asked.

"Who?"

"Her guardian."

"Aye, he came to the meadows." Derina looked up at the late afternoon sky, gauging the gray clouds for their watery threat. "He liked to stand in the rain sometimes."

"He doona like it anymore?"

"I have not seen him of late."

"He grieves."

She looked at the girl. "Why do you say that, Glenna?"

Glenna shrugged, pushing blond curls from her cheek. "When Lana and I exchanged places, I felt her inside me. For that one moment, we were as one with Valor. If the guardian feels anything of what she felt for him, he grieves now."

Derina suspected as much. " 'Tis forbidden for a guardian to take a mortal bride."

"Lana be no longer a mere mortal," the girl argued softly, "she be special, like me."

Unable to argue that point, Derina unknotted the rope holding the guardian's cuff to her belt. "The guardian has left you this silver gift." She held it out in offering.

"I doona want it," the girl rebuked.

"You refuse a guardian's gift, Glenna?"

"It be meant for her, not me."

"He asked me to give it to you. It be for you."

Hiking up her blue gown, she came over and took the silver cuff, her light brows puckered in a frown. She held it in her right hand, the thin bronze bracelets on her wrists chiming faintly. With the tip of a finger, she traced the intricate metalworking. "Oh, I doona want it," she cried suddenly, and flung it behind her, unsettling the horses.

Derina said not a word, but went and retrieved it. Very carefully, she secured the cuff to her belt. "Come back to my home, Glenna. The day wanes."

"I doona like a roof over my head. I need the sky and stars above me." She held out her arms, face upturned to the purpling sky.

"You canna stay here again all night," Derina admonished. It had been two months of this, hiding in the round house by day and wandering the lands by night.

"I must," the girl insisted.

Derina inhaled deeply, refusing to be frazzled by the whirlwind of emotions spilling out of the girl. "Tell me what troubles you."

Glenna buried her face in her hands, her bracelets gliding down her forearms. She shook her head despondently.

"Tell me," Derina urged.

"I am lost," the girl cried in a flood of tears and anguish.

"Lost?" Derina did not at all understand. She shuffled over to the distraught young woman and placed a comforting hand on the girl's slender shoulder. "Nay, Glenna, you have been found."

The girl pulled away. "I doona belong here. The colors be all wrong," she said tearfully. "The air smells wrong. Everything be wrong here."

Derina leaned heavily on her walking stick, her legs aching. "You must give yourself time to adjust."

"Adjust," she shrieked. "I will grow old here like you."

"Aye," Derina acknowledged slowly, memories of her youth returning and then floating away into billows of forgotten pain. "Here we all grow old, Glenna. It be the way of things."

"I want to go home."

"Home be here, Glenna," she answered carefully. "Your family be here, if you but let me introduce you to them. Rianon be with child . . ."

The girl shook her head in swift objection. "They be Lana's family, not mine."

"They could be your family," Derina offered sympathetically.

"Nay, I doona want them."

Her aged hands tightened about the knob of her walking staff, showing her tension. "What do you want then?" she asked.

"I want Valor. I wish to return to her. She be my beloved."

"Your beloved?" Derina repeated, not sure if she had heard right.

"She and I be one. I feel empty without her."

"Easy, child," Derina soothed. "Let us return to my

home and we be talking more about this."

"Can you help me, Derina?"

"Mayhap." She held out her hand to the girl. "Walk home with me."

The girl did not take her hand, but walked sullenly by her side back to the cottage. Derina was glad when the weepy-eyed girl chose to forego eating and retire early. She had much to do this eve, if she was going to tempt the wrath of the Gods and Goddesses.

Grabbing her walking staff, she went outside and lowered her frame upon a bench beside her pail of water. Adjusting her brown robes, she focused internally. Within her mind, she reached out, calling the territorial goddess, Blodenwedd, to her side.

Several hours later, when the stars came out in the night sky, her waiting ended.

"I HAVE COME AS YOU BADE, OLD CRONE," Blodenwedd said with annoyance.

Derina wished she had eyes so she could glower her dislike at the beautiful goddess standing in front of her.

Grabbing her walking stick, Derina stood on legs stiff with age. "Come," she commanded, and shuffled away from the doorway and the wild emotions of the girl sleeping on the bed of pelts within.

Her fey born visitor followed silently behind her.

A few horse lengths away, Derina stopped and faced the goddess. "Glenna wishes to return to Valor," she said, coming directly to the point.

"Why summon me?"

"You be a friend to the guardian." The goddess did not vow or disavow the statement and Derina continued with her request. "I wish you to take Glenna to Valor. Then, after the sword spirit reclaims her, I wish you to take Lana to Keegan, wherever he may be."

"Lana," the goddess said with strong irritation, her hatred for the sword host clinging to her every breath, her every heartbeat.

"Will you do what I be asking?" Derina inquired, unaware of the secret feelings of the goddess.

"The guardian be no more."

Derina was not sure she heard correctly. "Keegan be no more?"

"Punished."

"Who punished him?" Derina asked with outrage.

"High King."

"For rescuing Valor, battling invaders, and saving our lands?" She could not believe her ears. "Why?"

"Mating with a forbidden claíomh host."

Her heart sank. The olden ways had risen again to hurt those of a true heart. "Be the guardian alive, Blodenwedd?" she asked, fighting off her despair.

"No longer guardian."

"Be Keegan alive?" Derina jabbed her walking stick into the ground.

"He be Rain, not Keegan."

"I doona care what he calls himself. Be he alive?"

"Aye."

She breathed in a sigh of relief. "Blodenwedd," she made her request again, "I ask you take Glenna to Valor. I understand the magical sword be at Tara."

"Aye." The goddess's brows drew together skeptically. "Valor wants Glenna back?"

Derina shrugged. She could only hope. "Only Valor can decide that."

"When?" the goddess asked, her features set in a strange fierceness.

"Now," Glenna exclaimed, peeking out from the cottage's doorway and then joining them.

Derina could have never known the territorial goddess blamed Lana for the guardian's punishment.

CHAPTER 20

Lana felt strange, as if her body was not yet connected to her will. She knew she was in the underground vaults of Tara, a place of magic and unmoving shadows, of enchanted talismans, and of crystal altars.

Closing her eyes, she bowed her head. Blond hair swept forward, caressing her cheeks. She held onto that achingly familiar sensation. The link to the sacred feminine sword spirit, Valor, remained strong — yet a new change trickled within the breath and flow of her, something arresting and hopeful.

Her body wavering between glow and flesh, she rested on her right hip, legs tucked under the sweeping folds of a nearly transparent gown the color of sea foam. The gray floor beneath her was made of cold and flat stones, edges joined with green-gold moss.

She could hear Valor's vigil in the deep reaches of her blood, angry at her unassailable resolve, and yet grudgingly respectful of her strength of spirit. They locked wills, two beings, one of magic and one of flesh. Steadfastness and loyalty battled obstinacy and selfishness, neither one able, or willing, to give way to the other.

Lana wondered how she survived it, how she remained true to her heart and self. She wondered why the sacred feminine spirit allowed her the freedom to disagree, instead of squashing her down like an annoying insect. Mayhap the sword spirit needed her determination and strength of will in ways she did not understand or recognize.

Mayhap, Valor whispered in her mind. The tone came in waves of compelling silkiness. *Too much like the fiery-willed sorceress you be.*

Lana's lips curved at the hard won praise. She could hear Glenna's sweet voice too, a pleasant melody in her mind, both youthful and grateful.

"Lana," Glenna called softly to and within her. "I can see you."

Slowly, Lana opened her eyes to a world of bright amber and cool white radiance. Valor lay on the ground between her and a young blond woman who knelt in joyful alertness. The young woman wore a simple blue gown with a darker blue hooded cloak draped over her shoulders. On her small wrists, bronze bracelets gently rang with a musical tone, chiming in with the matching ones on her bare ankles. Tiny gold and silver beads gleamed in blond plaits framing an oval face graced with pink and rosy cheeks. The woman beamed, her full lips curved in absolute happiness.

"I am Glenna." She dipped her head respectfully, the beads in her hair reflecting the enchanted light growing and surrounding her.

"I am Lana of the *Tuatha Dé Danann*," Lana replied, and bowed her head in turn.

"I know. You are even lovelier than I imagined."

Lana smiled at the kind words. "So are you, Glenna. I am honored to meet you."

They were exchanging places, a dual gleaming, a willing acceptance of fate, obligation, and desire.

Glenna leaned forward, her features set in earnestness. "Please accept my thanks for keeping Valor safe. She is most precious to me."

"I know, my sister of the sword."

The young woman sat back, relief sweeping over her face, and Lana felt gladdened by it. She felt a strong kinship with Glenna, even though this was the first time they ever set eyes upon each other.

"I have worried for her safety."

"There was no need to worry. You, most of all, know Valor is strong." Lana gave the girl an equal study. They were drawn to each other. Sisters linked by the blood of the sorceress, they were separated only by the passage of time and events.

"True." Glenna laughed softly. "Valor is strong, but we, Valor and I, would have ended in the black waters at Dowth if not for your bravery."

Lana shrugged, feeling uncomfortable with such undue praise. "Bravery belongs to my guardian, Keegan. I dove into the waters only to retrieve you."

"We differ in opinion, my sister." Already Lana could hear Glenna's lyrical voice and Valor's strong tone joining and becoming one. "To hold your breath and put more of the straining upon your already damaged heart took great courage. Verra few have courage of the spirit, verra few have . . . valor." Glenna smiled warmly. "Valor says you will argue with me."

Lana bit back a smile. "True," she agreed. She was prepared to protest. She could hear the sword spirit's reluctant mirth within her, a relinquishing link not yet severed.

Never will we be truly severed, Valor echoed inside her, and Lana knew it would always be true. This thread of awareness would remain within her.

"Lana of the noble heart," Glenna coaxed gently, "Valor wishes to give you a parting gift for your bravery." The sparkling light surrounding her sister of the sword brightened, nearly blinding her.

Lana lowered her eyes. She did not want anything from the sacred female sword. She had her fill of Valor's dark experiences and memories, enough to last many lifetimes. She shook her head. "My thanks, Glenna, but I doona want anything from Valor."

"This you need," her sister of the sword said firmly, her physical form fading, except for the brilliance of her blue eyes. "This you want, Lana."

Lana could think of nothing she wanted in this life other than Keegan. She looked through her lashes at what remained of Glenna, and felt a deep wariness spread through her blood.

"You must trust me," Glenna said, her gaze soft and supportive. "This you want, my sister. Please trust me."

Lana nodded that she did, and then reeled back in shock.

A sudden hurt seared into her chest. It pierced her heart and knocked her breathlessly to her left side. Gasping for air, she clutched at her chest in distress, quivering in terror.

"Trust me," Glenna urged softly, almost pleadingly.

It felt like an open wound had been burned closed by the breath of flames, except it was inside her. Lana thought the end of her life had finally come. Then something magical happened. The searing pain receded like foamy waves upon a smooth shore, leaving a feeling of wellness and vigor in its wake.

"It be done," Glenna and Valor replied in one harmonious voice, reverberating inside her trembling body.

Lana struggled to push up to a sitting position. She felt lightheaded and disjointed.

"Hurts no more?"

Lana gave a slow nod, unsure of what just happened. She took a recovering breath and shoved hair out of her eyes.

"You be the last descendant of the sword, Lana."

"What?" Lana asked, fighting the lingering effects of the

disorientation.

"You must listen now, Lana. The time of pain be over."

Lana sat up straighter. Taking a deep breath, she gestured she was ready to listen.

"You be the last descendant of the sword, Lana. Never forget this."

"I will not ever forget," she said and then asked, "What have you done to me?"

"Healed your heart."

Overwhelmed by the possibility of it, Lana bowed her head and blinked back tears, but Valor was not yet finished with her.

"Listen well now, Lana. We must speak of what has happened. Your birth father be no more. He died from his wandering and foolish ways."

"My father?" Lana echoed in alarm, and looked up.

"Not the father at home, Lana," the dual voices reassured. "We speak of the one your mother took to her bed that long ago night, your true birth father. You understand this."

Lana nodded, the dread within her waning. *Aye*, she knew this. Valor's connection to all those carrying the blood of the sorceress flowed through her as well. When she first joined with Valor, all knowledge of the sacred sword spirit became hers. Her mother had taken a man other than her husband to her bed. That man had been a true blood heir of the sorceress.

"There be no other living heir, no other blooded kin of

the sorceress. All prospects for the future fall to you, Lana."

Lana swiped the tears from her eyes with the back of her right hand. "How do you know my birth father is dead?" she demanded.

"Valor knows," Glenna answered, her voice separating from the sword spirit's tone for just a moment. "She kept it from you for her own reasons."

Questioning the sword spirit to learn the reasons was hopeless, Lana knew. She turned away from the hurtful light, no longer able to see Glenna within its white embrace.

"What future falls to me, Glenna?" She hoped her obligations to the sword spirit were finished.

"You must give birth to the next daughter of the sword, Lana. "

Lana grimaced and turned away. "I canna do it," she replied.

"Why?"

"My moon time comes but rarely. The simpler of my tribe has said my body would never be able to carry a child. As a sick tree does not bear fruit, so too an unfit body does not bear children."

They ignored her. "Foolishness. Take a strong male to your bed. Valor wants her daughters."

"I am unfit to have children, Valor."

"Lie with a male, Lana." The joined voices were quietly amused, but final in their command. "Your body be healthy now and will accept a male's seed."

Lana immediately thought of Keegan. He was the only male she ever wanted in her bed. But why did she feel dread whenever her thoughts strayed to him?

" 'Tis time to go our separate ways, Lana of the noble heart."

In a burst of light, Glenna was gone, leaving only the shimmering blade of Valor on the ground before her.

Lana looked down at her hands. Was she finally free? she wondered. Had she awakened from this impossible existence of both dream and nightmare? Her thoughts returned to Keegan once more. *Punishment?* Had something happened to her guardian mate? Images in mist danced just beyond her memory. She could not remember, but it would come back to her. She felt sure of it.

Trembling slightly, she smoothed the glossy folds of the sea-colored gown across her thighs. She ran her hands up and down her bare arms and noted the absence of the silver dragonfly cuffs. She had no recollection of their disappearance. Had she lost them without knowing? Had Valor taken them because they were a fey gift of bride approval for a guardian of the waters? More likely that, she thought in silence. The sword spirit was immeasurably jealous of her hosts, fiercely resentful, and horribly vindictive when wronged.

Covering her eyes, she released a deep sigh, her lungs filling with the weight of her trepidation.

Another full breath came and left, unperceived and unrestricted.

Resting her hand on her chest, she inhaled deeply, filling

her lungs to a capacity never experienced before.

No tightness did she feel.

No discomfort.

Inside her body, the rhythmic beat of a healthy heart continued unhindered.

She did not wheeze.

Did not cough.

She did not feel weak or lightheaded.

Tears caught and gleamed in eyelashes, spilling like jewels upon her cheeks.

She felt whole and healthy, and with that came the feeling of value.

She was valuable.

Something else nudged the edges of her memories, too. It came through a veil of white mist and Lana drew back in horror. Eyes widening, she bit back a scream. *Keegan!*

"Destroyer of guardian."

Lana startled. Turning around, she searched for the chiding female voice. From the shadows, a willowy figure of white stepped forward. "I AM BLODENWEDD."

Lana immediately recognized the fey born goddess from Valor's shared memories. "They cut off his wings," she choked out, feeling jerked back into the nightmare.

"BECAUSE OF YOU," the goddess accused.

Lana shook her head in rapid denial. "Nay, I love him."

"Love?" Blodenwedd laughed caustically at her, her eyes gleaming with hatred.

Lana reached for Valor's hilt. "Tell me what happened, Valor," she demanded of the sword spirit. "What did you do to him?" Valor gave her the images that had been blocked from her perception. The sword spirit filled her mind with such vibrancy and jealousy it felt as if she stood beside him on that awful day.

Her guardian mate knelt willingly, wrists lashed to stone pillars.

A sword swung high, glinting the arrival of twilight, and then descended.

Wings and muscles cut, first one and then the other.

Blood splattered the sky and land.

Lana screamed . . . and Valor willingly released her.

The horrific images faded to grayness.

She wept uncontrollably, dragging in great gulps of cool air. She knew Keegan felt deserving of this punishment for his forbidden desire for her, but he was wrong, so terribly wrong. "How could you?" she spat out in grief, gripping Valor's hilt with the vengeance of one who had been deeply hurt. "You had no right to punish him." She smashed the sword on the ground in an outburst of temper and challenge. "No right. I initiated the mating, not him. He lay ill and I took advantage. I did it. You know the goodness of his spirit. How could you hurt him?"

Valor offered no remorse and Lana really did not expect any. Valor was a true dark feminine spirit, zealous in her jealousy. She looked down at her right hand, fingers pale and white wrapped around a spiral-cut bone hilt. "I wish I could hate you," she mumbled in desolation and ragged tears. "I wish I could hate you, Valor."

"Destroyer of Guardian."

Slowly, Lana looked up at the unkind goddess who stood watching her. She clung to the image of Keegan, knowing he lived, knowing he needed her, and tapped into her dark strength to overcome her anguish.

"Do you know where he is, Blodenwedd?"

"Think I tell you, ever?"

Lana climbed to her feet, the magical sword an extension of her right arm. Since joining with Valor, her spirit had become bold and courageous. No longer was she the innocent farm girl. She met the goddess's gaze and saw death watching.

"Blodenwedd, I give you fair warning," she said, her mind becoming clearer.

"Warn me?" the goddess shrieked.

"Aye," Lana replied coolly, "if you think me the frail girl I once was, you are sadly mistaken. I have lived within the sword spirit Valor, lived her memories as if they were my own, lived her intentions as if they were my own, wore her bloodshed as if it were my own skin. Do you think you can frighten me?" She held the enchanted blade with authority. "I know all about you, Blodenwedd. Valor has shared her memories with me."

"Memories," the goddesses said sarcastically.

"She says you are a selfish goddess capable of great hatred, but also of unusual sacrifice. Because of this, I will not hurt you. At least not yet."

The goddess shot her a furious glare. Besides beauty, Lana knew the fey born valued strength above all else, so it was what she showed. "Valor thinks you wish to kill me. That is why she insists I not release her." She balanced the sword easily in her right hand.

"Valor be wise, destroyer of guardian."

"Mayhap I am this thing you call me," Lana admitted reluctantly. "Never did I intend to hurt him, Blodenwedd. I would give my life for him. You must believe me."

"Destroyer."

The goddess made her judgment and nothing she could say would convince the perfect one otherwise.

"Aye, well," Lana sighed. There would be no reasoning with this one. She must go on the offensive. "Know this, Blodenwedd. If you do succeed in killing me, do you think you will ever be safe from Valor's wrath? What your high king did to my guardian mate is nothing compared to what will be done to you."

The goddess hissed at her, white teeth bared in recognition of her words. Lana felt certain Blodenwedd intended to exact retribution for the unfair punishment the guardian suffered. She could not fault the territorial goddess for it.

Turning her back on the irate goddess in a sign of dismissal, Lana knew she must keep up the appearance of strength and purpose. She walked to the large sword altar that cradled

Answerer. It was where Valor belonged.

"I love Keegan, Blodenwedd. I would never knowingly hurt him."

She stood in front of the crystal altar. Flowing weaves of amber and bronze webs draped its sides. Gently, she laid Valor next to the great defender, Answerer, the blade that inflicted only mortal wounds. She felt the goddess come up behind her.

Releasing Valor, she pulled her hands back to her sides.

Memories of all things linked to the sorceress wavered within her until only a single thread remained, a thread of unending awareness.

Above the altar, a single wall torch cast shadow and light upon the blades and the silence.

"Your fey defenders are beautiful," Lana murmured. "Keegan protected Valor and Valor protected our lands from the invaders. Come and look upon your defenders."

The goddess moved into her peripheral vision, her blond hair nearly as bright as sunlight.

Lana returned her attention to the exquisite weapons. They looked nothing alike. Answerer had a golden hilt and an elegant, leaf-shaped blade, epitomizing a weapon of a powerful male warrior deity, like Keegan. Valor's form was cast for a warrior goddess, her deadly blade longer and without a blood groove.

Lana watched Blodenwedd reach for Valor's hilt. Long, perfectly tapered fingers wrapped around spiral-cut bone.

The goddess pulled back with a startled cry as if burned.

Lifting her gown, Lana stepped back and bowed her head respectfully to the two great defenders of the fey born. Mayhap Blodenwedd understood what would happen to her if she let her hatred rule.

Lana glanced at Valor one last time. Resentment and bitterness mingled with a kind of regret she could not explain. Valor was part of her as Keegan was part of her. The two were forever enemies, but her heart would always decide her true choice. Her gaze rested on the fine magical craftsmanship of the slender blade. No one would ever know, nor would she ever reveal, Valor was the only sword which could defeat the great Answerer, the sword that inflicted only mortal wounds.

Lana met the goddess's vindictive gaze, sure in its judgment and blame. "If you will not take me to Keegan, Blodenwedd, may I ask you take me to Derina instead?"

✻ ✻ ✻

It took Keegan a long time to make his way back to the river valley and Dowth, the Faery Mound of Darkness. Spread across the rolling green landscape were sacred dolmans and freestanding stone circles constructed of the common granite boulders. No longer could he wink in and out of place, for they cut the magical part of him away and made him forever blemished.

He could not think of it without becoming sick inside, without laying blame and anger for what had been, in his mind at least, a just punishment.

He pulled on the worn sleeveless tunic. Once white and now gray, it covered his upper body in a withered fashion. He liked the cloth because it laced up the sides and front allowing him freedom of movement without affecting the few remaining bandages on his back. The breeches were old too, worn and thin across the thighs. Both garments he stole from some farm in his passing. They were pieces of mortal clothing, which would not bring attention to the wearer, and he preferred it that way. The boots were comfortable on his feet, unremarkable, and stolen, too. He carried a plain dagger at his waist, and nothing more for defense.

He always knew he would return to Dowth to retrieve the dragonfly cuffs. He wanted them for no other reason than to have them. He should have taken them initially, he thought in reproach, but his dull-witted mind had been too focused on doing Lana's bidding and getting Glenna to safety.

He walked through the tall grasses and came upon the mortal entrance to Dowth North. He lived from day to day, moment to moment, a dismal creature no longer valuable even to himself. Gazing down into the shadowy path, he felt his pulse quicken in memory and then entered. He chose not to take the feypaths of his kin. This path was the direct one to the Dowth's underground chambers.

When he came upon the twin pools, he paused to listen

to the unchanged and constant ripple of the waterfall. Somehow, he thought the black pools would be different, as he was different, but it was the same white foam and mist, the same rocks and crystal shores, and the same white bark trees weeping in the corner. The carcasses of the dead faeries were gone, he knew not where, nor did he care. The silver cuffs, however, remained where they had fallen from Lana's arms.

He walked around the pools, staying away from the cursed trees, and knelt beside the cuffs. They were still radiant, the delicate filigree and dragonfly motif still beautiful.

With both hands, he gently scooped them up, feeling the cool, smooth perfection in his palms.

The cuffs were fey born crafted. He wondered if they would respond to his request, or simply ignore him. Placing one reverently in his lap, he held a cuff over his right wrist and waited for the cuff's acceptance or contempt. Immediately, the cuff expanded in approval, fitting over bone and flesh, fitting his wrist perfectly. He reached for the second cuff and slipped it over his left wrist. It, too, enlarged in the same way, forming to his flesh, a proper fey born fit.

Keegan stared down at his wrists. Nostrils flaring, his jaw clenched. A river of rage rose up inside him and then, just as quickly, dispersed. Hands dropping to his sides, he rocked back to his feet.

He walked slowly around the twin pools, his future set in everlasting shades of disgrace and darkness.

CHAPTER 21

IN A FLASH OF LIGHT, Lana found herself alone and standing in front of Derina's home. Over her shoulder, the morning warmth of the sun and a new day spread across the land.

She silently thanked the Gods and Goddesses for Blodenwedd's restraint. The goddess's hatred emanated out of every single pore of her skin, and Lana knew she would always have an enemy.

Lana took hold of herself. She would not underestimate the greater battle to come, the battle for Keegan's heart. He had been terribly hurt, maimed in an unfair punishment she had caused. Mayhap he blamed her for it, mayhap even hated her. She had to find out, had to know if there was anything left of their love to fight for.

"Derina." She leaned into the open doorway.

When no answer came, Lana walked in.

The round house was empty.

Returning outside, she came around the back and found

the druidess sitting in her garden. All around her were fragrant plant beds and flat walking stones. In her hands, she held Keegan's sea cuff of silver.

"Ancient."

The druidess turned to her, her face blank. "Lana, is that you?"

"Aye." She held out her hands and then dropped them to her sides when the welcome did not turn warmer.

"Valor has released you?" the druidess asked.

Lana nodded and sat beside the druidess on the unfinished rock wall.

"Is that his cuff?"

The druidess handed it to her. Fey born crafted, the sea-etched cuff was as light as an oak leaf, the metalworking exquisite to the eye.

"He gave this to you?" she asked the ancient.

The druidess adjusted the draping of her brown robes over her skinny legs. "He bid me give it to Glenna because he could not give it to you."

"Glenna dinna want it?"

The druidess shook her head. "Nay, but then the guardian be not her beloved."

Lana nodded despondently. Keegan was her beloved. He belonged to her. Her gaze strayed to the meandering cow in the gently rolling meadow beyond.

"You will not return home, Lana?"

"Nay, I canna return to that life, Derina. Better they

think me traveling with Keegan and someday returning."

"Why did you come here?"

Lana hesitated. "Blodenwedd hates me and will not take me to Keegan. I am not even sure if she knows where he is anymore. I doona know why she relented and helped me." She shrugged. "I could only think of you and hoped . . ."

"What do you hope?"

"I hope you will help me find him. I know you be fey born, Derina." She smiled hesitantly. "Doona look so surprised. Valor told me."

"What does a sword spirit know of it?" The ancient scowled in displeasure.

"She has knowledge of many things."

"Knowledge," Derina huffed, waving her hand in dismissal. "She doona know all of it."

"Nay," Lana agreed, "nor would I ask."

The ancient reached for her walking stick and dug the tip into the ground with noticeable distress. "Now that you think me fey born, Lana, what do you want of me?"

"I need your help. I must find him, Derina. I must find Keegan."

"Why?"

Lana pulled back at the ancient's unusually callous tone.

"Do you not want me to find him?" she asked, hurt by one she thought a friend.

"Tell me why you must find him, Lana."

"I love him," Lana replied just as fiercely. "I love him and

I believe he loves me. With or without your help, I am going to find him." She stood up.

"Sit down." The druidess's demeanor softened. "That be all I needed to hear."

Lana sat down beside the druidess, overwhelmed with emotions. "I love him," she cried, her voice watery.

The druidess patted her knee in reassurance. "So, Blodenwedd refuses to help."

"Aye."

"What makes you think a crippled old crone like me can help?"

Lana looked into the empty eye sockets without reservation. "Keegan be of your bloodline, Derina, is he not? Direct-blooded fey born can sense each other more easily, Valor says."

"Valor says," the druidess muttered aloud. "The infernal deity thinks she knows more than most." She dug her walking stick into the ground with more irritation. "Valor says," she grumbled on in dislike.

Lana waited for the ancient to calm herself.

Derina looked up, her fingers clenching around the knob of the walking stick. "I suppose I must tell you, if you are to understand all of it."

Lana kept silent, her hands locked around Keegan's sea cuff.

"I remember that long ago day as if it be only yesterday, Lana. A dreadful rainstorm of lightning and thunder swept over the lands, turning the day to night. My eldest sister went into the sacred woodlands alone to give birth to her first child, but something went terribly wrong." She took a trembling breath and Lana covered the withered hand with her own, offering comfort.

"Go on," she whispered.

"I found my sister the next morning, dead. In her arms lay her newborn son. She had shielded him against her breast, protecting him from the fury of the rainstorm." She took a deep breath and tapped her finger on the silver cuff. "That sea wave cuff you cradle so gently, Lana, belonged to my sister."

"I am so sorry, Derina. I dinna know."

The druidess turned away. "His father be a guardian and I gave the babe into his care. That be the last time I had seen him, until he came to the tribe of men, full grown." She smiled gently. "He has the exact shape and shade of my sister's eyes. I knew him instantly."

"Does he know about you?" Lana inquired, already guessing the answer.

The ancient shook her head. "Nay, and that be how I wish it."

"I will not betray your confidence, Derina. Your secret stays with me." A wrinkled hand slid over hers and squeezed.

"He be hurt, Lana. I speak not of the scars on his back, but deep down in the magical reaches of him, a terrible sorrow dwells."

"I understand."

The empty eye sockets studied her in the long silence that followed. "Mayhap you do understand," the ancient said after a while. Pushing down on her walking stick for balance, she climbed to her feet. "Have you seen Lightning today?" she asked casually, seemingly changing the subject.

Lana stood too, a bit confused by the question. She took a quick look at the cloudless blue sky above and detected no coming storm.

"Not that kind of lightning, Lana." The druidess arched one white brow, waiting for comprehension.

Lana gave the wizened face a strong examination. "Lightning," she murmured, and then grasped the answer. "Lightning, my friend."

"I be finding it difficult to call that battle-scarred, bad tempered horse a friend." the ancient said warmly. "Follow the stallion, Lana, and you be finding your heart's desire."

Lana hugged the ancient tightly, holding on to the diminutive frame, feeling incredibly indebted and grateful.

"Easy," the druidess laughed, smoothly pulling away. "You be squeezing the air out of me."

"Derina, I . . ." Lana offered an apologetic smile.

"No harm done. Come."

A small knobby hand slid in the crook of her arm, turning her back to the cottage.

"Methinks you need to change out of that fancy fey gown if you be roaming the woodlands after a stallion. We wouldna want any of the men folk around here mistaking you for a faery now, would we?" the ancient laughed. "I have your old clothes inside, Lana. Your mother never reclaimed them."

Lana remembered she always left a change of clothes at the druidess's house. She allowed the ancient one to lead her at a slow pace even though she wanted to hurry.

"The clothes be in the back room, Lana."

Lana entered the cottage ahead of the druidess and found her worn brown tunic and breeches immediately. Quickly removing the gown, she placed it reverently on the bed of pelts. Turning, she slipped into her comfortable working clothes. The soft boots were familiar, too.

The druidess moved inside the room and touched something shiny on the corner shelf.

Lana looked up and was surprised to see the Tara brooch Keegan gave to her as a gift before their handfasting.

"I have kept the brooch safe for your daughter."

She frowned. "Ancient, I have no daughter."

"Yet."

Lana walked over and kissed the druidess's soft cheek. "My thanks, Derina."

"Off with you now," the ancient said, embarrassed.

Lana ran out of the round house and took off for the high meadows. Legs pumping, heart pounding in a strong beat, it was not long before she found the stallion.

CHAPTER 22

LATE IN THE NIGHT A mid-autumn rainstorm passed through the edge of the fey woodlands where Keegan made his home. High winds and torrential rains made the land tremble in homage before felling an ancient oak and moving on. The crash startled the numbness inside him, and he had gone to the doorway.

He did not know how long he stood in the entrance of his home, naked and waiting for dawn, but it felt like a long while to him. After a time, he leaned a shoulder against the door's wooden frame and folded his arms across his chest. The nightmares were less frequent, he thought with a sense of detachment. In the beginning, he walked the woodlands in isolation, a bitter and wounded animal, until finally he let go of that other life. He found a sense of solace in the simpler and slower ways. At least, that was what he told himself.

He closed his eyes wearily and listened to the hum and echo of daybreak. Pushing off the doorframe, he went back inside and slipped into a pair of torn gray breeches. He wanted to see the fallen tree. Venturing out on bare feet, mud and soggy grass slipped between his bare toes. The air felt humid, a residual of the last breath of summer warmth. He let his senses lead him to the downed tree, not far from his unfinished home.

Picking his way around the broken branches, he knelt beside the thick trunk of the fallen tree like a grieving friend. "Given up, old ruler?" he asked quietly, and nudged a piece of rough black bark aside. Swirling insects infested the tree.

Keegan replaced the bark and gave the tree a final pat. "Time to rest." The oak lived a long life and now must dwindle, as was the way of things, as he too would dwindle with time. Resting a forearm on his thigh, he looked up at the bright ribbons crossing the lightening sky. Another day had arrived.

Standing, he stretched his arms, testing the soreness of his scarred back. He caught a whiff of horse in the woodsy air currents. In the near distance, he heard the sound of hoofbeats approaching. Keegan looked down and allowed himself a small grin. Lightning had found him again.

Not far from the village, he had retreated to this secret place on the other side of the fey woodlands. It was a secluded spot near a tiny loch known to only a handful of trusted guardians and one sorrel stallion. He knew the other guardians would keep his secret, an honor among them. His guardian father, although they rarely spoke, had seen to the secrecy of his existence. As for the stallion . . .

"Early riser this morn, Lightning." The stallion emerged from the trees, sleek and well groomed, his brown eyes bright with life. He bobbed his head and then shied away from the fallen tree.

"Easy boy," Keegan soothed and stepped over the trunk. " 'Tis just an old tree whose end has come." He came up beside the horse's strong shoulder and stroked the muscular neck with fondness. "Nothing to be afraid of."

Lightning snorted in disagreement.

Keegan chuckled, enjoying the rare moments of companionship. "All right, you can disagree. Have you come for one of your apples?" He scratched behind the horse's left ear and received a grateful whinny.

"I hope you took great pains not to be followed. It might put a damper on my health as I am a banished fey born these days."

Lightning pawed the ground.

"Impatient, are you?" Keegan gave the horse a firm pat. "Follow me then."

Turning, he followed the path back to his home and walked around the back end of the circular gardens and a patch of purple foxgloves in full bloom. The round house stood near the loch. He had built it so he could gaze upon the clear waters whenever he wished. A place far from turmoil and emotion, he had found a small measure of peace in the growing of things.

The stallion followed close at his heels, sniffing at his

hips. He leaned over and grabbed an apple from the wicker basket beside his doorway.

"Is this what you are looking for?" The horse pushed at his hand with his muzzle. "Wait a minute, you old goat." Keegan removed the dagger at his waist. "Here, let me cut it in half for you." With a quick slash, he cut the shiny red apple and held one half up in his open palm. The horse's soft muzzle scooped up the offering and he held out the other half. It was gobbled up as well.

"I like apples, too," a familiar female voice said.

Keegan stiffened. Slowly, he looked over the stallion's smooth back.

Among the clustered purple bells of the foxgloves, a lovely, slightly damp apparition stood in a brown tunic and breeches. Sun-kissed hair cascaded in glorious wet waves down slender shoulders. Enormous dark eyes were watchful, full lips curved in a faint smile, unsure of welcome.

And rightly so.

Why should he welcome another fey born?

Anger coursed through his blood. He did not want to be found.

"I seem to have gotten caught in the rainstorm last night."

She stayed hidden amongst the foxgloves, *the lus na mban sidhe*, the herb of the faery woman, caught in the shadows of the morning light.

He swallowed hard and realized he could do nothing. Sheathing his dagger back in his belt, he stepped away from the horse.

It is not her, his mind insisted, resolute in grief, a flood of raw and painful feelings streaming through him.

He forced himself to kneel on one knee and bowed his head. "I am honored."

I am honored? Lana peered at him, too astonished to speak. His brown hair had grown longer, the red and gold strands glinting with remembered light. He looked virile and healthy, but there was a glaze in his eyes before he bowed his head, a spirit withdrawn and no longer touchable.

"Keegan?" she heard herself say.

"I am he."

She bit her lip. When he retrieved an apple for Lightning, she saw his punishment and felt queasy. Two identical red scars sliced down his shoulder blades. They were the length of a big man's forearm.

"Keegan, 'tis me, Lana," she murmured nervously, picking at the soggy laces of her tunic. She thought of what he suffered and her heart ached with shame and sorrow. "Do you not know me?"

"You are not her." He lifted eyes haunted with shadows and rage.

Grief pressed in upon her, and Lana walked the short distance to him.

Kneeling, she took his cherished face in her hands. "I have missed you," she said shakily. "Please, Keegan."

His eyes closed. It was as if he could not suffer to look

upon her, and she felt her insides crumble to tiny bits. She kissed each eyelid in desperate tenderness, tasting the saltiness of the tears he held back. She kissed his smooth cheek. She kissed his perfect nose and the delicious seam of his closed lips.

"Lana," he rasped, a deep hurtful sound given to her name. His eyes opened, cast in frozen silver. Long blunt fingers wrapped around her wrists, and shoved her hands away.

"You are not Lana," he stated dully. "You are not my bride. I am not fooled. Why are you here, fey born?"

"Keegan, what have they done to you that you doona recognize me?"

His eyes turned murky. "They clipped me."

Tears spilled down her flushed cheeks. "I know," she said in an agonized whisper just before a horse's delicate muzzle pressed to her temple.

"Lightning," Lana choked, barely able to respond to the animal. Reaching up, she touched a smooth forehead. "You must forgive me." She smiled sadly. "I have no apples drizzled in honey for you." She kissed the soft muzzle and quietly pushed the stallion away. "Please, not now."

Her guardian mate stared at his sea-etched cuff on her wrist. He wet his lips, his face deathly white.

Lana held on to her hopes and slowly removed the cuff from her wrist. "I believe this belongs to you." Reaching out as if she gentled a spooked horse, she removed her dragonfly cuff from his thick wrist. "Methinks the sea cuff looks better here on your wrist," she encouraged. She fit the sea cuff back over his right wrist where it expanded to a perfect fit, where it belonged.

Without thought, she slipped the dragonfly cuff back up her arm where it fit perfectly, too.

His gaze slowly dipped to the remaining dragonfly cuff on his other wrist, and he reached for it.

"No need for that, my love." She gestured. "You wear it for now."

Dark eyelashes lifted and Lana found herself gazing into a fierce storm of want and bitterness.

"Lana?"

"Aye, aye, 'tis me, Keegan." Her heart and chest felt tight. She saw he was looking at her jaw, where he made the mating bite of claim upon her.

She pulled her hair away and tilted her face. The physical sign might be gone, but the scent of his claim remained on her flesh, as it always would.

His jaw tightened with an undefined emotion. "Forgive me," he murmured and shifted back on one knee, putting distance between them. Bowing his head once again, he folded his right hand across his chest. "How may I serve you, *claíomh host*?"

He withdrew into himself, a forced separation, barely existing. Lana curled her fingers into her lap. "I am not a sword," she whispered achingly.

"Nay, you are not," he agreed.

She lifted her hand to touch him and then dropped it back in her lap. "This is not how it is supposed to be."

He stared at her, a translucency marring the perfection of his features.

The noise of the morning roared in her head. She felt her heart shrinking into nothingness.

He inclined his head. "How may I serve you, *claíomh host*?" He repeated his request in a low tone with no telltale sign of emotion.

Pale morning light fell across his face while his words echoed in her mind. *How may I serve you?*

She gripped her hands tightly in her lap, nails digging into flesh. "Well, you can take off those torn breeches for one thing and make love to me in the waters," she said it quickly, said it on impulse, and waited.

His beautiful eyes widened in surprise.

She fought too hard to have a normal life, a life with him. She could think of nothing else, wanted nothing else, and fought back a foolish burst of tears.

He continued to watch her steadily.

Valor taught her self-confidence and it was time she tapped into it. She absolutely refused to give up and let him withdraw into vagueness.

Lana rocked back on her feet and stood, the sorceress's strong and rebellious bloodline flowing hotly in her veins. "The day feels warm. These clothes are clammy and I have traveled far," she stated in the tone of a spoiled faery queen.

She looked toward the tiny loch. "The waters look inviting. Do you not think so, Keegan?" She began to undo the wet laces of her tunic, her fingers shaking at her unaccustomed boldness. She waited until her breasts nearly spilled out in his face before turning away and heading down the grassy slope toward the crystal waters of the loch.

After a moment's hesitation, she heard him follow.

Lana shrugged out of her clammy tunic. With a flip of her hand, she tossed the tunic over her shoulder, and heard it smack a large chest. Stopping near one of the few granite boulders dotting the shore, she leaned against it and removed her boots and breeches.

Two perfectly formed male feet took a position in front of her.

Lana lifted her head, straightened, and drew back. Her passion melted at the sight of the fury reflected in his eyes.

Her nerve and audacity evaporated into thin air.

"What else would you have them cut off me?" he said savagely.

Her hands flung to her face in a sob of misery. "Nay, Keegan," she cried. "Doona say this to me."

"They have cut away the magical part of me, Lana. Would you have Valor castrate me as well?"

She shook her head in horror. "Nay!" Her voice quivered. "I wish it had been me instead of you. I wish they had cut me!"

Driven by painful heartache, she dashed toward the loch

and away from the wrath in his face. The love they once shared was gone, and with it her hopes for a reunion.

Their love was gone.

Cut out of him.

Lana splashed her way into the cool waters. Shivering uncontrollably, she half fell, half swam toward the center, the ground slipping out from under her feet. The surface had reached her breasts before strong hands grabbed her shoulders and spun her around.

With tear-stained cheeks, Lana stared up into a tempest of rage.

Keegan stared down into his salvation.

"Never!" he snarled with the force of controlled emotions, and spread his fingers across her delicate cheekbones, cupping her face. "Never say that to me, Lana."

"I wish they had cut me in punishment. It should have been me! I kissed you!"

He shook his head. "Lana, you fed me when I hungered. Quenched the dryness in me. I knew what I was doing when I took your virgin sheath."

"Nay, Keegan!" Small hands grabbed his wrists. "My fault," she sobbed. "My fault."

Her eyes were dull with hurt and shame. He felt the brokenness inside him expanding.

"Nay," he whispered.

"You were weak and feverish, you dinna know what was happening."

He smiled gently. "I knew what I was doing, and a guardian is never weak, Lana."

He forced himself to release her then, and stepped back reluctantly. "The bottom falls away here." He gestured to his right. "Please be careful or Valor will have to punish me again when you sink."

She lifted hollow eyes to him and his own gaze blurred. He looked away. "Why have you come?" he asked.

He heard a small sniffle. "Valor released me, Keegan."

He closed his eyes.

"Did you hear me, my love?"

He heard her. The scars on his back began to itch.

"Valor freed me, Keegan. I am free."

"Why?" The one word burst out of him like the torrent of an angry river. He looked back at her, made himself stand still, made himself continue to breathe.

"Glenna wished to be returned to her beloved. She is the sorceress's first granddaughter. You brought her to Derina to heal, remember?"

"I remember," he murmured.

"Do you remember giving Derina your silver sea cuff? You asked her to give it to Glenna because you could not give it to me."

He nodded, a quaking spreading through his limbs.

"Glenna dinna want the cuff, nor did she want the life you and I sacrificed to give her. What she wanted was to be returned to her beloved."

"The men of her time are all dead, Lana."

"Her beloved is Valor, Keegan. Valor is Glenna's mate."

"The sacred feminine sword spirit?" he heard himself ask in astonishment, afraid to accept what that meant.

"Aye, Valor is Glenna's chosen mate. Love exists in many forms it seems, and I am most gladdened that it does. With the help of Derina and Blodenwedd, Glenna has returned to her beloved mate as I am attempting to return to mine."

He could not dare hope she wanted him as he was now, a broken and blemished creature.

"Keegan?"

He swallowed hard. "Aye." His voice cracked.

"Are you my beloved?" she asked softly.

He could not respond.

"I love you, Keegan."

He raked a trembling hand through his hair. "Valor has released you, Lana?"

"Aye, my love." Tears slipped down her flushed cheeks. "I would never have willingly put you in danger. You must believe me. I dinna know our mating would lead to such punishment and pain. Please, Keegan, can you ever forgive me?"

The numbness inside him twisted. "There is nothing to forgive. I knew what I was doing." He looked away. "I wanted you, and I took what I wanted."

"I have wanted you since first I saw you."

His gaze slid back to hers, and he felt a physical pain of longing.

"Keegan? What is it? What tortures you so?"

He said the horrific fear aloud; his breath caught and locked in his throat. "I am blemished, Lana."

Her lips curved in understanding.

He searched her face. "I am blemished. Did you not hear what I said? I am blemished."

"I heard you, my love. Now, I can have you." She lifted her hand and rested it gently on his chest. "You are a mighty guardian of the fey, and I a mere mortal. Do you not see? We are equal now. You are a bit less magical, and I a bit more." She smiled. "You are not blemished, Keegan."

His skin tingled where she touched him, his heart swelling with a desperate hope.

"I am the sorceress's last blooded kin. Do you know what that means?"

He could only nod. His mind seemed to have stopped working.

"Valor asked me to give birth to her daughters of the sword. Our daughters, Keegan." Her voice quivered with the emotions boiling in the cauldron inside him.

"What better way to take retribution, my love, than to have the white blood of a powerful fey born guardian flowing in the veins of our children."

"I am no longer a guardian, Lana."

"You are First Guardian of the Waters," she countered strongly. "I will not hear otherwise from you, or anyone."

"I have no wings," he tried to explain, but she did not let

him finish.

"Let me see the scars, my love."

He froze. He did not wish her to see the brokenness of him, and stepped back reflexively, sending ripples through the water.

"Nay, Keegan." She reached for him. "Doona ever fear my rejection."

She walked around him.

His hands clenched.

Gentle hands pushed his hair aside, spilling it over the front of his left shoulder.

He shut his eyes.

Soft palms rested on his hips.

He prepared for her reaction of horror, his spirit folding in upon itself into utter darkness and despair.

And then . . .

Supple breasts pressed into the curve of his back.

Warm, soft lips kissed his mutilation.

By the white moon!

He gulped, an excruciating relief tightening his chest.

"I love you," she said against his scarred flesh. "These are battle scars of a war met with valor and victory. Doona ever hide them. You should be proud, for they are beautiful."

She pressed her soft mouth upon him again. There, where it had hurt and bled, first one side and then the other, her touch strangely quickening.

He forced air out of his lungs. "Lana, stop, I am . . ."

"No more pain, Keegan, only pleasure. Only pleasure will you feel here."

Her hands were tender on his flesh.

Her tongue, sweet torture . . .

Turning in her arms, Keegan captured her mouth with his, reclaiming his heart's desire.

"I love you," he said feverishly against silken lips, needing her taste inside him. "I love you, Lana." His hands buried in her tresses and he kissed her, inhaled her, and remembered all that she was.

Lana's heart soared with joy.

She wrapped her arms around his corded neck and kissed him back, meeting his passion and drinking deeply of his excitement. He tasted of rainstorms and thunder, of sweet apples and crystal lochs, but most of all he tasted of their love.

She could not get enough of him, and pressed closer.

Her right leg brushed against a muscular thigh and she felt the pulse of his arousal against her stomach. She wished his wet breeches gone and curled her leg around his, moving up and riding his thigh.

He moaned in her mouth and she took advantage, suckling his tongue, taking what he offered, what she needed to live and survive, him and only him.

He shuddered and she thrilled to his response, thrilled in bringing him pleasure.

In her brief joining with Valor, she received knowledge of many things, including the many ways in which to arouse a male. Her left hand locked around his nape for balance. She shifted sideways against him and boldly trailed her right hand down his chest. He was her one true love and suffered greatly for it. Never again would he know that kind of pain. She would make him forget all of it and fill his life with only joy and pleasure.

The muscles of his stomach were firm and strained beneath her fingertips. While she feasted on his mouth, she played with the band of his breeches, dipping her fingers beneath, knuckles sliding against warm, pulsating flesh, reaching lower . . .

Keegan's breathing hitched with a wild hunger, his body pulsing with a demand to mate. Desire and urgency flooded his blood, storming and releasing intensities he thought were dead. Reaching under her arms, he lifted his fair bride out of the water, his mouth closing over the nipple of her left breast while he headed toward the shallows. With one arm locked around her for support, he used his free hand to mold her breast, fitting her better into his mouth. His tongue flicked across her sensitive nipple and she moaned soft and long. A knee jammed into his stomach, and he released her breast only to latch onto the other one.

Lana flung her head back, gasping for air, absorbed by the hot wetness suckling at her breast. His tongue rasped over her nipple and she writhed uncontrollably in his embrace.

When they came to the shore, he laid her down upon the grass, his mouth still suckling her, water licking her legs.

He removed his dagger and breeches somehow. His mouth created a craving so intense her womb hurt. He nibbled the underside of her breast, her ribs, and downward . . .

Lana buried her hands in his hair, pulling him back up, impatient and hungry for a full joining with her guardian mate.

She shifted under him, her legs moving alongside his outer thighs.

The hot length of him pressed against her inner thigh and she tilted her hips up invitingly. Her guardian mate needed no further invitation. His body moved above hers, a graceful predator, pinning her hips.

His mouth lowered and nibbled at her jaw where he claimed her with a mating bite long ago. She arched under him, eager fingers digging into his shoulders.

His warm mouth slid to her ear.

"Claim me, Lana," Keegan breathed roughly.

"To you am I bound." His beautiful mate said the Claim of Binding words, words he thought never to hear. "To honor. To twilight. To land."

In one swift thrust, he entered her, burying his thick root fully into her tightness. She gasped in pleasure at the sudden invasion of him, and Keegan gloried in the sound and feel of her.

Hot.

Liquid.

Fire.

He moved slowly for her benefit, her pleasure, his body

listening and responding to the flow of hers, his beloved.

In.

Out.

Slower.

Deeper.

Longer strokes . . .

Lana wrapped her trembling legs around his moving hips and pulled his head down to kiss him, to inhale her love's living breath. He was hard and hot within her, a surging of solid male stretching her with delicious pressure, consuming her.

A tidal wave of craving washed over her, a building storm of want and need.

The weight of him.

The taste of him.

The magic of him.

His hips shifted to a different rhythm, a more urgent and untamed demand. Large hands wrapped around her bottom, tilting her hips further upward.

Lana couldn't breathe from the exquisite force moving between her thighs. The bright white turbulence growing within her womb began to unravel into a spiraling spasm and then, when she could no longer breathe from the fire and force of it . . .

Keegan knew she was ready.

Clenching his teeth, he thrust deeply into her and stopped. Closing his eyes, he *melded* with his mate in the way of the guardians, blood to blood, spirit to spirit, taking her over the cliffs, and into the wild hot rapture of a true guardian mating.

He heard her cries of ecstasy and basked in them, the sweet sounds of her like music to his ears. With one final thrust, he sent his seed into her womb and laid his claim within her for always and the forever time.

He belonged to her now.

Eyes closed, his head slowly lowered to her shoulder of its own accord. Body trembling with blessed exhaustion, he slid, boneless, to her side.

She gave him a calming within his spirit, a lost magic returned, and he would love and cherish her without end. Keegan snuggled in close, holding onto her, his most valuable and beloved bride.

"I have given you a daughter, Lana," he whispered huskily, and then slipped into slumber, a rest long overdue.

Lana smiled and caressed the smoothness of his cheek. She, too, snuggled in close and closed her eyes. She had no doubt he gave her a daughter and would continue to do so, at her most frequent urging.

EPILOGUE

ANOTHER SPRING'S PROMISE RETURNED TO the lands, sharing and savoring warmth with blooms of life in bright wild colors.

Lana placed the Tara brooch back in her daughter's wooden box for safekeeping and walked out of the cottage. She headed for the large rowan, which kept the back of their home in shade. Dense white flowers clustered upon upturned branches. She ran a hand along the jagged green-brown bark. The trunk was wide and thickened with age.

Today, like most days, she wore a comfortable tunic and breeches, her hair in tight plaits behind her ears. "Where is our daughter?" she asked, moving to the stone wall her guardian mate built behind their home.

"No doubt, still swimming with our son," her beloved responded, freeing the two brown oxen from the yoke of their plough. "Did you find the brooch?"

"In her bed again, wrapped in cloth. She must have slept with it."

He chuckled and nodded.

"I worry she will stab herself with it."

"The brooch will never hurt her, my love."

Lana watched the play of muscles across his bare back as he worked, the horrible scars thinned with the passage of time. As usual, he wore only a pair of low riding breeches during the warm months.

She looked in the direction of the sea. "The children love the waters. They are very much like you."

He slapped the animals' rumps to herd them into the green pasture. "Are you saying I need to bathe?"

"Aye," Lana laughed softly. Indeed he did, covered in dirt and soil from a full day of toiling in the fields.

"Do I stink?" he asked, glancing at her with a twinkle in his eye.

"Never, my love."

He laughed knowingly and closed the wooden gate to the pasture. Her guardian mate would always smell of rainstorms.

Lana smiled warmly. She adored him. His once pale skin turned golden this spring, disguising the truth of his faery blood. Red and gold fire streaked his long brown hair, which he wore in plaits now, like herself. She learned he loved to be part of the growing of things and often watched his delight in the sniffing of fragrant blooms and herbs. In the eve, he shed his clothes, not that he wore much these days, and took long swims in the sea. Sometimes she wondered if the water faeries ever spoke to him, but never would she ask. That life lay behind them.

They returned to the land of men a few summers before and settled on a piece of rich farmland near her family and the sacred fey woodlands.

At the prompting of the other guardians, the Faery King had given pardon to her guardian mate, though he could no longer be what he once was, and that suited them well enough.

To her, Keegan would always be fey born, always a bit mysterious, even though they were farmers now, setting ancestry in the land. The magic within them was forever resident and pulsing, as was their love for each other.

Her guardian mate came up beside her on silent step. Folding his arms across his chest, he leaned a hip against the trunk of the rowan tree, his lips curved in a sensuous smile.

"Should we not call the children back?" she asked. "They have been playing in the sea all day. Their skin will be wrinkled."

" 'Tis not the first time. Besides, Derina sits on the shore with her basket of food. They are safe."

"I know," she murmured in agreement. She gazed down at the silver cuff on his right wrist, a fey born etching of sea waves. It remained there always, as the dragonfly cuffs remained upon her arms, a lingering of the past and enchantment of their flesh.

"This morning, I saw you give our children three large fey apples."

He chuckled low and nodded. "For my favorite stallion; I think you know who I mean."

She laughed softly, too. "Lightning. Methinks that horse be a long-lived fey born. He appears almost ageless."

"It would not surprise me in the least if he was. And like any true fey born, he chooses to show up at the most inconvenient times."

Lana's eyes sparkled in devilment. "Is this an inconvenient time, my love?" she inquired in a sultry tone.

His head tilted, brown lashes lowering over eyes turned smoky with desire. "There is a brook in the woodlands," he offered in a seductive caress. "Care to bathe me, my love?"

Aye, she thought, her mind momentarily slipping back to the past. He was so beautiful, his spirit steadfast and true. There were no reasons to what had happened. Only an acceptance of inner peace, pushing the scars into faded memory. He chose a mortal life alongside hers, rich in emotions and experiences.

She healed too, a final acceptance of inner worth and understanding. Value came from one's self. Never should merit be sought in another's eyes. Wholeness, she had come to realize, always came from within.

Except now, while her body quickened in response to his desire, she knew the enchantment that had once brought them together held little sway in their love and devotion for each other.

He watched her for a long moment and then offered his

hand.

Lana recognized the slow heated grin and slipped her hand into his much larger one. Her body went fiery with excitement as it always did when he touched her.

He swept her up in powerful arms and murmured huskily against her neck, "I thirst for some magic, my love."

Wrapping her arms around his strong neck, she proceeded to nibble at the exquisite contours of his left ear. "So do I, my love."

- The End -

NOTES ON TEXT

Bodhran - A Celtic war drum.

Báisteach - Rain.

Claíomh - Sword.

Dana - Universal mother goddess.

Daoine Sidhe - Faery folk.

Duil - Desire.

Dúnmharfóir - Murderer.

Eire - Ancient Ireland.

Fey - Faeries.

Feypaths - Underground secret passages created by faeries.

Fortnight - Fourteen days or two weeks.

Fir Bog - Belgians, mystical settlers of Connacht, known as the bag men.

Formorians - Sea raiders.

Freagarthach - The Answerer, a powerful sword and one of the talismans of the faery realm.

Months - Aibrean (April), Bealtaine (May), Meitheamh (June), Mean Fhómhair (September), Deireadh Fhómhair (October)

Sennight - Seven days or one week.

Sidhe - Gaelic name for the faeries in both Ireland and the highlands of Scotland.

Teastaigh - Madness and want.

Temair na Rig - Tara of the Kings.

Torc - A neck ring, commonly made of gold or bronze.

Lus na mban sidhe - The herb of the faery woman.

Tuatha Dé Danann - Collective term coined in the Middle Ages for the people of the goddess Dana.

Undines - Water faeries.

AUTHOR'S NOTES

Myth, magic, and archaic legacy are open to many interpretations. Most historians believe ancient Ireland was invaded and settled by successive tribes over different periods. The book, *Leabhar Gabhála* or *Lebor Gabala Erren* — the "Book of Conquests" or the "Book of Invasions of Ireland" — contains the stories of these successive invasions and settlements. Some believe this book does more of the retelling of legends than of truths — I will let the wiser of us decide.

Another resource for *Fey Born* comes from the *Cath Maige Tuired*, The Second Battle of Mag Tured (Moytura), translated by Whitley Stokes in 1891. This story centers mostly on the race of Irish deities or faeries, known as Tuatha Dé Danann.

I found the ancient text at:
http://www.ancienttexts.org/library/celtic/irish/2nd_moytura.html.

There are many other sources offering analysis and the

retelling of those times. Myth and the real world could be argued from many points of view. I invite you the reader to draw your own conclusions.

Remarkably, some of the locations in *Fey Born* continue to exist today. *Knowth* and *Dowth,* the Faery Mound of Darkness, are passage tombs in Ireland. They are located north of the River Boyne. Official tours are available from the Brú na Bóinne Visitor Centre, although *Dowth,* at the time of this research, was closed to visitors.

As always, any incorrectness in my portrayal of the times of ancient Ireland are, of course, like the fantastical notions, very much my own.

Also available from Medallion Press,
R. Garland Gray's first novel:

PREDESTINED

PROLOGUE

EIRE
LONG AGO

THE PEOPLE SPEAK OF IT at night, in hushed whispers,
away from the non-believers.

It is an old Irish legend come down from the north.

On the last eve of the full moon when spring and
prosperity had reigned, the first generations of the
Tuatha Dé Danann became the faery folk. The people
named them the *Daoine Sidhe*, their tongues pressed to
the roof of their mouths in speech. The "Deena Shee,"
they said, the dwindled gods.

Before enlightened memory, the *Tuatha Dé Danann*
had shed their mundane mortality like unwanted
cloaks seeking divinity and their own forever.

Others of the tribe struggled to remain mortal,
resisting the temptation that would change their destiny evermore.

Still others wavered in twilight, caught between

two worlds, both mortal and faery.

Myth says the *Tuatha Dé Danann* are the faeries. It was said that one, separate and apart, would save them all.

CHAPTER 1

DRUMANAGH, EIRE
KINDRED, RUINS OF A FAERY FORTRESS

HE FELT SLUGGISH AND GRAY, locked in a cold oblivion not of his making. Drugged eyelids crusted open, struggling for focus. Shadows lingered beyond the candlelight in the crumbling tomb of the ancient faery fort.

Tynan shifted cramping muscles. Iron manacles dug into the raw flesh of his wrists and ankles. Painfully, he lifted his head and surveyed his surroundings. He lay on his back on a sacrificial altar of stone, naked and chained, an offering to the otherworld gods, he supposed, his mind still foggy. They had extended his arms above his head and spread his legs apart; leaving him vulnerable.

His head fell back with a heavy thud. He wished he could wake up from this dark dream.

"Doona fight so; let the drug release you."

He startled at the soft lilting voice, so out of place here. A small figure came into view and Tynan blinked to bring the hooded shape into focus.

"Where am I?" he asked. His voice sounded rusty to his own ears.

"They brought you to the lower tombs of Castle

Kindred." The figure moved to stand near his hip, an obscure form carefully crafted to hide the identity of the woman within.

"How do you feel?" she asked.

He felt blurred and queer inside. His body ached in places it had never ached before. The last thing he remembered, dusk had fallen while he bathed in the woodland stream. Low ceiling and stone walls surrounded him now. The damp air attested to the nearness of Eire's wind-swept sea. Black candles burned low in stone crevices, oblivious to the moisture that would extinguish their flames forever.

A movement on the floor caught his attention. He lifted his head. *"Aile Niurin,"* he muttered. Hell Fire. Red beady eyes blinked brazenly back at him before scurrying beneath soiled straw.

"They are only rats looking for food. They will not harm you, warrior. If you feel you can, drink this." She held a flask out to him. "There is little time before they return."

Tynan tried to see the face behind the enticing voice, but the hood's drape hid all features.

"Who comes?" he asked.

Small hands held a silver flask out to him.

"What is in it?" he asked, leery of any offering.

"Water and a crushed apple."

He frowned with indecision, not trusting but needing nonetheless.

"It is safe, warrior," she reassured. "I prepared it myself before coming here." She took a sip from the flask to prove it.

He nodded, too thirsty to argue and opened his mouth.

She supported the back of his head. Fingers buried in his hair, shifting the black length so it spilled down the stone at his shoulder.

"Slowly, warrior."

The flask touched his cracked lips. Tiny beads of apple slid down his raw throat. The unexpected tartness of the fruit quickly revived him, his mind finally clearing. When finished drinking, he pulled away.

The hooded figure just stood there, watching him, a slight tilt to her head. The scent of lavender teased his nostrils. "Let me see you."

She shook her head and took a small step back. " 'Tis safer not to see my face. If my Roman master found out I ventured to the tombs, he'd order me flayed."

"You are a slave, then?" Tynan could not hide his surprise.

"Aye, to the Roman Centurion that holds this ancient place."

"Do Roman centurions allow their slaves free reign?"

"I am trustworthy and given freedom as long as I remain within my master's boundaries."

"Your master's boundaries do not include the tombs."

"Nay."

"Yet, you are here."

"Aye." She nodded slowly, no doubt wondering where these questions were leading.

He had but one focus lately. "Do you know where the Roman Centurion is holding the faeries?"

The hooded figure stiffened and shook her head. "I doona know anything about that."

Tynan wasn't sure if he believed her.

She turned to the back corridor where voices could be heard.

"They come, warrior. I must leave."

She walked around the altar, and Tynan grabbed a piece of coarse gray cloak. "Who comes?" he demanded.

"The Sorcerer and his minions. They search for the Dark Chieftain of Prophecy."

The woman tugged on her cloak. "Please release me, warrior. If you live, I will find a way to help you."

If I live? He had no intention of dying. Tynan released her. "Hide yourself."

Slipping the silver flask within the folds of her robe, she became part of the darkness, silent and gone as the moments from which she had come. He wondered briefly if he would ever see her again, ever gaze upon her features, but then pushed those thoughts quickly aside for the air became foul with the smell of garlic and sweat.

"The dark sovereign has awakened."

Tynan peered into the shadows trying to locate the owner of the male voice. *One thing felt certain, his captors knew his name.* Tynan meant dark sovereign among his people.

"Are you the Dark Chieftain of Prophecy?" an older man's voice inquired with a touch of excitement.

"Are you the Sorcerer?" Tynan countered instead. A cloaked man came to stand at his head, face hidden by the drape of the hood. *Does everyone wear hooded robes and cloaks here?*

"I have gone by many names in this life: *Yn Drogh Spyrryd*, Evil One, Dark Druid, but Sorcerer is the name I answer to now. Do you answer to the name of Dark Chieftain?"

Lord Tynan, the Dark Chieftain of the *Tuatha Dé Dananns*, calmed, for his captors did not know whom they held. In his mind, images of purple light and elfin faces flashed and swirled. The imprisoned faeries had become aware of his presence from within the sacred walls of the ancient faery fort.

"Silence will only cause you pain, warrior. I have brought many men down to the tombs to be tested. All have died."

Calloused fingers grazed his temple and Tynan turned away, gripping the manacles.

"Your eyes are faery marked with the color of amethyst, warrior. It is a sure sign of the fey heritage in your blood. Mayhap, my search is finally over."

Tynan ignored his captor's ramblings and tried to see the man's face behind the hood. The rough stone of the altar scraped his bare back. He caught sight of a strong chin and long, black hair, streaked with winter's gray.

"Curious of my face, warrior?"

"Evil has many forms," Tynan answered.

"Think me evil, do you?"

Crooked fingers placed a seventeen-inch black sword on his chest, the blood groove encrusted with lime. Dried leaves draped the double-edges of the iron blade. Tynan shifted, only now becoming aware of the two servants who had stood in the back, out of his line of sight.

The air stirred above him. He looked down his chest. The ancient sword quickly took on a threatening quality. A burning sensation spread into his flesh. He yanked at his chains. "What sorcery is this?"

His captor came around and stood by his shoulder looking down at him, trying to see into his very soul.

"Your blood belongs to the faeries, of that I vow."

He was more mortal than faery thanks to his father's betrayal. "Many of my tribe show the faery claiming in their eyes."

"Not like yours. I think you are their chieftain."

Tynan did not reply.

"Tell me, who is the territorial goddess? I have searched widely for her. The fates are spiteful and keep her hidden."

"The great Evil One cannot find the territorial goddess?" he goaded, trying to turn his captor's interest away from the goddess. All knowledge of her had been lost years before, yet he alone must be the one to find her.

"Tell me her name." The Sorcerer made his demand with spittle and venom. "Tell me or I will spell-bind you in darkness and silence."

"Your threats are weak. I will tell you nothing,

Evil One."

"So be it. You are no different than the others before you and so shall suffer for it." the Sorcerer raised his hands and began to chant, something murky and unholy and unrecognizable.

A blood-freezing cold washed over Tynan's face. He reared up in surprise, yanking at the manacles binding him.

The world writhed and slithered into dark and silence.

Slowly his sight winked out. Blind.

Sound wasted away and became only silence. Deaf.

"Nay!" He struggled to breathe in the eternal night and cold stillness engulfing him. His heart pounded erratically in his chest, fear and terror overwhelming him. He felt suspended, lost in a vast ocean of freezing quiet and living blackness.

"TYNAN," the imprisoned faeries trilled in his mind. "HURRY AND FREE US FROM THIS DARK PLACE."

Tynan's jaw clenched.

"DARK CHIEFTAIN. THE EVIL ONE CANNA VEIL OUR FEY GIFT TO YOU. YOU BE OF OUR BLOOD. SEE THE SHAPES WITHIN THE DARKNESS. LOOK INTO IT WITH FEY SIGHT AND KNOW THAT YOU BE NOT ALONE."

He swallowed hard and focused as his fey brethren decreed.

Suddenly within his blindness, gray shapes moved. He could see form and movement, a living grayness etched with a male's red heat. His faery sight allowed him to see beyond the vileness of the spell, but he could not see details and he could not see color. He could not see the face of his tormentor.

The Sorcerer pulled back his hood and scowled down upon the sweaty warrior. "Willful. This one shows more strength than most."

Laying his hand beside the warrior's right temple, a sickly smile curved his lips. He opened his fist and released the black spider. "Let us see what he thinks of my creature."

The warrior jerked his head away and the Sorcerer grinned in delight. "Feel the spider at your temple? It feeds upon the senses. It is an ancient creature, spellbound in the old way of magic and obscurity."

The Sorcerer knew the warrior could no longer hear him. Still he spoke, relishing in the sound and echo of his words in these olden tombs. "Live in this world of undying night and silence. Let your senses feed the spider's incessant appetite. In time, your fear shall breed and betray you and then you will tell me all that I need to know."

Chains clanked loudly with the warrior's inner battle and a kind of glee gripped him. "So, the terror begins . . ."

The Sorcerer motioned his servants to leave him. Leaning over, he cupped the warrior's chin harshly, holding him fast, his thin lips inches from the warrior's ear.

"Do you want the answer to your freedom?" He

asked with cruel intent. "It is the true kiss of a faery."

He released the warrior and cackled in the way of those doomed. Gazing in satisfaction upon his prisoner, the Sorcerer pulled up his hood and walked away, back to the unending corridors below the ancient castle, back to the unending searches for salvation.

✱✱✱

Tynan blew air out of his lungs. The spell stealing his senses both terrified and enraged him.

"FREE US. NOW." The faeries drummed in his mind, endless demands laced with bad-temper and selfishness.

Jerking the chains, he flung back his head in bitter exasperation. First, he must free himself.

ISBN #1932815821
ISBN #9781932815825
Jewel Imprint: Amethyst
US $6.99 / CDN $8.99
Available Now
www.rgarlandgray.com